Sue Minix is a member of Sisters in Crime, and when she isn't writing or working, you can find her reading, watching old movies, or hiking the New Mexico desert with her furry best friend.

A Chapter on Murder

SUE MINIX

avon.

Published by AVON
A division of HarperCollins*Publishers*
1 London Bridge Street
London SE1 9GF

www.harpercollins.co.uk

HarperCollins*Publishers*
Macken House
39/40 Mayor Street Upper
Dublin 1
D01 C9W8
Ireland

A Paperback Original 2023

2

First published in Great Britain by HarperCollins*Publishers* 2023

A catalogue copy of this book is available from the British Library.

ISBN: 978-0-00-858468-9

Typeset in Sabon Lt Std by Palimpsest Book Production Limited,
Falkirk, Stirlingshire

Printed and bound in the UK using 100% Renewable Electricity
at CPI Group (UK) Ltd

This book is produced from independently certified FSC™ paper
to ensure responsible forest management.

For more information visit: www.harpercollins.co.uk/green

To Dawn Dowdle,
the hardest working superhero I know.

CHAPTER ONE

The first Saturday in December was famous for two things in Riddleton, South Carolina: the Christmas parade and the kickoff of the Home and Business Christmas Decoration contest. And contest didn't come close to describing it. In this tiny town, the competition was more Thor versus the Incredible Hulk, than Snow White versus Cinderella. All for a gold-colored plastic trophy and the right to strut like the only rooster in the henhouse until next year. I had no room to judge, though. That trophy would look great on my mantel. If I had a mantel.

My best friend, town librarian Brittany Dunlop, and I had camped out in front of the still unadorned windows of my bookstore, Ravenous Readers, waving at the passing floats. Although floats might be a generous portrayal. Mostly, they were garland-and-banner-laden pickup trucks with regular folks standing in the beds wearing their gaudiest Christmas sweaters and reindeer antlers, waving, and throwing candy canes into the crowd. Still, it brought the community together, which was a good thing in a place like this.

Brittany snagged a foot-long peppermint stick

1

before it crashed into my front door. She did a little celebration dance, her flyaway blond hair airborne as if she was standing behind a jumbo jet on the tarmac with its engines running. Her caesious-blue eyes twinkled in the sun, the tip of her tongue protruding from her rosebud mouth, as she waved the prize overhead.

As the last float rolled by, Brittany poked me with her peppermint stick. "It's ten thirty, Jen. We should hustle to the diner, before it fills up."

My empty stomach rumbled. "Sounds great. Let's go."

My protector, therapist, and companion since we'd been seated next to each other in kindergarten, I couldn't imagine a minute without Brittany in my life. Not to say we hadn't had our rough patches. Like when she started dating my ex-boyfriend, Stan Olinski. We always worked it out, though. The pinky-swear we'd made twenty-five years ago on that first day of school ruled over all: Dawson and Dunlop together forever!

We zigzagged through the crowd, past the police station and the town hall. The flag Santas attached to the black wrought-iron lamp posts fluttered under the sunny, sixty-degree sky. Safe to assume the only snow we'd have between now and the big day would come out of a can, sprayed on storefront windows. The more desperate might throw tubs of the fake stuff on their roofs. Nothing like Christmas in the South. You could have it any way you wanted.

Brittany twirled her peppermint stick like a baton as we walked. "The parade wasn't too bad this year."

"No, not at all." I sidestepped a family of four who

believed their tax dollars had purchased them the whole sidewalk. "I miss the days when your parents took us to Blackburn for the big one, though."

"I looked forward to that trip all year." She elbowed me. "Remember the time you got lost?"

"I wasn't lost. I knew exactly where I was. Chasing the reindeer balloon that kid let go of. I almost had it, too."

Brittany pushed up the sleeves of her Santa sweater as the temperature climbed. "Too bad my dad didn't. His face turned so red, I thought he'd explode when he realized you weren't there."

"Yeah, and you cried for an hour."

"I was seven and scared. I thought you were gone forever."

"Maybe, but it was only five minutes tops."

She stuck out her lower lip. "Well, it felt like forever."

I draped my arm around her shoulder as we hit the sidewalk in front of the diner. "Thank you. I missed you too."

"Oh, you did not!" She pushed me away, laughing.

The Dandy Diner's Christmas window featured apron-adorned elves flipping burgers on a snow-topped grill. Mrs. Claus mixed a milkshake with one hand and filled a glass at a soda fountain with the other. The door depicted Rudolph in a server's smock carting a tray of food and drinks to the glass on the opposite side, where Santa enjoyed a loaded cheeseburger he held with both hands. Not a bad paint job for a former bank loan officer from New Hampshire. Proprietor Angus Halliburton might've missed his calling a second time.

Brittany and I snagged a corner booth under a nineteen-forties-era advertisement for Lucky Strike cigarettes. It reminded me of the old black-and-white movies I loved so much growing up. The only things missing were William Powell and Myrna Loy chugging highballs while they solved the *Thin Man* mysteries.

Behind the front counter, Riddleton's own Santa, Angus, directed his workshop of waitstaff, busboys, and cook elves.

I reached for a menu. Brittany snatched it out of my hand.

"Hey, what gives?"

"You don't need that." She tucked a stray hair behind her ear. "We both know what you're going to order."

"Oh yeah? What?"

"A cheeseburger, fries, and either a chocolate shake or a Mountain Dew. Right?"

"Not necessarily. Now, hand it over."

She raised an eyebrow and slipped the menu into my outstretched hand.

I studied it, knowing full well she was correct.

Our waitress, Penelope, brought us water and took Brittany's order for a chef's salad with ranch dressing. When she finished writing, she turned to me and asked, "Today a shake day or a Dew day?"

Brittany pursed her lips, suppressing an I-told-you-so smile.

I narrowed my eyes. "A shake day, but instead of fries, I'll take an order of onion rings. Thank you." Actually, I wasn't crazy about onion rings, but I had to make my point somehow.

I slid the menu back into its slot, and we all giggled.

4

Penelope shook her head and returned to the counter to give the grill cook, Marcus Jones, our order.

Portly Angus stopped at our table with his arms akimbo. A macho Weeble. "Jennifer Dawson, I'm still waiting for you to tell me when your new book is coming out."

"It'll be out in April. Soon enough for you?"

He smiled. "No, but I guess it'll have to do."

"If it makes you feel any better, I'm already working on book three in the series." Well, I typed chapter one on a blank page, anyway.

"That's great! When's that one due?"

My cheeks heated. "No due date, yet. I'm hoping *Twin Terror* will sell as well as *Double Trouble*, and the publisher will want another. I need to be prepared, especially since meeting deadlines isn't one of my strengths." I'd had so much trouble finishing the second book, my publisher had threatened to sue me for breach of contract to motivate me to write the thing. To be fair, though, a lot had happened in that year. My boyfriend left me, Brittany's fiancé disappeared and I moved back home to support her, I almost died investigating the murder of the original owner of the bookstore, unofficially, of course, and I was kidnapped looking into another. Plenty of fodder for a new book, but little time to write one. "I don't want the *Davenport Twins Mysteries* to be the shortest series on record."

Angus grasped my shoulder. "You'll be fine. I have faith in you."

"Thanks." My cheek fireballs ignited again. Hard to adjust to having people around who believed in me. I'd get used to it, though. Eventually. "What have you been up to?"

He rocked back and forth on his heels. "I've decided to promote Marcus to assistant manager."

"Are you kidding? How terrific!" Marcus had a rough beginning in life, but, after his release from a five-year stint in prison for armed robbery, had turned things around. He and his two young daughters had moved to Riddleton, and Angus had hired him as a cook last summer. Despite his early mistakes, he'd become an honorable man, and I was proud to call him my friend.

"He's doing an awesome job, and he has a good head on his shoulders."

"I think it's a smart move," Brittany said.

"Can't wait to see his face when I tell him."

Brittany gave him a thumbs-up. "He'll be thrilled. Anything to give Larissa and Latoya a better life than he had."

I grinned at Angus. "What're you going to do with all your free time?"

"What free time?"

"When Marcus takes over the diner."

He chuckled. "That won't happen any time soon. He still has a lot to learn."

I waved a hand at him. "He'll catch on fast, don't worry."

"I know. It'll be wonderful to spend less time behind the counter and more with my customers, though."

I leaned back against the wall beneath the Lucky Strike sign and stretched my legs out on the bench. "You mean collecting gossip, right?"

He pushed my feet to the floor and squeezed in beside

6

me. "I don't gossip. I gather valuable information for future reference." He smirked. "Besides, I've helped you out a time or two, haven't I?"

Angus's so-called news had come in handy more than once, I had to admit. "Very true."

Angus squeezed out of the booth and eased away from the table. "Well, I'd better get back—" His foot slipped on a dropped fork, and arms circling wildly all the way down, he landed flat on his back. Apparently, this Weeble *did* fall down.

I scrambled out of the booth to his side. "Angus, are you all right?"

"I'm fine." He massaged the back of his skull. "I'll probably have a nasty headache, but other than that, I'm okay."

Rapid footsteps sounded behind me. I turned as Dr. Ingrid Kensington reached us from her table by the door. "What happened?"

"Angus was showing off his moonwalk and slipped on a fork." I picked up the bent hindrance. "Apparently, neither one came out intact."

Red-faced, Angus imitated a beached whale, trying to sit up.

Ingrid put out a restraining hand, her dark skin glistening in the fluorescent light. "Hold on, luv. Let me check you over. Ensure you didn't break anything."

"I'm fine! I don't need a doctor, unless you specialize in bruised egos. Or cracked tiles."

"The tile's fine. And even if it wasn't, it would be easily fixed, then Bob's your uncle. Just allow me a look anyway. It'll make me feel better."

Angus peered up at her from the floor. "I don't have an Uncle Bob."

She laughed and shook her head, short loose curls bouncing. "It means everything will be sorted." At Angus's puzzled expression, she continued, "Fine. Everything will be fine."

Ingrid, town doctor and part-time medical examiner, had moved to South Carolina from London, and she often dropped words on us we'd never heard before. However, listening to her mellifluous accent was like eavesdropping in the servants' hall of *Downton Abbey*. Without all the drama.

She poked and prodded Angus's neck and ribs, then ran her hands over his limbs. "Any pain anywhere? How about your breathing?"

"I'm okay, I promise." He tried to get up again.

Ingrid held him back. "Hold on. Just one more thing since you hit your head." She held up a finger. "Follow my finger with your eyes only."

She moved her finger back and forth and he tracked it.

When she finished, she asked, "What were you doing before you fell?"

"I was telling Jen and Brittany about how important my information-gathering is. See? I'm fine."

"All right, then. I can't find any evidence to the contrary, so I concur."

Angus collected the offending fork and scurried back to his position behind the counter, rubbing the back of his head. Intermission over, the symphony began anew. Ingrid slid into our booth beside Brittany and stole an onion ring off my plate. Penelope had dropped off our food while we tended to Angus.

"How are things going with you and Marcus?" I asked, offering her another one.

"Pretty well, I think." She nibbled at the breading. "I like him a lot."

Brittany nudged Ingrid with her elbow. "Like or love?"

Ingrid blushed and looked away.

Brittany and I high-fived and said, "Love!" at the same time.

"There's nothing to be embarrassed about," I said. "We're happy for you. Marcus is a great guy. You could do a whole lot worse."

"So could he," Brittany added. "I think you two make a lovely couple."

"Thank you." Ingrid picked at her unpolished thumbnail. "I hope you're right."

"Of course we're right." Brittany laid her napkin beside her half-finished salad. "If you'll excuse me, I need to use the little girls' room."

Ingrid stood and Brittany slid out of the booth.

Another onion ring disappeared into Ingrid's mouth. "So, Jen, where's Eric taking you for your birthday next weekend?"

"We don't have any plans I'm aware of. Besides, I don't even want to think about it."

Ingrid tilted her head. "Why not? How old are you going to be?"

"Thirty. I'm supposed to be an adult now."

"Who decided that, luv?"

"I don't know—my mother, my editor, society? You name it."

Ingrid snorted. "Since when do you care what other people think?"

Great question. Was that really who I'd become?

As Brittany approached the booth, she pointed

toward the diner entrance. "I wonder what that's all about."

Outside the front door, my boyfriend, Detective Eric O'Malley, stood nose-to-nose with his partner, Detective Francine Havermayer. And neither one seemed happy.

CHAPTER TWO

My German shepherd, Savannah, who I stopped to pick up when I left the diner, towed me into the bookstore at eleven forty-five. We had to open a couple of hours late because the parade route ran right by the store. Charlie Nichols, our barista-in-chief as he liked to call himself, had set up the coffee bar, but I didn't see him anywhere. Lacey, in her red Ravenous Readers polo shirt and khaki pants, was dusting the cherry bookcases that lined the walls. Above each case, a carved wooden plaque identified the genres in alphabetical order.

Lacey waved her feather duster at me from the Mystery section—the last category before the stockroom—then went on to the cash register to retrieve a dog treat. Savannah's mother, Princess, had saved my life after I'd almost drowned investigating the murder of Ravenous Reader's original proprietor, Aletha Cunningham, who left me the bookstore in her will, last year. Princess's owner had gifted me a puppy to keep me out of trouble. A nice thought, but an impossible task.

Savannah created nose-print art on the showcase glass, as Lacey fished for the bag of bacon-flavored

11

snacks. A game she particularly liked to play when riding in the car. Fortunately, she couldn't reach the windshield or back window. Otherwise, I'd be driving blind.

While I could ignore the expressionist paintings on my car windows, the bookstore had to be at least presentable. I hustled past the butcher-block tables, surrounded by well-padded chairs, into the stockroom for glass cleaner and paper towels. As much as Lacey loved having my dog around, cleaning up after her was too much to ask of anybody. Savannah was definitely a full-time job. Ironically, the clutter that consumed my apartment mostly belonged to me.

The last smudge removed from the case displaying bookmarks and book lights for night owls, I returned the cleaner to its shelf while Lacey flipped the sign on the entryway door to "Open."

Charlie—wearing skintight leather pants, a lavender satin shirt, and purple, glittery, platform shoes—bustled through with a box of pastries from Bob's Bakery across the street and set the carton on the counter. "Whew! I made it barely in time. Do you see that storm rolling in?" He gestured toward the front.

I arranged the croissants, shaking my head. Disco Charlie was back. But I knew who he was when I'd hired him. A good guy with unique taste in clothing. Whatever made him happy made me happy, as long as he continued to do his job.

I took a few steps up the aisle, and anvil clouds skidding across the blackened sky came into view. Lightning snapped in the distance, accompanied a couple of seconds later by rumbling thunder. The storm was about two miles away and moving fast. Savannah squeezed under the table closest to my leg. "Well, there goes our morning business."

Lacey pointed toward the horizon. "Not necessarily. It's clear over there. It's only another pop-up thunderstorm. Should be over in a half hour, give or take."

"I hope so. We actually broke even last month. I'm hoping for a better December with the Christmas rush."

Lacey tucked the puppy treats away. "I think the Jen-solved-another-crime boom has passed. Why don't you go see what Eric's working on, so you can interfere?"

"Ha ha." My adventures during the investigation after the chief of police was murdered last July had attracted the curious in droves. Terrific for the bottom line, but the prospect that the only way the bookstore could stay afloat was if people in Riddleton died, and I hunted down the killers, nauseated me. It was a gruesome idea, actually. Were we South Carolina's Cabot Cove? Nope. Jessica Fletcher solved a new murder every week. I could barely do my laundry every week. Actually, I could barely *find* my laundry every week.

Charlie slid the last tray of blueberry muffins into the display case. "Traffic is picking up some. We're going through coffee like we're a camel's watering hole. I have to refill the urn three or four times a day."

I poured myself a cup out of said urn. "That makes sense. We're crowded all the time now. The free Wi-Fi did what it was supposed to do: bring them in."

"Yes, it did." The bells hanging over the front door jingled, and Lacey turned. "The problem is they're not buying anything. They drink coffee and play on their phones or laptops for hours." She left to greet the customer.

13

"You see that too, Charlie?"

He straightened the collar of his paisley shirt. "Pretty much. In fact, they're even using fresh cups for refills rather than topping off the ones they have. Plus, creamer and sugar or sweetener. Stir sticks, napkins. But I did make two dollars in tips last week." He laughed.

Not a productive way to run a business. "What if we charged for regular coffee like we do the specialty coffees? Not a lot. Only enough to cover expenses. And free refills if they use the same cup."

Lacey returned from guiding a fiftyish woman with a vanilla-blond bob to the Biography section. "What's only enough to cover expenses?"

I exchanged a glance with Charlie and took a deep breath. "We were talking about selling regular coffee instead of giving it away. Or perhaps offering freebies only to people who buy something. The way we do things now, so many people are drinking it, it's costing a fortune. If we sell it, it would offset expenses and more people might buy the specialty coffees instead."

She looked from me to Charlie, then back again. "You're not serious."

"Why not?"

"Because it's not what Aletha would've wanted."

Resting my hands on Lacey's shoulders, I said, "Aletha wanted the place to thrive. To encourage kids to read. That was the focus of the essay she wrote to win the Your Life Contest, which provided the money to open the store in the first place. The only way to achieve that goal is to make enough money to stay open. The payments from the contest aren't going to continue forever. In fact, we only have three more coming."

She stepped back. "There has to be another way."

14

I folded my arms across my chest. "I'm listening. Whatcha got?"

"Nothing right now. Give me some time to mull it over."

"Fair enough. What do you think about charging for Story Time? We had twelve kids last Saturday, which means twelve crowns, twelve boxes of crayons, and two dozen cookies. Not to mention plates and napkins. And all their parents did while you were reading was commandeer all the tables, surf their phones, and drink free coffee. We have to do *something*."

Tears pooled in Lacey's eyes. "I understand, but this isn't the answer. Aletha opened the store to turn kids on to books. That's *why* she won the contest for Pete's sake. You think people will bring their preschoolers here if they have to pay? No way. They'll take them to the library, where their children are entertained for free. And just because they don't buy anything on Saturday morning doesn't mean they don't come back later."

Savannah poked my hand and whined at my feet. I scratched her behind the ears as the storm arrived. "You're okay, little girl. Everything's all right."

Lacey squatted to rub her under the chin. Savannah licked a tear off her cheek.

I crouched beside them. "How about we table this discussion for now? See what else we can come up with. Does that work for you?"

Lacey nodded and kissed Savannah on the top of her head. "Sweet dog you have here."

"Yeah, she's sensitive like her mother."

Charlie and Lacey burst out laughing.

When Charlie moved out of earshot, Lacey took my elbow. "I don't have a pleasant way to say this, Jen, so

I'm just going to let it out. I agreed to help you make Aletha's dream a reality. I can't work here if you're going to make changes that contradict what she wanted. I'm sorry."

How can she say that? I counted to ten. Anger would help nothing.

"I understand." Losing Lacey would be a huge blow. But so would having to close the store altogether. Apparently, I had two choices: come up with a solution Lacey could live with or learn how to run the bookstore without her. Perhaps I needed to do both.

As Lacey walked away, the blond woman approached. "Hi, Jen! You don't know me, but I loved your book."

I'd never get used to being accosted by strangers after the success of my first mystery novel. "Thank you... um..."

She extended her well-manicured hand. "Lula. Lula Parsons. I'm the secretary at St. Mary's."

The Catholic Church? Nope, I definitely didn't know her. "It's very nice to meet you, Lula. I'm glad you enjoyed the book. The next one will be out in April." Might as well beat her to the question.

"That's wonderful! I can't wait to read it."

My cheeks and ears burned. At this rate, I could double as a barbecue grill next summer. "I hope you enjoy it."

"I'm sure I will. I'd better get back to George, my husband, now. He's at the diner and gets grumpy when I leave him alone in public too long." She waved and scooted out the door.

Charlie leaned on the pastry case and whispered, "You know, someone told me she had a baby in high school, and nobody knew who the father was."

16

"So what? You sound like Angus."

"He's the one who told me. I just thought it was interesting. Usually, the father's the boyfriend or something, but she didn't have one."

"What are you thinking? Immaculate conception?"

He opened his mouth to say something, then thought better of it and returned to straightening the cinnamon raisin croissants on their tray.

The rain trickled to a stop as Eric burst through the door like Clark Kent when he couldn't find a phone booth. He was a tall, scrawny redhead, who carried a freshly minted gold detective's badge from the Riddleton Police Department. And my boyfriend.

He wore a navy-blue sport jacket and slacks with his white button-down sealed at the neck by a red and blue striped tie. Opie Taylor in his Sunday-go-to-meetin' clothes. I peeked behind him, looking for Aunt Bea in her flowered hat. Nope. She must be waiting in the car.

He grabbed me around the waist, kissed me, then nuzzled my neck. "Mmmm. You smell good."

Ears burning again, I untangled myself. "I didn't know you had a shampoo fetish."

He waggled his eyebrows. "There's a lot of things you don't know about me."

"And I'm not going to find out now, in the middle of the bookstore."

"Okay. My secrets will keep." He reached for a coffee cup. "How's your day going?"

I sidestepped to allow him free access to the urn. "Not too bad. Why are you still all dressed up? I thought you were off duty after the parade."

He blew steam from the top of his drink and ventured a sip. "I was supposed to be, but something came up."

17

"Is that what Havermayer was talking to you about?"

"Yeah, there was a scuffle at the diner last night. Nobody was hurt, but Olinski told us to look into it anyway."

I refilled my cup. "A scuffle? What happened?"

He leaned in. "Marcus's old cellmate showed up, and they got into it. According to the patrol report, Marcus went over the counter after the guy, and Angus had to break it up. I haven't spoken to him yet, so I have no idea what it was about."

Funny, Angus never mentioned it. "Huh. When I first met Marcus, he told me the guy, Travis something or other, I think, had helped him survive his time at Broad River Correctional. Sounded like they were friends to me. Why is Olinski so concerned?"

"Well, for starters, Marcus is still on probation from his role in Aletha's death. If he's been hanging around with a known felon, it's a violation." He leaned on the counter and scrutinized his coffee as if the answer to my question floated in it. "I'm guessing the first thing Olinski wants to find out is if it's a continuing association or just a one-time thing."

I scowled. "No way Marcus would mess up his life. What's the deal with the other guy—Travis what's-his-name?"

"Travis Underwood. He was gone by the time the officers arrived, so no idea. I hope you're right about Marcus, though." Eric set his cup down. "Well, I'd better head over there and get his side of the story. I'll call you later."

I kissed him goodbye, waited for the butterflies in my stomach to alight, then went back to work.

I'd finished setting up the semicircle of chairs for

18

Story Time when the first kids came in. In each seat was a paper crown for them to color and wear home, along with a small box of crayons. The ten to twelve children that showed up on Saturday mornings these days were a massive boost from the one to four we'd had only a few months ago. Aletha would be thrilled. Did I dare risk mucking it up?

On the seat of Lacey's throne lay a copy of today's selection: *How to Babysit a Grandma*. The table beside it held several copies of the book for purchase by parents after the session. Maybe someday they would.

I examined the life-sized giraffes bracketing the rainbow-colored Ravenous Kids painted on the back wall.

What do we do, guys? How do we fix this?

The giraffes kept their solutions to themselves.

Lacey was right, of course. Aletha would never have agreed to the changes I'd proposed. But Aletha wasn't here now. If the store failed under her reign, she'd only have had to live with the knowledge her idea didn't work. If I failed, I had to live with the knowledge I'd let her down. A heavy burden to bear. I had to do whatever it took to ensure success.

I helped Charlie deliver cookies as the children took their seats. Savannah wandered from child to child, receiving pats and hugs while she decided which kids were likely to drop the most cookie crumbs. She settled in front of Riddleton mayor Veronica Winslow's three-year-old twin boys, Peter and Parker.

"Morning, Mayor. How are you?"

Veronica flashed her green eyes at me. "I really wish you'd stop that. I'm not the real mayor. Not yet anyway."

"Sure you are. The council selected you when the

19

last one imploded, remember? And you qualified for the runoff election."

"Of course, but I won't feel like the real mayor until I'm elected by the people. The council only picked me because they couldn't agree on anyone else. And I didn't get more than fifty percent of the votes on Election Day."

I poured her a coffee. "True, but neither did anyone else. Including Bob Yarborough. I don't think you have anything to worry about, though. Everyone I know will vote for you."

She added sweetener and cream to the cup. "Still, I have to survive Tuesday's runoff first. Bob makes some marvelous doughnuts. I'm betting he's generated quite a following."

My mouth fell open. "You honestly think people are going to cast their ballots for baked goods over common sense? You've done a lot for the town in the past five months and anybody paying any attention at all knows it."

"I'm not so sure about that, but thanks for the pep talk. And thank you for agreeing to host my party Tuesday night."

"You mean your victory celebration?"

She tucked a stray strand of auburn hair behind one ear. "I certainly hope so."

Charlie walked by on his way into the stockroom. "I'm going to take out the trash. I forgot to do it last night. Would you mind keeping an eye on the front?"

I waved goodbye to Veronica, and headed toward my office. "Sure. Just let me grab my coffee." Before I made it to my still steaming cup, however, Charlie returned.

"Hey, Jen, I can't open the back door."

"Is the lock stuck again?"

"No. I turned the knob and pushed, but it won't budge."

I followed him to the door, which led to the alley containing the dumpster. The black plastic trash bag rested on the floor. I grabbed the doorknob, which turned effortlessly, but when I tried to move the door, it resisted. "That's weird. Maybe the storm blew something against it. Let's go check it out."

He accompanied me through the store and out the front, trash bag in hand. Splashing through the remains of the brief but fierce storm, we ducked around the corner to the alley behind the building. By the time we approached the back door, my feet were soaked through. Sticking out of the alcove was a pair of legs, wearing sopping-wet jeans.

"Good grief! Somebody's leaning against it."

Charlie shook his head. "I'll roust him out." He stretched to tap one sneaker with his platform shoe. "Come on, buddy, wake up. You have to go."

I eased past him, then froze. The man's empty brown eyes stared straight ahead. His rain-soaked, white oxford had five bloody slits in the chest and abdomen, which had spread into pink stains. His face was unlined, but he had a sprinkle of gray in his tightly curled brown hair. If I had to guess, I'd say he was in his late forties.

"Charlie, he's not asleep. He's dead."

CHAPTER THREE

Charlie gawked at the body, slack-jawed, and dropped the trash bag at his feet. The plastic split and a cardboard coffee cup rolled out. On the side of the cup, facing me, Aletha sat in her chair, reading her book, with "Ravenous Readers" floating above her head. I almost heard her soothing voice saying, "It's going to be all right, Jen." Too bad I didn't believe her.

Charlie covered his mouth with a shaky hand, eyes bugging out of his head.

I froze while my stomach threatened to disgorge my breakfast. I pressed my lips together and breathed until the sensation passed. How could this be happening again?

My inner mystery writer took over. I clapped to break Charlie's trance and pointed to the cup. "Hey, pick that up before it contaminates the scene!"

His eyes widened again, and the blood drained from his face. He collected the cup and bag and deposited them in the dumpster. "Sorry. I've never seen a dead body before."

After a peek at the man's close-cropped brown hair and unblinking chestnut eyes, the picture of the last murder victim I'd discovered flashed into my brain. I swallowed back the bile rising into my throat. "Wish I could say that." I pulled my phone out of my pocket. "Do you recognize him?"

After several swallows, Charlie's mouth worked, but nothing came out.

The electronic deaths he inflicted every day in his computer games hadn't prepared him for the real thing. Then again, how many people ever saw a deceased person outside of a funeral home? Because of being pulled into two murder investigations, this was my fourth. Lucky me.

But this guy wasn't only another corpse in an alley. He was somebody's husband or father or son. Maybe all three.

Deep breath in, slow breath out.

I called 911.

A minute later, two uniformed officers bustled out the back of the police station next door. One of them was a new guy I hadn't met yet. The other was Zach Vick, son of Riddleton's former police chief, who carried a roll of crime scene tape. He nodded to me. We'd met during the investigation into his father's death last July. Actually, to be more accurate, he'd stalked me throughout. It was all good in the end, though. I found the killer and twenty-one-year-old Zach stayed out of trouble.

Zach's partner took the roll of plastic tape and gave Zach instructions I couldn't hear from where I stood. Zach herded us back to the end of the alley like a navy-blue clad Australian shepherd. The requisite cop notebook made its appearance. "Which one of you found the body?"

Charlie was still perfecting his fish imitation, so I

replied, "We both did. We came out to investigate what was blocking our back door."

"Any idea who the victim might be?"

Besides another dead person somehow connected to me? An Irish dance troupe rehearsed in my stomach, and I crossed my arms. "No. I've never seen him before. Have you, Charlie?"

He clamped his mouth closed and offered an almost imperceptible head shake. His sweat-soaked satin shirt adhered to his torso, highlighting a slightly rounded belly. Not too bad for a fella whose exercise routine consisted of gunning down imaginary enemies with his keyboard and strolling to the refrigerator for another Red Bull between rounds.

I shifted my weight from one cold, squishy Nike to the other, desperate to go home and change my shoes and socks. Not likely to happen any time soon, however.

"When did you last use this door?"

I glanced at Charlie.

He shrugged. "I'm not sure. Sometime yesterday."

Zach scribbled in his notebook. "Did you hear anything unusual out here this morning? An argument maybe?"

"No. I didn't hear a thing." My detective brain kicked in. "Are you sure he was murdered where we found him? There doesn't appear to be a lot of blood. Maybe he was brought here after the fact."

"The blood was probably washed away by the rain. But, even if that isn't what happened, why dump him here? Leaving a body right next door to the police station strikes me as someone begging to get caught."

"Beats me. Guess that's one of the things you'll have to figure out."

Zach banged his notebook closed. "All right. I'm sure the detectives will have more questions for you, so stick around. They'll be here shortly."

Goodie. Another round of Havermayer accusing me of murder. No guarantee she would, but if she followed her routine, a big red "S" for suspect was about to be painted on my forehead. Which really stank, since I'd just managed to scrape the last one off.

Charlie swayed, and his color hadn't improved, so I sent him back to the store before he passed out. The dance troupe in my belly broke into a new number, and Jell-O had replaced my legs, but I was stable compared to my previous experience finding a corpse. At least it wasn't someone I knew this time. That helped too.

Eric hopscotched around the puddles down the alleyway from the diner. I suspected his loafers weren't much better at keeping his feet dry than my Nikes. Likely he missed his duty boots right about now. And the thick wool socks he wore with them. I doubted he'd be willing to give up his promotion to get them back, though. Nor should he, since he seemed born to be a detective. Of course, that could simply be my pride talking.

He smiled discreetly and waved at me, slid under the crime scene tape, and approached the legs jutting out of the tiny alcove. Zach handed him an evidence bag that appeared to contain a scrap of paper, although I couldn't tell for sure from the wrong side of the yellow line. Eric glanced at it, then stared, slack-jawed, in my direction. I waved. He jutted his chin and flashed a smile, which quickly faded as he examined the man propped against the door.

Zach's report complete, Eric carried the bag to where I stood. "What do you make of this?" he asked and showed me the plastic sack.

Scrawled haphazardly across the torn scrap of notebook paper was:

JEN DAWSON
RAVENOUS READERS.

"Where did it come from?"

"Zach discovered it in the man's shirt pocket. You sure you've never met him?"

This is crazy! Why would a murder victim have my name in his pocket?

"Positive. But this might explain why there's no blood at the scene."

"How so?"

"He could've been knifed someplace else and managed to stagger here to find me before he died."

Eric ran a hand over his orange buzz cut. "More likely the rain rinsed it away. Along with any other evidence, I suspect. The man was stabbed five times. That means a whole lot of blood loss. He couldn't have gotten very far."

I agreed. Eric was thinking like a detective. As much as I hated to admit it, Havermayer was training him well. "Something to keep in mind, though."

"Right now we're looking at it as a robbery gone wrong since he doesn't have a wallet or phone, but don't worry, we'll investigate all possibilities. And when I say 'we,' I mean the police department. You have to stay out of this one." He held my gaze.

"Of course." No chance I'd involve myself this time.

Interfering in police investigations was like scraping away with a dull razor, and I'd already had too many close shaves.

Charlie came around the building carrying two cups. His color had returned, and he no longer appeared on the verge of collapse. He offered me a coffee. "What're you looking at?"

"Thank you." I showed him the slip of paper.

"Whoa! Where did this come from, and what would he want with you?" He took the bag for a closer look. "That handwriting is sort of familiar. I'm sure I've seen it before."

Eric retrieved his notebook from his inside jacket pocket. "Do you remember where?"

"Not off the top of my head, but it'll come to me. Let me think on it a while."

"Don't think too long. Havermayer's going to want answers when she gets here."

Charlie scrunched his eyebrows together. "Well, I can't give her what I don't have. And no amount of bullying is going to help. I'll let *you* know as soon as I figure it out."

As if they'd spoken her name three times into a mirror, Detective Havermayer appeared on the police station steps. She turned her head, and her gaze bored into me. No point in trying to hide. She could spot me at the Macy's Thanksgiving Day parade.

Havermayer descended the stairs and strode to where Zach, still combing the body for clues, dropped something else into a plastic bag. He handed it to her, and she held it up, turning the sack one way and then the other. She patted him on the shoulder and headed in our direction. Lovely to learn she could be friendly

27

when she wanted. I'd never experienced that side of her myself. Probably never would.

Her immaculate black suit and crisp white blouse sheathed her in a cloak of professionalism. Until she opened her mouth. "I should've known you would beat me here, Jen. If there's a murder victim around, you're never far away."

I felt the big red "S" reappearing on my forehead. "Happy to see you too, Detective. And someone dumped the body at my back door. If I hadn't beaten you to it, you wouldn't even know it was here."

Havermayer narrowed her eyes. "Do you recognize this?" She displayed the bag containing a small rectangular bottle of clear liquid Zach had given her.

"No. We don't sell anything like that in the bookstore. Check with Bannister's Bar and Grill. Could be a shot of vodka or something."

"All their liquor has to be consumed on the premises."

Charlie gulped his coffee. "I have an idea what it is," he said in a tiny voice. "It's holy water from St. Mary's. It usually has a label, though. I guess it fell off."

We all turned to stare at him.

He raised his hands. "What? I grew up Catholic. Every time we relocated, my mother would collect some of the stuff from the local priest and sprinkle it around the house to drive out the evil spirits. She brought me an identical bottle when I moved into my apartment. I still have it somewhere."

"Can we take a look at it?"

"Sure, no problem."

Havermayer sent Eric and Charlie to retrieve the holy water from Charlie's apartment in the same building as mine. I hoped, for his sake, Charlie's apartment wasn't as cluttered. If he couldn't find his bottle, Havermayer might use that as an excuse to treat him as a person of interest, even though he was the one who had brought it up in the first place.

Chief Olinski came down the steps as Havermayer dispatched Zach and his partner to interview the people in the bookstore. I couldn't imagine any of them being involved, but the detective followed the rulebook religiously. It was one reason she hated me so much. Playing by the rules was never one of my finer attributes. I wouldn't call myself reckless, but she treated me like a cliff diver who'd never learned how to swim.

Hands stuffed in his pants pockets, Olinski sauntered in my direction. The four gold stars on each side of his navy-blue shirt collar glittered in the sunlight finally peeking through the clouds. Unlike the wrinkled suits he wore as a detective, his uniform was starched and pressed, a knife-edge running down his trousers. He must've fallen into Havermayer's mangle iron.

Olinski and I had a tangled history, beginning as the couple most likely to marry after high school and ending with him as my best friend Brittany's boyfriend. However, we'd moved past the he-hated-my-guts-for-refusing-to-marry-him stage last year and now maintained a civil, bordering on friendly, relationship.

"Hey, Jen. Found yourself another one, I see." His mouth smiled, but his eyes didn't.

"More like stumbled over. Not exactly what I had scheduled for my day." I studied the scuffs on my sopping-wet Nikes. "I think a finder's fee is in order, don't you?"

"Not really." His gaze caught mine. "It looks like a

29

botched robbery, so, you're going to stay out of this one, right?"

"That's the plan."

"Good. Keep it that way." He turned and trudged back to the station.

He came outside just to tell me that? I'd have thought the chief of police would have better things to do. Not Olinski, though. He'd take advantage of any opportunity to put me in what he considered my place. However, my place was wherever I said it was, whether he liked it or not.

When Ingrid, wearing her proverbial medical examiner hat this time, came around the corner to examine the deceased, I intercepted her. "Busy day, huh?"

"Unfortunately, yes. How are you holding up, luv?"

I rubbed the back of my neck while the dancers in my belly took up clogging. "As well as you might expect. Getting a little annoyed with tripping over dead bodies." I attempted a smile. "I don't have your fascination with them."

"Ingrid!" Havermayer called from beside the body. "Over here."

We exchanged glances, and Ingrid dipped under the tape. I followed, and she stopped me. "Not this time, luv. You're a person of interest."

"I guess that means I can't observe the autopsy either."

"Afraid not. You sure you don't have a fascination for dead bodies?" Ingrid laughed as she set her bag down next to the body and went to work.

The police combed through the newly vacated store for the second time in a little over a year. So much for our Saturday sales. Sunday, too, probably. What did they expect to find? We found the guy outside, and whoever he was, he had nothing to do with Ravenous Readers. If they believed it was only a robbery, they had no reason to search my store. However, he had that paper with my name on it in his pocket. Was that why someone killed him? To keep him away from me?

Ridiculous. The only thing that note accomplished was giving Havermayer another opportunity to be wrong about me being involved in a murder. I'd think she'd be tired of that game by now.

On the other hand, I always ended up in the middle of these things. Perhaps she figured sooner or later she'd be right.

Except I had no intention of ever being in a position where I had to kill someone again. The one time I'd taken a life was when Aletha's killer tried to kill me, too. Even Detective Starchy hadn't been able to argue with the district attorney's determination. I suspect she tried everything she could think of, though.

Meanwhile, each hour the store remained closed diminished our chances of having better sales in December than in November. With luck, it would only be a day or two. I'd been looking forward to helping people pick out the perfect gifts for their reading relatives.

I headed back to my office and opened my laptop. Havermayer had let Charlie and Lacey leave, but I was stuck here for the duration. Might as well try to make the best of it. I pulled up the "Untitled" file and stared at the flashing cursor under Chapter One.

Various permutations of the first line of my new novel ran laps around my head. It was a subject I'd contemplated for much of the last two weeks without success. This was supposed to be the third book of the *Davenport Twins Mysteries* series, and I remained mired in the Wambaw Swamp, keeping an eye out for alligators.

Savannah dozed in her bed beside my chair. I suspected she'd be the only one getting any sleep tonight. If the past was any example, my dreams would be filled with grotesque amalgamations of all the dead bodies I'd seen in the last year plus.

The police were finishing up when Eric tapped on the doorframe of my office. "I almost forgot to tell you. I was going to make a reservation at that fancy restaurant in Blackburn for your birthday. You know, the one in the old train station? What do you think?"

Crap. That was the place guys took their girlfriends to propose. He couldn't be planning something like that, could he? I wasn't ready.

Nah. He probably only wanted to take me someplace nice for my birthday.

However, I couldn't take that chance.

I wiped my palms on my jeans. "Listen, we don't have to do anything special. Let's grab a burger and watch a movie, okay?" Exactly what we always did. "Or we could go to Sutton for Chinese. What do you think about that?"

He twisted his lips and studied the scuffs on the tops of his shoes. "If that's what you really want to do. I'm trying to do something romantic, and I feel like you're pushing me away."

"I know. I'm sorry. I don't know why I do that." I cared about him and wanted to be closer to him, but every time he stepped toward me, I stepped back. What was I afraid of? Another relationship disaster. My track record was unimpressive. Three boyfriends, three catastrophes, three heartbreaks. Three strikes and you're out, right? I took his hands and gazed into his emerald eyes. "I swear I'm trying, but when we get close, I panic and bolt. Please, give me a little more time."

He sighed, kissed my cheek, and strode out the door. *Way to go, Jen.*

CHAPTER FOUR

Sunday morning dawned cloudy and gray, the wet air drilling into my bones like a dentist run amok. I huddled in my jacket. Savannah pranced and dawdled by turns as I shivered around the block. Today was an inside day.

The police search ended late in the afternoon yesterday, having produced zero results. I still couldn't fathom what they'd expected to find. Simply because the guy carried a slip of paper with my name in his pocket didn't mean I had anything to do with his death. What did they think? I murdered him in the bookstore and then dragged him outside to point the finger at myself anyway? Havermayer probably ordered the search to annoy me. Wouldn't put anything past her. I'd still love to know why she hated me so much.

I could blame no one but myself, though. I'd agreed to the search. It seemed the easiest way to get Havermayer off my back. Given the mess they left behind, I should probably rethink that strategy next time. Better yet, I should skip the "next time" altogether.

I turned my coffee sweet and beige as Savannah scarfed down her breakfast, then sat by her bowl and begged for more. Oliver Twist in a German shepherd suit. A visible ribcage had replaced her Mount Whitney-sized puppy belly, but the vet, Dr. Felton, assured me she'd fill out soon. With luck, before someone called the ASPCA. I saved my grocery receipts just in case.

Desperate for a distraction from the whole found-another-dead-guy situation, I grabbed my "Creativity Begins With Coffee" mug, settled at my desk, and opened my laptop. The blank page with Chapter One at the top appeared on the screen. The flashing cursor beneath taunted me. Perhaps I needed to give up on a perfect first line for the moment. One would come eventually. Or not. Either way, there'd be an opening sentence. Just not necessarily the eye-popper I'd hoped for.

In *Twin Terror*, the teenage stars of my mystery series, Dana and Daniel Davenport, had buried their father, brought his killer to justice, and begun their freshman year of college. In book three, they would embark on their latest adventure when a classmate was murdered on Homecoming weekend. But first, I had to get them there.

Of course, I could just write the pep rally scene where the murder occurred since I knew what would happen, and fill in the rest later. Whatever I needed to do to put words on the page. I'd spent enough time staring at blank screens writing the last book to consume my entire lifetime allotment.

Perhaps I should randomly type and see what came out. A little free association. *Who knows?* I could channel Edgar Allan Poe. Better yet, Agatha Christie. Or both. That might be interesting. *The Telltale Heart* starring Hercule Poirot and Miss Jane Marple. Nobody had to know they weren't twins.

Get serious, Jen.

Even though no official deadline existed, the publisher wouldn't trust me to finish the project if the first draft wasn't written when the second book came out. I'd let them down continually while writing that one. Not this time, though. This time, I had my life under control. Nothing would stand in my way.

A sea of blue and yellow filled the parking lot outside the football stadium. Dana wrapped her jacket tightly around her against the chilly October evening and wondered how on earth Daniel had convinced her to accompany him to the homecoming pep rally. Her twin could be quite persuasive when he wanted to be. Dana would much rather be curled up in front of the fire with Harry Potter, sipping chamomile tea made from Mrs. Barlow's secret recipe.

Where was her brother? He'd disappeared into the crowd the moment they'd arrived. She craned her neck, trying to spot him. It should be relatively easy as he stood head and shoulders above most of their classmates. Including her. Dana rose on her tiptoes, then

My phone rang. I had to learn to put the thing on silent while working. I picked it up, and MOM split the screen. Our weekly Sunday morning call.

"Hi, Mom! How are you?"

She sighed. "Not bad. A little tired. How's my favorite granddaughter?"

I rolled my eyes and shook my head. "Savannah's fine. She's sleeping off her breakfast on the couch."

"That's my girl. Just like her mother."

"I don't nap nearly as often as I used to, thank you very much. How's Gary?" My stepfather was diagnosed with colon cancer last summer.

"He's having a decent day today."

During surgery, the doctors had found the cancer had spread to his liver. "His chemo is going well?"

"He's managing. We won't be able to tell if the treatment is working for a few more weeks, but the doctor is optimistic."

"Terrific! You should try to get a little rest while he's feeling better."

"I want to spend as much time with him as I can."

She loved him. If only I could share the sentiment. I'd come a long way, however. At least I didn't actively hate him anymore. Not that he didn't deserve it after the way he'd treated me when I was growing up.

Why couldn't I forgive him? Perhaps it was things like when he'd grounded me for two weeks because Brittany and I had dinner before going to the movies when we'd told him we'd see the film first. We'd missed the beginning and went to the second showing instead. *Big deal*.

Of course, there was also the time he locked me in my room for six hours because his grilled-cheese sandwich was too brown on one side. He remembered to let me out just before my mother got home, though.

Mom continued, "Why don't you bring Savannah over and spend the afternoon with us? We can have a cook out and watch movies. You always enjoyed those old pictures he loves."

Not always. It depended on how many beers he'd had. "I'll think about it, Mom. I need to write, and I have a lunch date with Eric."

"How is he? You know I really like him. I think he's good for you. Not like those other boys you've dated."

Boys? Come on, Mom, I'm almost thirty. My stomach sank at that thought. "That's true, he's a sweetheart." I'd had only three other relationships in my whole life. All miserable failures. Sometimes I wondered if the issue was me. As much as I'd like to believe myself blameless, the problem couldn't possibly be all of *them*.

That might be the reason I couldn't commit to Eric. I was protecting myself from another potential romantic catastrophe. However, keeping up my defenses could end up causing the relationship failure I was so desperately trying to avoid by pushing Eric so far away he might not come back. A no-win situation.

"I'll tell you what. Let me do some work and maybe we'll come by this afternoon."

"Please try. We need to talk about what we're going to do for your birthday. We can have a party. Invite all your friends."

"I'm not in high school anymore."

"No kidding. Grown people enjoy birthday parties too."

Grown people. When did I become a grown-up? Next Sunday when I turned thirty. "I'll think about it. Besides, there's a lot going on around here right now."

"You mean the man they found dead yesterday?"

The gossip train had already run off the rails. "Among other things."

"What does that have to do with you?"

"Hard to say at this point. We discovered him leaning against the back door of the bookstore, and he carried a slip of paper with my name in his pocket. The police think he was robbed and fought back, but clearly, I'm involved somehow. I'm not sure how yet."

"You have nothing to worry about, right? You didn't kill him." She coughed into the phone. "You're not thinking about playing detective again, are you? Remember what happened last time. You got kidnapped, for God's sake! And the time before, you almost drowned."

"I remember. And no, I'm not jumping into it." *Assuming I'm not already involved.* "I won't get the full picture until we figure out who sent him to find me and why."

"You mean when the police find out, right?"

"Of course. Why do you say that?"

"You said 'we.'"

I stared at the ceiling in exasperation. "It's only a figure of speech."

"All right. Go do your writing so you can have dinner with us. Gary would love to see you."

Ha! "In other words, he'd love to see Savannah."

"She makes him happy." Mom sniffled.

My heart melted. "I know she does. We'll come by later, okay?"

"Thank you."

I laid the phone down on the desk and held my head in my hands. If Savannah could bring a dying man a little joy, I'd take her. On second thoughts, I could call an Uber for her. However, my stepfather might not send her home again. I'd have to go, if for no other reason than to ensure I got my baby back.

I turned to my computer, reread the last few lines of the manuscript, and finished the final sentence where I'd left off when my mother interrupted me. I had to apply myself. I had to be a disciplined writer this time. No matter what.

Two more pages hit the "saved" file by the time I needed to put myself together for lunch with Eric. We'd first planned to go to Sutton, but after yesterday's events, we decided to stay in town. He had to remain available for the investigation. It was just as well. I wanted to catch up on my writing since I'd finally gotten started.

I threw on jeans and a baby-blue blouse, then fussed with my cowlick-riddled hair to no avail. No matter how many times I combed and brushed, wetted, combed, and brushed again, the strands still stuck up everywhere. So, I dabbed on some gel and ran my fingers through it to give the appearance I'd stuck my tongue into an outlet. If you can't fix it, make it look like you did it on purpose.

When I came out of the bathroom, Savannah waited by the front door, so I clipped on her leash, and we toured the neighborhood. Not quite what she had in mind, but no way she'd be allowed to join us on a crowded Sunday afternoon. Angus would likely have a doggy bag made up for her by the time I was ready to return home, though. That would take the sting out of my leaving her behind. I dropped her back, then tossed her a chew stick to keep her spirits up until I got home again.

I strolled through the chilly, damp air down Main Street toward the diner on the corner of Pine. The Goodwill store encompassing the entire block between Oak and Pine had jumped into the Christmas contest fray with a window depicting Santa rolling a bowling ball toward ten elves lined up as pins. Mrs. Claus cheered him on, and Rudolph, Dasher, and Prancer held balls, awaiting their turns. A Muzak rendition of "Silent

Night" spewed from an outdoor speaker, and on the sidewalk in front of the store, a Salvation Army Santa huddled next to his donation pot, hands stuffed in his pockets, too cold to ring his bell.

In the warmth of the restaurant, Eric had somehow secured a corner booth under retro posters of a woman holding a pack of Virginia Slims, with the words: "You've Come A Long Way, Baby!" on one wall and an early model Mustang convertible racing a horse across the desert on the other. I loved that car. Maybe someday when I was rich and famous I'd buy one. *In my dreams.*

A grin lit up his face as I meandered through the tables draped with garlands and filled with folks looking to recharge after church.

I dropped onto the bench across from him. "How'd you manage to snag a corner booth? This place is packed."

He tugged on the lapels of his sport jacket. "I know the owner. He hooked me up."

My chest filled with warmth. "Nothing like a man with connections!" I glanced at Angus behind the counter, directing his staff through their Sunday symphony. "I guess Havermayer's already put you to work today."

"The autopsy results came in. I went over them with Ingrid."

"Anything interesting?"

Eric sipped his water. "What we expected. Exsanguination caused by being stabbed five times. She did rule out robbery, though."

He bled to death. No surprise there. "Oh? How?"

"I can't say. Something she found in the autopsy."

41

Curious. "Now we need to determine who cut him and why."

"What do you mean 'we'?"

Him too? "I didn't mean it that way. Relax. *You* have to figure it out. Better?"

"Much." He pulled a couple of menus from the holder, handed me one, and glanced at his. "What're you going to have?"

Finally, someone who didn't assume I'd order the same thing I always did. Now I had to prove him right. "Excellent question. What's the lunch special today?"

He waved his menu to catch Angus's eye. "Let's find out."

Angus nodded and sent over Penelope, who extolled the virtues of the chicken-fried chicken patty smothered in white gravy. My cholesterol went up ten points just listening to her. We chose bacon cheeseburgers and fries instead. Not much better health-wise, but infinitely more satisfying to my taste buds. And the same thing I usually ordered without ordering "the usual." Win-win.

Penelope returned with my Mountain Dew, and I savored the first sip, letting the syrupy sweetness roll around my tongue. The kick would come later as the caffeine did its job. "Did Ingrid find anything else noteworthy this morning? What kind of blade was used?"

"It was about five inches long and thin, like a steak knife, only not serrated."

"Nothing unusual. Sounds like a crime of opportunity. The killer grabbed the first thing handy."

"That's a bit of a leap. I didn't say it *was* a steak knife, only that it was like one. He could've brought the knife with him. Besides..." Eric took a long swallow of his Pepsi and shook his head. "Never mind. Forget I said anything."

"What?"

He sighed. "Ingrid did find something strange, but we're not releasing the information to the public. I can't tell you."

"Seriously? I'm your girlfriend, not some bum on the street."

Penelope brought our food, and we added ketchup and salt to all the proper places.

Eric swallowed his first fry, then said, "You're just going to ask Ingrid, aren't you?"

"Yup."

"What if she doesn't tell you?"

I shrugged. "Then she doesn't tell me. It's not like I'm going to run off and investigate this thing, but anyone would be curious. Especially a mystery writer." I dunked a fry into my puddle of ketchup. "Of course, you guys need to solve this fast. As long as people think I might be involved, my store is losing business."

"What do you mean?"

"The guy was found propped against my back door. He had my name and the name of the bookstore in his pocket. People are assuming we had something to do with his death, which will most likely hurt our sales."

He smirked. "That's ridiculous."

"Is it? You know how people think."

"Either way, my telling you what Ingrid discovered won't alter that."

"True." I attempted a beguiling smile and waggled my eyebrows. "But it would make me happy."

Eric guffawed, spraying a half-chewed French fry onto the table.

43

So much for beguiling.

When he controlled himself, he took my hands and said, "Let's change the subject. Have you given any more thought to how you want to celebrate your birthday?"

Here we go again. "Yes. I'm going to find a cave to hide in until it's over. Maybe I'll draw stick figures on the wall for future generations to interpret."

"What's the big deal? Your birthday comes around every December. Why's this one such a problem?"

The number thirty attached to it. "Nothing. I don't understand what all the hoopla is about. If it's just another birthday, why not treat it that way?"

"What do you mean?"

Penelope caught my eye. I held up my empty glass for a refill.

"My mother wants to throw me a party. Last year, she almost forgot my birthday altogether, and this year she wants a big to-do. What's up with that?"

He shook his head. "You need to ask? She loves you."

"So, she didn't love me last year?"

He sighed. "No question she did. But, perhaps, with your stepfather being sick and all, she's realized how important family is. Did you ever think of that?"

More like she's ready for grandchildren. "Yes. Well, no. It never occurred to me. You think that's what happened?"

I waited while Penelope swapped my empty glass for a full one and left the check near the edge of the table.

"No idea. Definitely something to think about, though."

My top teeth trapped my lower lip. "Fine, I'll think about it. Will you come?"

44

"Sure, if I'm invited."

"Of course you are. Why wouldn't you be?"

He shrugged and studied his fingernails. A ping from his phone interrupted us. He glanced at the screen and looked up at me.

"What's going on?"

"The victim's been identified as Travis Underwood."

My mouth fell open. "Marcus's cellmate?"

"One and the same."

My stomach dropped as I swung my head toward the grill where Marcus was loading hamburger patties. His simple new life was about to become a little more complicated.

CHAPTER FIVE

I wanted to ask Marcus about his friend, but the restaurant remained way too busy, so I headed for the bookstore. The police search had left a mess, though nowhere near as bad as last time. When investigating Aletha's murder, the cops had torn the place apart, searching for clues to her killer. Her husband, Tim, and I had spent several hours putting everything right again. That was my first experience with a homicide investigation. An event I'd hoped never to repeat. No such luck.

This time, I wasn't sure what they were looking for in Ravenous Readers. Despite the note in his pocket, Travis Underwood had never entered the store, that I knew of, and I'd never met him.

No telling with Havermayer, though. If her sole purpose was to irritate me, she had succeeded. As usual. My office and the stockroom got the worst of it. The two places Travis was the least likely to have been, but the most likely places to find evidence if one of us had killed him. They confiscated the computer again, but we didn't use it much day-to-day. They'd bring it back eventually. Until then, we'd muddle through.

I sorted through the morass of papers on the desk to determine whether anything was missing. Truth be told, though, it seemed much the same as normal. Little chance I'd notice what they'd taken. Guess I'd find out when they brought it back. Perhaps they'd pay the bills for me.

The absent computer got my brain hamsters running on their wheels. We rarely used the thing, but what if we devoted our website to more than advertising our location and listing our inventory? What if we sold books on it too? We could even sell on eBay or Amazon. I kept an underutilized computer geek on staff already. Time to put Charlie to work. Lacey couldn't possibly object, could she? I'd find out tomorrow.

Aletha had asked a lot when she left me the bookstore. I knew nothing about running a business. And, although she never said as much, I felt the need to run it the way she would have, without knowing what changes she might've made along the way. A frustrating endeavor, given the adjustments necessary to make the store successful. No point in worrying about it now. When I'd accepted the keys, I'd accepted the responsibility.

I arranged the clutter into piles to deal with later. My standard cleaning routine. Scotch tape reattached the posters to the wall where the police had pulled them down to examine behind them. They were thorough, if nothing else. They'd also removed the desk drawers and riffled through the file cabinets. I put everything back into its typical chaotic order, then moved on to the stockroom.

Books covered every inch of the shelves, and the empty cartons they'd come out of lay everywhere. I carefully repacked them one by one, swept the floor, and took out the trash. At least there were no surprises in the alley this time. The crime scene tape remained in place, and I slid under it to reach the dumpster, sorry I didn't get to see Havermayer riffling through the refuse without getting dirty. She probably palmed the chore off on Eric, though. Another rookie detective task.

I gave up on cleaning at three, and figured Marcus might be available to talk, so I wandered back to the diner. He was leaning on the counter, deep in conversation with Ingrid, no more than six inches between their faces. The way they stared into each other's eyes spoke volumes. I hesitated to interrupt.

"Hey, Jen! I didn't expect you to show up here again today."

I turned to see Angus removing his condiment-splattered apron.

"I wanted to chat with Marcus if he had a spare a minute, but I see he's busy."

"He's always busy these days. Can't say I blame him, though. She's smart, attractive, and kind-hearted. He could do a whole lot worse." Angus winked.

"No doubt. Then again, so could she." Marcus—tall, and slim but muscular, with close-cropped hair and a pencil-thin mustache, which gave him a dignified aura—seemed a perfect match for Ingrid's down-to-earth personality.

Angus patted the counter. "Have a seat. I'll bring you something to drink."

I slid onto the stool two down from Ingrid. They had to come up for air sooner or later.

Ingrid broke first, resting her hand on mine. "Hullo, luv. How are you?"

"Not too bad." Eric had told me during lunch she'd

spent the morning autopsying Travis, but if I asked about the results, she'd shut me down. Daniel Davenport, the social twin, would make conversation and hope she brought the subject up herself. I followed his lead. "Just finished cleaning up the bookstore after the police search yesterday."

Angus returned with my Dew. "Did you enjoy your lunch with Eric?"

"How are things going with you two?" Ingrid asked.

"Not too bad. We're taking it slow."

Angus barked a laugh. "Slow? More like glacial."

My ears fired up again. The coals should be almost ready. "That's not true."

"Oh yeah? When was the last time you had a proper date?"

"Define proper."

"You know, dress up in fancy clothes and go someplace other than your apartment or his to eat something besides a hamburger you picked up from me on the way home."

"Since Antonio's closed, there isn't anywhere in Riddleton to eat besides here, and Eric's too tired at the end of the day to go to Sutton or Blackburn. Detective Havermayer's his trainer, and she's running him ragged."

Ingrid smiled. "Poor chap got promoted into being a rookie again, didn't he? That must be such a bee in his bonnet after all this time."

"Exactly. She's got him doing everything. You just can't give some people power. Especially Detective Starchy."

"Detective Starchy?"

"That's what I call Havermayer. She could fall into

a pigsty and come out without a speck of mud on her clothes. Stiff as an ironing board, with the personality to match."

"What does the chief say about it?"

"Eric hasn't talked to Chief Olinski. He says that's the way it is when you're training someone. He used to break in the new patrol officers and gave them all the grunt work, too. I guess he had the same philosophy as Havermayer."

I poked at the ice in my glass with the straw. Angus got the hint and poured me another.

Ingrid examined me thoughtfully. "You know, I don't believe this has anything to do with Eric being too tired. I think the problem is you."

I scowled. "What are you talking about? I'm perfectly happy with Eric."

"My point exactly. The only way to be perfectly happy in a relationship is to not really be in it."

"What are you saying?"

"You're bricking it, luv. Scared to death of being vulnerable."

Seriously? Did everyone think they knew me? "Can we please change the subject?" I hated when my friends ganged up on me. Especially when they might be right.

Ingrid and Angus exchanged glances.

"Eric told me you finished the autopsy this morning." Ingrid tugged down her pale-green scrub top. "Did you know Mr. Underwood?"

"No, we'd never met." I glanced at Marcus. "At least not while he lived."

Marcus grabbed a towel and wiped the counter beside Ingrid's teacup, his liquid-brown eyes moist. "He was my friend."

Ingrid took his hand and squeezed.

He stopped cleaning and lowered his head. "The last thing I told him was get out and don't come back. Then I tried to hit him."

"What were you two fighting about last night?" I asked in a low voice.

"It was stupid. Something that happened in prison years ago. He dragged it up again for some reason."

"Can you tell us about it?" Ingrid asked.

"Nothing to talk about. It was an incident when I was at Broad River I had nothing to do with, but he bothered me about it anyway. I don't even understand why he decided to bring up ancient history like that."

I took a swallow of Mountain Dew. "Do you have any idea why someone would want to kill him?"

Marcus shook his head. "No, unless he brought up the past to the wrong person."

"What do you mean?"

"Travis was in for a long time. He saw a lot and heard a lot. Made some friends and a bunch of enemies. Maybe he approached somebody else with something they didn't wanna discuss after he got out. He knew too many secrets. Some people might not've appreciated that very much."

Ingrid and I exchanged glances. Marcus wasn't making a whole lot of sense at the moment.

I asked Ingrid, "Did the autopsy tell you anything interesting?"

She shook her short, loose curls. "Nothing I can disclose, but I can say, he wasn't murdered by some random ex-con with a beef. Unless the ex-con happened to be some kind of medical professional. Does that ring any bells with you, Marcus?"

"A couple of doctors passed through during Travis's time, but not while I shared a cell with him. I remember him telling me they mostly kept to themselves. Didn't bother nobody. He certainly didn't mention trouble with either of them."

"Would he have told you if he had?" I asked.

"I don't see why not. We told each other everything. Lots of time to kill, you know?" He flashed his perfect, white teeth.

I suspected that while Marcus told Travis everything, the street might've only run one way. "Why was Travis in prison, Marcus?"

He frowned. "Manslaughter, but he was innocent."

Ingrid sipped her tea. "Don't they all say that?"

"*I* never did, but a lot of guys do. I believed Travis, though. Somebody killed his girlfriend one night after he dropped her off at home. He was the last one to see her, and he didn't have an alibi, so they came at him hard. Kept him in a freezing room for eighteen hours with no food or water until he finally told them what they wanted to hear. They wouldn't even let him go to the bathroom."

"Couldn't his lawyer get the confession thrown out?" I asked.

"He couldn't afford no *good* lawyer, so he got a public defender. The dude had never tried a murder case before, and the prosecutor wouldn't deal since Travis confessed. Travis never stood a chance. The jury took two hours to convict him. And probably only that long because they wanted the free lunch. He got twenty years, and he got out on parole after fifteen."

I could say nothing about a failing criminal justice system where things like that happened more often than we wanted to admit. Or even knew about. "I'm sorry, Marcus. It sounds like he was a good guy who got a bad deal."

Marcus shook his head. "You know what the worst thing is? Before we started arguing last night, Travis told me he thought he'd found out who really killed his girlfriend. He heard somebody else confessed, and the Blackburn cops didn't check into it because they'd already closed the case. They didn't care that Travis might be innocent. He said he was gonna do something about it. I tried to talk him out of it, but he wouldn't listen."

Huh. Perhaps Travis confronted the real murderer, and the guy silenced him. Or worse, what if one of the police officers had shut Travis up to cover his mistake? A possibility I didn't want to examine too closely.

"I hope you told all this to the police."

"I did, but I'm not sure they believed me."

Savannah leaped with joy when I got home, and while she no longer had razor-sharp puppy teeth, keeping extremities out of the way remained a good idea. I put my hand out, palm down to claim my space, and she turned circles, propelled by her wagging tail, instead of trying to touch my chin with her nose. Whoever invented dog training deserved a Nobel Peace Prize. Life was certainly a lot more peaceful around here than it used to be.

We headed out into the dense, damp chill for a walk, only long enough to take care of business. The sun had deigned to show itself at last as the clouds drifted apart without having unleashed any rain. No complaints from me. Winter storms led my top ten list of things I'd happily live without forever.

While Savannah scratched and sniffed at the base of

her go-to oak, I mulled over my conversation with Ingrid and Marcus. Why did Ingrid ask Marcus about doctors? She clearly believed Travis was murdered by a medical professional. What did she find to lead her to that conclusion? Something about the injuries, probably. Perhaps the killer left a sponge in one of the wounds.

Safely back in our well-heated apartment, Savannah snagged her favorite stuffed monkey and ran the Riddleton 500: around the living room, down the hall to the bedroom, across the bed, back down the hall, and around the living room again. And again. And again. Almost knocking over my tabletop Christmas tree on the last lap. I retreated to the safety of the kitchen and grabbed a Mountain Dew out of the fridge, feeling sorry for the guy who lived directly below us. He'd never complained, though. He must be hard of hearing.

Tongue hanging out of her mouth, sides heaving, Savannah skidded sideways into my shins and dropped the toy on my Nike with a grunt.

"Had enough, little girl?"

She slid down to the cool linoleum, a puddle of drool collecting between her front paws. One spot that no longer needed mopping. I tossed her a treat and carried my drink to the desk, Ingrid's questions ricocheting around my skull.

I tried every permutation of "why would a medical examiner believe a victim was stabbed by a doctor" that came to mind. All I got was: how to defend against a knife attack, how to hold a knife, and a litany of individual cases, none of which applied. Perhaps I could somehow convince Ingrid to tell me what she'd found. Not an easy feat, I suspected. She was tight-lipped as a clam when she wanted to be.

It was just as well. I needed to stay out of the investigation. What began as idle curiosity often pulled me into deep water, and I didn't swim well. It didn't matter what Ingrid meant. I'd let her and the detectives fight that out. I would mind my own business and focus on my book and bookstore. I refused to put myself or Savannah in jeopardy anymore.

Might as well head over to Mom's and give Gary some extra time with Savannah. Something constructive to do. I called to see if she wanted me to pick anything up on the way.

She answered on the first ring. "Hi, honey. I can't talk right now."

My belly flipped. "What's going on?"

"We're at the hospital. Gary started throwing up and couldn't stop."

"I'll head over to keep you company."

"No, don't bother. They gave him something that appears to be working. I think they're going to admit him overnight to keep an eye on him."

"Are you sure you don't need me to bring you anything? Some food? Clothes?"

"I've been keeping a bag packed for emergencies, and I'll grab something to eat in the cafeteria. I have everything I need."

"Okay. If you think of something, call me."

"I will."

I set the phone down and looked at Savannah, stretched out on the couch. "Well, kid, seems like we've got some free time on our hands."

She yawned and covered her eyes with her paw. I was on my own.

Voices in the hall outside my door drew my attention

an instant before the knock. The door opened as I got there, and Brittany poked her head in, blocking the opening against the yipping and wagging dog.

"Hey, we stopped for barbecue in Sutton and ended up with a bunch more than we can eat. You hungry?" She shook her head. "Silly question. You're always hungry. Come on over and hang out with us. We're just gonna watch a movie and chill. Savannah's invited for cleanup, of course."

Did I want to spend the evening with Brittany and my ex-boyfriend Olinski? The enticing aroma of barbecue wafted into my apartment, making my mouth water. "Sure, why not? We'll be over in a sec. Need me to bring anything?"

"Just whatever you want to drink."

"Be there in a minute."

Brittany left and closed the door.

Did I really want to do this? It should be fine, though. Olinski and I had called a truce for Brittany's sake. We could have a nice, relaxing evening together as friends.

"Come on, little girl. Let's go get some grub."

Her ears perked, and she bolted toward the door, paws barely touching the floor.

CHAPTER SIX

I tapped on Brittany's door and walked in with Savannah on my heels. Brittany and Olinski were in the kitchen, holding hands and gazing into each other's eyes over the Styrofoam containers dotting the counter. I could grab the food and leave, and they'd never notice. My stomach clenched. Jealous? Of what?

Brittany would always be my friend, no matter what. Our friendship began the first day of kindergarten when the teacher sat us beside each other. If she hadn't dumped me by now, she never would. And no doubt I wasn't interested in rekindling my relationship with Olinski. So, what was my problem?

I killed time checking out Brittany's Christmas decorations. A six-foot tree filled one corner, and she'd covered it with lights, tinsel, and every ornament she'd ever had, including the giant book-on-a-hook her father had given her when she was ten. She knew even then she'd spend her life surrounded by books. On the table beside the tree rested the hand-painted nativity scene she'd purchased at the Christmas bazaar at St. Mary's last year.

The distraction did nothing for my discomfort,

though. Perhaps I envied the relationship itself rather than the individuals involved. When was the last time someone had gazed into my eyes that way and meant it? Eric would if I'd let him, but every time he tried, I looked away. Did I really have a fear of intimacy, as Ingrid suggested? Nah. I just wasn't ready yet. Why was I suddenly worried about all this, anyway? Probably hungry.

Savannah made a beeline for her favorite "aunt," breaking up the lovefest. Brittany required both hands to fend off the onslaught. However, I'd taught her how to claim her space, so Savannah settled for an ear scratch and a kiss on the head. I should be a dog trainer. The job seemed much easier than writing books or running bookstores. All I needed was a handful of treats and a mischievous dog. Piece of cake.

Olinski looked on with an idiotic grin not directed at Savannah. Had he ever regarded me that way? Perhaps initially, when he was determined to go further than I was ready for. Certainly not by the end of our relationship. The last facial expression of his I remembered was a sneer of frustrated anger. And that lasted for ten years.

We'd finally made our peace, however, and I approached the kitchen with a smile. The aroma of fresh barbecue sent my salivary glands into overdrive. "Hi, guys."

Olinski opened containers. "Hi, Jen. Thanks for bailing us out. We couldn't decide whether we wanted mustard-based or tomato-based sauce tonight, so we got both. Way too much food for only the two of us."

No such thing. Olinski could eat the whole pig and still have room for dessert. Even if he'd slowed down some since his football days, he still had two inches of gut hanging over his belt courtesy of his new desk job and old appetite. A bad combination.

"Thanks for inviting me." Savannah poked my hand. "Excuse me. Us."

Olinski handed me a plate amid a burst of laughter.

We loaded up barbecue, potato salad, and coleslaw and settled in the living room. The lovebirds staked out Brittany's floral-print couch, and I dropped into the matching armchair on the other side of the glass-topped coffee table. Savannah parked at my feet but kept a vigilant eye on all of us. Well, our plates anyway. No falling scraps would hit the floor on her watch. The carpet was safe for democracy.

The barbecue was melt-in-your-mouth tender. While I preferred tomato-based sauce, I sampled both, and they each had my taste buds dancing a jig. We shoveled food like firemen on a steam engine until our bellies bulged. I actually considered refilling my plate but decided the meal wouldn't be nearly as tasty coming back up.

The leftovers, scraped onto a dish for Savannah, disappeared instantly. Cleaning up was a true team effort. Brittany washed while Olinski dried, and I repackaged the remains destined for the refrigerator. Savannah pushed her empty plate around the floor, then settled on her haunches, satellite-dish ears perked, eager for a refill. I scratched under her chin. "Not this time, kiddo."

When we flopped back into our seats, I put out a feeler. Possibly a stuffed, relaxed Olinski would let something slip. "How's the investigation going, Chief? Anything new and exciting?"

He sighed. "Really, Jen? Can't we enjoy a meal together without you badgering me for information that's none of your business?"

So much for stuffed and relaxed. Some things would never change.

"We found the guy propped against our back door. The store's been closed since then, and I spent all afternoon cleaning up the mess your people left behind. Sounds like my business to me."

"I disagree. I'm sorry about the mess, but that's how these things go."

"Maybe so, but I'm at least entitled to learn if you found anything in my store, aren't I?"

Olinski grinned. "Don't worry. If we found anything, we'll tell your lawyer."

Since when did I have a lawyer? "Gee, thanks."

Brittany laid her hand on Olinski's knee. "All right, you two, enough is enough. There will be no arguments tonight. I have spoken."

Olinski and I glanced at each other and shrugged. I wasn't aware we'd been arguing. I asked a question, and he answered me. If that was Brittany's definition of an argument, then ninety percent of my conversations were adversarial. Possible, I supposed, but not likely. Even if the discussions involved Olinski.

Brittany stood and went to the kitchen. She pulled a bottle of wine and a beer out of the refrigerator. "How about we all relax a little?"

Hmmm. Olinski was the beer drinker. Maybe I could encourage him to drink enough to let something slip. "Hey, Britt. You have any salted nuts?"

She lifted an eyebrow. "No. Sorry. Since when do you eat nuts?"

"I don't know. Just a craving, I guess."

"Oh? Something you'd care to tell us?"

"Good grief, no, I'm not pregnant."

She smirked. "Too bad. Eric would be a great father."

"Hey, what about me?"

"You'd be a great father, too." Brittany poured wine into two glasses and carried them, along with the beer, back to the couch. Handing one glass to me and the beer to Olinski, she said, "All right, let's get something straight. You two have to learn to get along. For my sake, if nothing else. I'm not listening to you squabble whenever we're all together."

I sipped from the glass of white Moscato. "Yes, Mother. I'll behave."

Olinski took a large swallow of his Michelob and belched. "Absolutely. Just for you, dear."

Shaking her head, Brittany snagged the remote from the coffee table and searched Netflix on the twenty-seven-inch flat-screen attached to the wall. "What are you guys in the mood for?"

We shrugged again. Perhaps Olinski and I still had a few things in common.

"Never mind," she said. "I'll pick."

While Brittany hunted for a movie that appealed to her, I turned to Olinski. "How's Eric doing as a detective? Havermayer complaining about him yet?"

"Not at all. She thinks he has potential."

"High praise from her."

He shook his head. "You need to give her a break. She's an excellent detective."

"If you say so. And I'll give her a break when she gives me one."

"She likes to push your buttons."

No kidding. "She's an expert."

He drained the last of his beer and stood. "Anyone ready for a refill?"

My glass was still half-full, and Brittany hadn't touched hers. We both shook our heads.

I didn't remember Olinski as much of a drinker when we dated, but that was back in high school. People changed. Maybe he would need no encouragement from me. Two or three more bottles, and I might pry some information out of him.

Brittany finally settled on *Catch Me If You Can*, a favorite we'd all seen. That worked for me. We could talk and not lose track of the story. I only had to wait for Olinski to polish off a couple more beers.

Olinski had started on beer number four, and fake Dr. Abagnale was hiding in his office when I tentatively broached the subject of the investigation again. "Did you ever find out what Marcus and Travis were arguing about the other night?"

"Not really. Marcus said it was nothing. An old prison thing Travis brought up."

"He told me the same thing."

Olinski set his bottle down on the coffee table. "You're not going to leave this thing alone, are you?"

"Marcus is my friend, and his ex-cellmate's body literally landed at my back door. And the guy was apparently looking for me when he died. What would you do in my place?"

"I'd let the professionals handle it."

"Baloney."

His mouth fell open. "What? I've never lied to you."

"I don't think you'd sit back and let others decide

your fate. Why do you expect me to do something you never would?"

"Because you're not me."

Brittany winked at me and turned to Olinski. "Why don't you tell her what she wants to know? She's going to find out, anyway. And get herself in trouble in the process."

"I can't do that."

"You mean you'd rather see her be kidnapped again or killed? Because that's what's going to happen, and you know it."

I held my breath while they talked about me like I wasn't there.

Olinski emptied his beer and grabbed number five out of the refrigerator. "C'mon, Britt, you're asking too much."

She smiled. "Don't forget, last time she dragged me along for the ride. And I ended up needing surgery on my ankle."

Dragged her along? No way. She'd insisted on coming with me. It wasn't my fault we were abducted and almost murdered. Besides, I got us out of trouble, didn't I?

Olinski waggled his eyebrows. "Yeah, and I got to carry you up and down the stairs the whole time you used those crutches."

Brittany's eyes widened. "Seriously? That's what you remember? I spent six weeks on those things. I was miserable."

He hung his head and peered up at her from under the bushy black caterpillars living over his eyes behind his black-rimmed glasses. "You're right. I'm sorry. But what does that have to do with this case?"

"I don't want to have to go through that again. You're aware somebody has to keep an eye on her."

"Hey, wait a minute," I said. "I don't need a babysitter. You wanted to come with me."

She put her forefinger to her lips.

I shut up.

"Fine." Olinski released a hard breath and considered me. "What do you want to know?"

I forced myself to sit still, although my impulse was to bounce up and down like a two-year-old being offered an ice-cream cone. "What did Ingrid find in the autopsy? She questioned Marcus about possible medical professionals imprisoned with him and Travis."

"Why would she ask that?" Brittany asked.

"My question exactly."

Olinski reintroduced his glasses to the caterpillars. "Because of the stab wounds."

"What about them?"

He leaned forward and looked directly into my eyes. "We're not releasing this information to the general public, so it can't leave this room. Understood?"

The evidence must be important. The only reason they would tell no one is if it was something only the killer would know.

I crossed my heart and nodded.

"The wounds were carefully placed to miss all the vital organs. Ingrid suggested that only a doctor could be so precise. And there were hesitation marks, so she thinks it's someone who cared about him or someone who'd never done anything like this before. Or both."

Huh. That eliminates Marcus as a suspect, since he credited Travis with getting him through his time in prison, and he'd never injured anyone. He went to prison for armed robbery but never fired the gun. He was a good person, and he'd never jeopardize his family or his freedom, especially with his mother gone. Who'd take care of his daughters? They'd end up in foster care. Somebody else had to be responsible for this.

Something in Olinski's face told me he was holding back.

"What else did she find?"

"He had a puncture wound in his upper left thigh. Her swab tested positive for ketamine."

Holy crap! Travis was drugged and *then* stabbed. Where would someone get ketamine? From a vet. Or a drug dealer. Really, anywhere these days. "Who are you thinking about as a suspect?"

Olinski crossed his arms. "Uh-uh. I'm not telling you that so you can run off and start interrogating people."

"Who, me?" I batted my eyelashes. "I'd never do that."

"No, of course not."

I turned away from his smirk, unable to keep a straight face myself. He had it wrong, though. I never interrogated people. I only asked pointed questions I expected immediate answers to. That wasn't the same thing at all.

CHAPTER SEVEN

I opened my eyes Monday morning to Pat Benatar running with nighttime shadows and Savannah casting one over my face. How long had she been staring at me, hoping I'd wake up? I reached out to pet her, and she pranced away, flew off the bed, and galloped into the living room. My German shepherd either needed to go out, or she was starving to death. Probably both.

After gathering the pile of sweats off the floor beside my bed, I dressed on my way to the front door, pinballing off the hallway walls to keep my balance. My dog sat with her brown nylon leash hanging out of each side of her mouth, her bushy tail sweeping the carpet. That answered that question.

In the kitchen, the coffeemaker gurgled right on schedule, filling the apartment with the magical aroma second only to puppy breath on my list of favorites. I fished my Nikes out from under the couch, and Savannah waited patiently as I clipped the lead to her matching collar. I almost missed our tug-of-war sessions before she'd learned to control herself. Almost. I didn't miss the puppy-tooth slashes on my forearms.

Following a stroll around the block filled with stops and starts, Savannah crunched her kibble, and I savored my first cup of the day. Coffee was like those potato chips that once advertised, "You can't eat just one." The first round was always the best, however.

I carried my steaming mug to my desk and fired up my laptop. Still no sign of the perfect first sentence for my novel, so I returned to the pep rally scene. Dana had finally found her social-butterfly brother and worked on convincing him to let her go home. Daniel was determined to socialize his introverted twin sister whether she wanted it or not. Enough conversation, time for some action.

> Dana grasped her brother's hand. "Daniel, you're going to have to accept that even though I'm not like you, it doesn't mean I have something wrong with me. You don't have to fix me, because I'm not broken."
>
> "I know, sis. I just want you to be happy."
>
> "I am happy. In fact, I'm so happy—"
>
> A scream split the air, and kids ran in all directions. Dana took off toward the sound, Daniel following close behind. They pushed through the shocked, silent crowd. Beside the bleachers, head cheerleader Sharon Simpson lay staring blankly at the sky, blood pooling beneath her head.
>
> Dana pressed two fingers into Sharon's neck. She looked up and shook her head.
>
> "Daniel, call 911! I think she's dead."

All right, I'd dropped the body. The core of any murder mystery. Now I had to run the Ws—who, what, where, when, and why. I'd already covered where, when, and what. That left who and why. The fun part. The obvious solution was another cheerleader wanting to move up in the pecking order. Except it was too easy. Although it would be the perfect misdirection, which was a terrific way to keep the twins occupied for the book's first half.

At the moment, though, I needed to hit the showers. I had to go to the bookstore. Another confrontation with Lacey over making changes Aletha might not have agreed with wasn't high on my to-do list, but online sales might solve all our problems. Or at least put a dent in them. I couldn't ask for more than that.

The hot water pelted my neck and shoulders, the tension swirling down the drain into the Riddleton sewer system. If only there was a way to stop it from bouncing right back out again. I shampooed and massaged my scalp, hoping to stimulate brain function. A healthy dose of creativity might fix my issues, both real and fictional.

Dried and dressed in jeans and a Gamecocks sweatshirt, I attacked my mulish hair with the blow-dryer. A pointless endeavor. No matter how wonderful my hair looked when I finished, it would collapse into a skintight helmet within thirty seconds. Except for the cowlicks, of course.

I saddled up Savannah, and we cantered past the Goodwill-cum-North Pole bowling alley. The speaker blasted "O Come All Ye Faithful" while the sidewalk Santa clanged his bell at us. I managed a return wave before my German shepherd pulled me away to investigate a random smell in the street by the curb. I eased a pang of guilt over not contributing anything to

Santa's pot with my intention to give him a check on Christmas Eve instead. That made more sense than donating whatever little bit of change I had in my pockets every day. Easier for him to count, too.

We crossed Pine Street and stopped in front of the town hall. Across the road, Bob's Bakery was overrun with customers. Picking up snacks to nourish them while they waited in line to vote in the runoff tomorrow? Or getting a last-minute feel for who they would vote for. I hoped the Riddleton electorate couldn't be swayed by overfilled donuts and mouthwatering hot ham and cheese croissants for Veronica's sake.

Average height and average build, fifty-two-year-old Riddleton native Bob Yarborough was an average guy whose only claim to fame required flour, sugar, and eggs to bring to life. He had no campaign slogan, no platform, and no agenda. Bob didn't need any of those things. He grew up with most of the people who'd be casting votes. And he stood an excellent chance of being our next mayor.

Unlike Ravenous Readers, Bob had already decorated for the contest. The front window had a mural with elf-hat-clad chocolate chip cookies flinging muffins at each other on a layer of spray-painted snow. Along the top, Santa tossed fruitcake bombs out of his reindeer-drawn sleigh. The hats must've had Kevlar linings.

When Savannah and I crossed the threshold into the bookstore at nine fifty-five, Cowboy Charlie jingled past on his way to the bakery. "Hold on there, Hoss." He tucked his thumbs into his gun belt, complete with an empty holster tied to his thigh. "I'm going to get the goodies."

"Bob's is packed right now. You might as well hold off a while."

"What about the cookies for Story Time?"

"Do we have any left from Saturday?"

"A few, but they're stale."

"You think a three-year-old will notice?" Squatting to give Savannah a chest rub, I checked out the still-deserted sidewalk. "We don't usually get a lot of children on Monday, anyway, and I have a feeling we're gonna be slow today, what with the murder and all."

He nodded. "Perhaps you're right. I'll wait a little longer. Maybe the bakery will clear out by then."

"And we'll have a better idea how many, if any, kids we'll have."

I flipped the door sign to "Open," and we trooped inside. Savannah took off to find her favorite treat dispenser, Aunt Lacey. Charlie and I moseyed over to the coffee bar to check out the stock, his spurs clinking with each step. As he'd said, a few cookies were left, but they hadn't weathered the weekend well.

Lacey led a leaping Savannah out of the stockroom while Charlie and I debated the merits of selling our leftover cookies to the NHL for use as hockey pucks. We relegated them to the trash can instead.

I took advantage of the customer dearth to call a quick staff meeting. We settled into seats at the round table by the kids' section. Queen Jennifer and her knights. I didn't dare say that out loud, though. Charlie would come in tomorrow wearing a full suit of armor, which would be much noisier than the spurs.

"I wanted to talk about our conversation on Saturday. Things got a little heated and—"

"I'm so sorry," Lacey said. "I was way out of line."

"Don't worry about it. I expect you to speak your mind, always. We all want the bookstore to succeed, and your objections helped me come up with a way to boost sales we can each live with. I was taking the easy way out. You forced me to consider other alternatives."

She smiled. "I'm glad. But I want you to know I wouldn't have quit. I love this place too much. I owe it to Aletha to see this through."

"That's great. As long as you understand we might someday have to make changes Aletha wouldn't have liked in order to keep the store open."

Lacey nodded. "I know. I only hope it never comes to that."

"Me, too."

Charlie waved his ten-gallon hat. "Yippee ki-yay, we're all friends again. Now tell us your idea!"

"All right, calm down, cowboy. I think we should sell books online."

Lacey sat back in her chair. "You mean like on Amazon?"

"Amazon, eBay, even our own website. What do you think, Charlie? It would be your project if you want."

His face lit up. "Are you kidding? Dang, skippy, I want it!"

I dropped my forehead to the table, grateful he didn't have a plug of tobacco in his cheek. Otherwise, his statement would've been followed by a spit and a wipe. Fortunately, the front door opened before I had to respond.

Veronica Winslow came in with her twin boys. "Hey, y'all! We reading a story today?"

Lacey stood. "Absolutely. Come on in."

"Where is everybody?" she asked, looking around the store.

I chuckled. "I think this *is* everybody. I guess everyone else is scared of the boogeyman."

The twins' eyes grew wide and they hurriedly looked around.

Lacey took the kids, and Charlie scooted across the street to pick up the cookies.

Once we were alone, Veronica said, "I'm afraid you might be right. I've heard some buzz about people not wanting to come here because the killer might come back. You know, they supposedly return to the scene of the crime."

"They've been watching too many movies. Besides, they haven't established this *is* the scene of the crime. The victim may have been transported here after the fact."

"Could be, but you know how people can be. They're afraid of their own shadows."

I nodded. "What about you? Do you think you should have your victory party at the diner, instead? Angus is already doing the food, so he wouldn't have much trouble adjusting if you wanted to change the venue."

"No way. My people will come here if I ask them to. There's no evidence you had anything to do with that guy's death. I'm not going to punish you for something out of your control. Besides, somebody has to show everyone else there's nothing to fear."

"I appreciate that, but if you change your mind, it won't hurt my feelings."

"Thank you. However, the 'Ronnie for Riddleton' campaign will be here at six p.m. sharp tomorrow night to wait for the returns."

"We'll be ready for you. Who knows? With luck, they'll find the murderer by then, and it won't be an issue."

She held up her crossed fingers and strolled to the back, where her children were rolling a fire truck back and forth to each other. Savannah lay with her chin on her paws, brown eyes following the tiny vehicle, waiting for her chance to steal it.

Perhaps I needed to help move the investigation along. If customers really wouldn't come in until someone found the killer, we had to unearth the culprit fast. Otherwise, the store might fail before we could put any of our new plans into place. And, if I was the one who found him, it might start another sales boom.

But what could I do? So far, the only suspect was Marcus, and I refused to believe he could be involved. No chance he'd risk returning to prison and leaving his young daughters to the perils of the foster care system. Mary Washington, the woman they lived with, who watched the kids after school when Marcus had to work, was a spry ninety-five, but still way too old to be their full-time caretaker.

What other information did I have? According to Olinski, the doer had carefully placed the stab wounds to avoid all vital organs. Ingrid believed a doctor would be required to accomplish that. However, Ingrid was the only doctor in town. Would she have murdered Travis because he was threatening Marcus? Did she love Marcus enough to put her career and all her plans for the future at risk? She'd uprooted her entire life to come here. I couldn't imagine her throwing it all away. There had to be another answer.

I still had no idea who wrote the note found in

Travis's pocket, so the only other hint I had was the bottle of holy water. Charlie had produced his, which had cleared him from suspicion. Perhaps Travis really did want to sprinkle the stuff around his new apartment. Or it might be a clue as to who murdered him. I had to go to the source. This afternoon I'd visit St. Mary's and talk to Lula. I doubted they had so many people asking for holy water she wouldn't remember Travis.

The door bells jingled, and Eric poked his head in. "You busy?"

Charlie squeezed by him, carrying the box he'd picked up from Bob's. We still only had the two kids for Story Time, so he could handle it without my help.

Butterflies soared in my belly. "No, what's up?"

"Nothing. I had a minute to kill, so I thought I'd pop in and say hello." He took my hands and planted a kiss on my lips. "Hello!"

"Hi, there." I turned his hands over and traced the lines on his mildly calloused palms. His fingers were strong yet gentle. The butterflies fluttered. "What are you up to today?"

His green eyes glistened. "We're going over to search Travis's apartment. Hopefully, we'll find something to lead us to his killer."

"That would be nice. I'd love things to get back to normal around here."

He looked around the empty store. "I see what you mean."

"Any luck with narrowing down the suspect list?"

"Not yet. We're still processing the note, and the prints on the bottle came back to the parish priest. No surprise there."

The door flew open, and Havermayer stepped in, completely ignoring me. "Eric, let's go. Move your butt."

He winked at me and scooted toward the exit. "Yes, ma'am."

CHAPTER EIGHT

St. Mary's Catholic Church was born in the 1840s as a nondenominational, one-room shack next to the stables holding the replacement stagecoach horses. A place for weary travelers to pray they'd survive attacks by Indians, bandits, or runaway slaves. Not that Indians or slaves were a real problem, but better to cover all bases, just in case.

Today, the building stood two stories high with an attached rectory, encompassing most of Riddleton Road between Oak and Park. The parking lot separated it from the only other structure on the block, which was the doctor's office and morgue. I tried not to read too much into that.

I climbed the half-dozen marble steps leading to the hand-carved, wooden double doors. The imposing edifice loomed, stained-glass eyes peering into my soul. My stomach roiled, and cold fingers tripped down my spine. Odd. My upbringing had included no religious indoctrination, but this wasn't the first time I'd ever entered a church, only the first time I'd had the sensation I might not come out again.

Get it together, Jen.

Deep breath in, slow breath out.

As I reached for the brass handle, the door flew open, and my heart zoomed into my throat. I jumped back, kicked myself in the ankle, and landed on my bottom. Good thing my butt was well-padded these days. Nothing injured but my pride.

A tall, thin man wearing all black, except for the visible square of the white collar around his neck, stepped onto the landing. "Oh, dear! Are you all right?" He reached out a hand.

I grabbed it, and he hoisted me to my feet, much stronger than he appeared. My cheeks and ears burned. "Thank you, Father. I didn't mean to make such a dramatic entrance."

A slightly crooked smile split his smooth-skinned face. "I'm sorry I frightened you. I'm usually seen as a somewhat benign figure. Good to know I can still scare someone off their feet when I need to."

The priest had a sense of humor. Nice.

He held out his hand again. "I'm Father Mathews."

A gold watch glittered on his right wrist. The padre might be a lefty. Or he could just be weird. "Jen Dawson." I shook his hand, his grip firm but not overpowering. "I own the bookstore over on Main Street."

"Very happy to meet you, Ms. Dawson."

"Nice to meet you, too, Father Mathews."

"My given name is Henry, but most people call me Father Hank. How can I help you?"

Hank? More suited to a mechanic than a priest. His parents must've had a different vision for his future.

"I imagine you've heard about the murdered man found behind my store Saturday morning?"

He nodded. "Hard to keep a secret like that in a town like this."

"Well, the only items in his possession were a note with my name on, and a bottle of holy water from your church. I was hoping to ask you a few questions to find the connection."

"I'll be happy to assist if I can, but I can't imagine the two are related." He reached for the door handle with a bandaged left hand. "Please, come inside."

Perpetrators of knife attacks often cut themselves. I wanted to ask how he'd injured his hand, but without becoming the next victim. How would Daniel approach this question? Carefully.

"That hand looks painful. Are you all right?"

His face reddened. "I'm fine. Feeling foolish, actually. I left a knife point up in the dishwasher the other day and cut myself taking it out. Should've focused on my task instead of planning Sunday's sermon in my head."

"I do stuff like that all the time."

"You're a writer, aren't you? I think our secretary has mentioned your book."

"Apparently, she's a fan. We met the other day in the bookstore."

He opened the door and gestured for me to enter. I stepped into the sanctuary, and the icy fingers returned. I shivered. Directly ahead, a life-sized crucifix, illuminated by a lamp, hung on the wall between two identical stained-glass windows depicting the Madonna and Child. A table to one side held brass-and-glass candle holders with several lit candles. A row of glistening, solid oak pews dominated either side of an aisle leading to the tabernacle. Impressive but innocuous. Why was I so creeped out?

Father Hank motioned toward a staircase guarded by a lustrous balustrade leading to the second story on my left. I started up the steps, careful to keep to the protective runner in the middle. At the top, I found offices on either side with open doors and a closed door between. Bathroom, most likely. In the office on the right, Lula Parsons chatted on the phone behind a small, wooden desk.

The priest led the way into the office on the left, the walls lined with bookcases and religious memorabilia. An oriental rug covered most of the scuffed, hardwood floor.

He stepped behind the desk, removed his jacket, and hung it on the back of the padded, swivel chair. I settled into the wingback opposite.

"So, what can I tell you, Ms. Dawson?"

"Jen, please."

He nodded.

"Did you know Travis Underwood?"

"Actually, I did, although this was the first time I'd seen him since he was a child."

I leaned forward in my chair. "Did he stop coming to church?"

"He did. A long time ago. Travis was a good kid. One of my altar boys, in fact. I left soon after, though, so I was rather surprised to learn the path his life had taken."

"I can imagine. Any idea why he took such a drastic turn?"

Hank frowned. "People whispered about trouble at home, but obviously I wasn't privy to much of the gossip. Nor did I want to be."

"Of course not." I smiled. "Besides, why receive

information secondhand when you hear it directly in the confessional, right?"

"Right. The perfect place to learn everyone's secrets." He leaned forward and clasped his hands on the desk. "Anything you'd care to share?"

Was he serious? "I... um... I'm not Catholic."

"That's okay. I take pagan confessions, too."

My mouth fell open.

Booming laughter resonated off the walls. "Gotcha."

His impish charm reminded me of my ex-boyfriend Russell. I hoped the resemblance ended there. Either way, I was in no danger of being seduced by charisma this time. Even if I had lousy taste in men, I wasn't foolish enough to fall for a priest. Especially one old enough to be my grandfather.

"What did Travis want the holy water for?"

"He didn't say."

"A friend of mine has the theory Travis wanted to free his new apartment of evil spirits."

"Possibly. Some people use it that way." Hank glanced at his watch and rose from his chair. "Goodness, I didn't realize it was that late. I'm sorry, but I have an appointment with a homebound parishioner."

I stood. "I don't want to keep you, but I do have one more question if you don't mind."

"Certainly."

"I mentioned earlier that Travis also had a note in his pocket with my name on it. Apparently, someone directed him to me, and he died on my doorstep. Do you have any idea who might've sent him my way? Or what he wanted from me?"

"I'm afraid I don't know anything about it."

"Thank you for your time, Father."

He put his hand out.

I shook it and started toward the door. "If you don't mind, I'd like to say hello to Lula while I'm here."

"Not at all. Make yourself at home."

"Thank you."

He trotted down the stairs, and I tapped on Lula's doorframe.

No longer on the phone, she glanced up. "Hi, Jen! Did you come to bring me a copy of your new book?"

Shaking my head, I said, "I wish. Soon, though."

She pointed to the folding chair in front of her desk. "Please, come in."

I settled on the lightly padded seat. "I was in the neighborhood, so I thought I'd say hi."

"I'm so glad you did."

Lula's desk was cluttered in an organized sort of way. A computer monitor and keyboard encompassed the center, surrounded by invoices. Bill-paying day. Photographs in plain silver frames, angled so they could be seen from either side of the desk, decorated each corner. One of whom I assumed was her husband, George, glowering into the camera, sat beside a photo of two boys and a girl dressed for church. Next to it was a picture of George in battle dress with an armband displaying a red cross. The frame on the other side showed Lula and Hank standing in front of St. Mary's.

"Your children are lovely. How old are they?"

"Those are my sister's kids. I've never had any, although we wanted them."

So much for the rumor mill. "I'm sorry."

Her eyes took on a faraway look. "It's okay. Motherhood wasn't in God's plan for me."

81

No bitterness. No regret. Only peace. That kind of faith was rare. I envied her.

"This is a beautiful church. I've never been in it before."

"I've been a member all my life. My parents first brought me here as a baby. This is my second home."

My belly tightened. A second home? I was still searching for my first. "That's wonderful. Especially since you're able to work here, too."

Lula sat back and smiled. "My first and only job. Are you aware of the history of this place? It's quite an interesting story."

"Only that the structure has been here since before the town was built."

"The church was also a stop on the Underground Railroad in the eighteen fifties."

I took a sharp, deep breath. "Really? I had no idea."

She popped out of her chair. "We have a whole network of tunnels under this building. Do you want to see them?"

People in Riddleton had helped free slaves before it was even a town? This could be an excellent backdrop for a novel. "Definitely! Thank you."

We headed down the stairs. I stayed by the wall to escape the temptation of depositing fingerprints all over the gleaming banister. Finger-painting without the mess. I'd grow up someday. Just not today. I wasn't quite thirty yet.

The pews on either side of the aisle lined up like soldiers in formation to guard the tabernacle. When Lula dropped to one knee and crossed herself at the end of the walkway, I bowed my head. While religion had played no part in my life, I respected her right to her beliefs.

She smiled as she stood and gestured toward a door on the side wall of the nave. "The entrance is in there."

I followed her through the doorway into a kitchen. A countertop, sink, and dishwasher lined one wall. The refrigerator and a small four-seat table took up the other. Clean, white four-inch tile covered the floor, with a blue, four-by-eight throw rug obscuring the center.

My shoulders dropped. I couldn't say what I'd expected, but this wasn't it. "The kitchen?"

Lula laughed. "Move the rug."

I slid the runner to the side, revealing a two-foot-square wooden hatch with an inset iron ring. I peeked at Lula, eyebrows raised.

"They found this around the turn of last century. Most folks forgot all about it. Go ahead. Open it."

I pulled on the ring, and the board came up on well-oiled hinges. Damp air wafted off the earthen walls, carrying mold and mildew. Narrow wooden steps descended steeply into the darkness. Someone would have to be desperate to tackle those stairs. "Have you gone down?"

"We use one of the rooms for storage, but I don't think anyone's explored the tunnels in a very long time." She peered into the hole. "Father Hank has ventured around some. I haven't worked up the courage yet. You know, small spaces and all that."

My heart raced. "Do you mind if I take a look?"

"Not at all. You'll find a light switch hanging at the bottom of the stairs. Apparently, the tunnels were used by rumrunners in the twenties, and they strung light bulbs along the walls. I have no idea where they come out, though. Somewhere in the woods, I'd imagine."

I lowered my feet into the hole until they made contact with a rung.

"Be careful," Lula said. "Rumor has it a frat boy went down there on a dare in nineteen twenty-seven, got lost, and was never seen again."

Maybe that was the source of the chill I'd had when I'd entered the church. The ghost of a lost kid from a hundred years ago. I shuddered.

"Don't worry, I won't go very far. I just want to see what it looks like. I have an idea for my next book."

The rough surface of the ladder grated against my hands, and I avoided sliding them down the wood. Too tricky to type with a fistful of splinters. The air grew wetter and cooler with each step, and the light from the kitchen faded ten steps down. I shivered in my sweatshirt, although I couldn't tell if the reaction was from fear or cold. Probably both. Still, I pressed on. Another sacrifice for my writing.

Seventeen steps later, I reached solid ground. The black was absolute. I saw nothing, heard nothing, felt nothing. An antebellum sensory deprivation tank. I craned my neck to see how far down I'd come. A tiny square of white broke the darkness.

I slid my hands along the wall on each side of the ladder. No light switch. I turned around and reached for the opposite wall. Something touched my hand in midair. I jerked back, banging my head on the staircase. My heart stutter-stepped.

Deep breath in, slow breath out.

I rubbed the back of my skull as my ears strained for any sound. Nothing. Whatever the thing might be, it couldn't be alive. Nothing could move that silently. It must be the light switch, hanging from the kitchen floor above. Reaching out, I fought the urge to pull away when I bumped it again.

Holding the contraption with one hand, I flipped the toggle with the other. Dim light illuminated a passageway behind me. I turned and stepped into the tunnel.

A warren of passages branched off in all directions. One wrong step, and I'd become a rat in a maze. Which one had the cheese at the end?

I turned right and followed the low-wattage bulbs on wires tacked to the boards shoring up the hard-packed walls. My lungs struggled to pull in the thick air, and moisture adhered to my skin like sweat.

A short way down, an opening appeared on my left. I peered into the darkness, barely making out a room full of folded tables and chairs with cardboard boxes scattered throughout. The storage room. No wonder Lula didn't want to come down here. She'd probably be expected to clean up the mess.

A little farther down the passage, more tunnels branched off. I stayed in my lane. The best way to avoid losing my way. About a hundred more steps and the tunnel ended at a solid clay wall. A diversion. How many of the other tunnels were dead ends?

The only way to find out was to try them all. Not a project I'd volunteer for anytime soon. Someone had to have mapped the shortest way out, but that person was long gone.

I doubled back to the stairway entrance, turned out the lights, and climbed up to the kitchen.

Lula sat at the little table, sipping coffee and thumbing through a magazine. "Did you have fun?"

"Absolutely!" Excitement warmed my face. "I could spend the rest of my life exploring."

Lula's eyes twinkled. "Make enough wrong turns and you just might."

"Don't worry, I'd leave bread crumbs. No birds to eat them."

"Maybe, but the mice might."

We laughed.

A sudden, pressing urge to go home and write pushed me toward the door. My plans for the third book had taken a hard left turn.

CHAPTER NINE

Savannah, attached to my side like a conjoined twin, let me oversleep Tuesday morning for the first time since I'd brought her home fifteen months ago. My little girl was growing up. Light filtered through the bedroom curtains, casting muted shadow monsters on the wall. The clock on the nightstand flashed 8:47.

I stretched my arms overhead, and my German shepherd flopped her head down on my chest. I scratched her behind the ears. "Good morning, sleepyhead. Forget to set your alarm?"

Her bushy tail thumped, and she yawned, showing off all forty-two teeth. Nothing like a face full of dog breath first thing in the morning. When I pushed her snout away, she leaped to her feet and pulled the pillow out from under my head.

"All right, I'm getting up."

When I swung my legs off the side, she flew off the bed, pillow bobbing, and ran head-first into the doorjamb. I laughed until my ribs ached while she sat and blinked at me.

"You okay, Doofus?"

As soon as I reached for my sweats, she took off for the kitchen. I'd take that as a "yes."

After a quick trip around the block, I nuked my first coffee of the day and settled at my desk while Savannah slept off her breakfast. But before my first word graced the screen, the phone rang. Eric's academy picture popped up.

I answered. "Hey, how's it going?"

Eric chuckled. "You mean me or the investigation?"

Smart aleck. "Whichever one you want to talk about. You called me, remember?"

"Only because you were supposed to call me last night and didn't."

"I'm sorry. My writing brain took over, and it was late when the thing finally let go. I didn't want to wake you."

"You should take breaks once in a while. You'll feel better. Besides, a phone call only takes a few minutes, and I'd rather talk to you than sleep."

"Thank you." Eric was sweet, but now I felt guilty about not calling him. Why couldn't he understand the real world faded away when I was writing? I rarely got on a roll, so I had to take advantage when I did. "I'm sorry I didn't call. It wasn't because I didn't want to. I was in the zone and lost track of everything else."

He breathed into the phone. "I'll get used to it, I guess."

Terrific. More guilt. "Can we please talk about something else?"

"Like what?"

Anything that didn't make me feel bad about myself. "Whatever you want. How was your day yesterday?"

"Productive. I learned a lot. You know, Havermayer's a first-class detective."

I sealed my lips against a laugh. He was already upset

with me, no need to hurt his feelings again. Besides, I didn't understand her as a person. She'd never allowed me past her unyielding facade. "I'm glad she's helping you. Are you feeling better about the training? You were a little discouraged there for a while."

"I am. I think I'm going to be a decent detective one day. I might not be as proficient as Havermayer, but I'll get the job done."

"You'll outshine Havermayer. You're good with people, she's not."

"Honestly, Jen, something about you rubs her the wrong way. She doesn't react to anyone else the way she does you."

Huh. "Why, do you think? She's been like this since the first time we met. I never had a chance to do anything to upset her."

"All I know is, every time I mention your name, she becomes irritated and changes the subject. Sometimes I wonder if she feels threatened by you in some way."

"That's ridiculous."

"Maybe so, but something's going on."

I stuck a refill in the microwave. "Well, why don't you use your newfound detecting skills, and find out what her problem is? I could live with not always feeling like she's out to get me."

"I'll see what I can do."

"Thank you." I opened the microwave door mid-beep and removed my steaming mug. "I went to church yesterday."

No response.

I checked my phone to ensure the connection was open. "Did you hear me? I said I went to church yesterday."

"I heard you. I just didn't believe my ears."

A little cream and sugar, and I declared my coffee ready to drink. I blew across the top and took a sip. "Yup. I stopped by St. Mary's to ask about the holy water Travis had."

"Jen, stay out of the investigation."

Oh, brother. "What? I'd never heard of sprinkling holy water around your house to drive out evil spirits. I was educating myself."

"Sure, you were."

"Well, do you want to know what I learned or not?" I imagined him rolling his eyes.

"I want to hear anything you want to tell me."

Now, I did the eye roll. "Well, the first thing I discovered was that Travis used to be an altar boy for Father Mathews, and shortly after Mathews left, Travis's life fell apart."

"What're you getting at?"

"I'm not sure, but it's worth looking into, don't you think?"

"I'll talk to Havermayer. What's the second thing you learned?"

"The church was once a stop on the Underground Railroad. There are all kinds of tunnels underneath. Isn't that cool?"

"I guess."

I sighed. He could be a real downer sometimes. "Come on. Where's your sense of adventure? Think of all the exploring we can do."

"Sorry, I'm busy thinking about all the trouble you might stumble into. You do manage to find it everywhere you go."

"That's what you love about me."

He chuckled. "So you keep telling me."

I had to wonder, though, if he loved me. The real me. He thought he did, but the longer we were together, the unhappier he seemed. And the unhappier he was, the tighter he held on. But I needed the easygoing, easy-to-be-around guy I'd fallen for despite myself.

I'd worked hard to keep him at arm's length and failed because he always had my back no matter what stupid thing I'd done. He was always there for me. I wanted to do the same for him, but nothing made him happy anymore.

We disconnected the call, and I tapped Brittany's college graduation picture. No way would Havermayer look into anything I found interesting. Even if it might break the case. Did Father Mathews kill Travis because of something that happened twenty years ago? Perhaps, if Travis was threatening to out him now. It depended on what had actually occurred back then.

Either way, my research guru would dig up the truth. She loved to remind me that she didn't have access to anything I didn't, but she always found the things I couldn't. Guess I should've taken that optional class on research methods in college. I was too busy being the whiz-kid writer. My, how things could change.

Brittany agreed to help, as I'd hoped she would. We went through a rough patch last summer when she started dating Olinski, and I'd made some new friends. The dynamic of our relationship had changed multiple times over the years, but we always adjusted in the end. Dawson and Dunlop together forever.

I returned to staring at my laptop screen. Still no sign of the perfect first sentence, but I'd killed off the head cheerleader, and Dana and Daniel were on the case. They'd had their first run-in with Detective Abernathy, who gave them the standard reminder to leave it alone, knowing they wouldn't. If they did, I wouldn't have much of a story.

The tunnels under the church poked at the back of my mind, but I still had no idea what to do with them. Better to let it percolate for a while and see what came out. Until then, I'd stick with what I had. I could always shift the dead cheerleader from book three to book four if my subconscious generated something better.

My project right now was to find an acceptable reason for the twins to be involved. Neither of them had any particular relationship with the victim, and Dana hated cheerleaders in general. Well, maybe not hated. She just wasn't as impressed with them as they were with themselves. Honestly, I doubted anyone could be. The high-school caste system had existed since the birth of high schools. And cheerleaders and football players always rested at the top.

I tapped on my keyboard, building the deceased cheerleader's backstory, including a burgeoning relationship with Daniel. At the moment, the history made sense, but I'd have to see how it read after I let it simmer for a while. My words often rearranged themselves into drivel when I wasn't looking. It seemed like it anyway. Most likely, they were drivel to begin with. That's what revisions were for.

When my stomach reminded me I'd fed it only coffee all morning, I leashed Savannah for a trip to the diner for lunch. With luck, the place would be empty enough for her to join me. If not, I'd have to drop her off at the bookstore. I kept my fingers crossed for a "locals only" crowd. As the town mascot and Angus's favorite customer, no resident would ever rat Savannah out to the health department. Not if they ever wanted to frequent the Dandy Diner again.

I checked out the bowling Santa on the Goodwill window vibrating to the raucous sounds of "Grandma Got Run Over by a Reindeer," and waved to the sidewalk bell ringer as we passed. He smiled and tossed my German shepherd a treat he dug out of his pocket. She caught it in midair and carried it with her to the restaurant.

Havermayer and Eric brushed past me as I opened the door. Havermayer glanced down at the dog and shook her head, while Eric avoided my questioning glance, his shoulders slumped. They hadn't been here for the food. I'd have to ask Eric about it later.

When I stepped inside, Angus was alone, wiping down the front counter, to which he'd tacked entwined green and silver garlands. I scooted onto a stool. Savannah settled at my feet.

"What did they want?"

He set up a mug and poured coffee. "They asked me questions about Marcus and Ingrid."

"Marcus and Ingrid? What were they fishing for?" I glanced around the empty room. "Where *is* Marcus?"

"They've been interrogating him since last night. He's still at the station."

My first sip went down like a boulder in a landslide. "What do they want with him?"

"As far as I can tell, they found some letters Marcus wrote Travis after he got out of prison about something that happened while Marcus was still inside. They wouldn't give me any details. Just asked if I knew anything about it."

"Do you?"

"No, Marcus never talked about his time in jail, and I never asked. According to the detectives, though, an inmate died, and Marcus was involved somehow."

The detectives. It was the first time I'd heard Eric referred to that way. I suppressed a smile. "I can't imagine how. Marcus doesn't have a violent bone in his body."

"No, but prison has a way of putting people in violent situations. Who knows how he might've reacted when threatened?"

"Still, there's no way Marcus murdered Travis. He'd never do anything to destroy all the work he's put in since he was released. And he just doesn't have it in him."

Angus came around the counter to occupy the stool next to me, and give Savannah a plate of scraps. "They found his fingerprints on the note with your name on it."

"That could mean anything. Or nothing. Nobody but Marcus has any idea why he referred Travis to me." And, strangely, Marcus never mentioned he'd spoken to Travis about me. Why wouldn't he tell me he wrote the note? And why did Travis want to talk to me? As usual, many more questions than answers. "Did Havermayer say when they were going to release him? Has he been charged with anything?"

"No, not that they mentioned. I got the sense they were holding him for as long as possible in case more evidence turned up."

"Like what?"

"No telling. They weren't finished examining everything they found in Travis's apartment yet."

Savannah swallowed the last of her snack and poked

me in the leg for more. I scratched behind her ears, knowing that would only hold her off for so long. "What were they asking about Ingrid? Surely, they can't believe she's involved."

"Havermayer asked me about their relationship. How close they were. I almost got the idea she was asking if I thought Ingrid would kill for him."

"I can't see that happening. Ingrid has worked too hard to get where she is. She wouldn't throw it all away."

"I'm not saying that's what she meant, only how it felt to me. I'm not sure what she was after to be honest with you. It was weird."

"Did she say anything about what they found that led to those questions?"

"Of course not. You know how she is."

Unfortunately, I did.

The door opened, and Nancy, my hairdresser from the Snip & Clip, came in with another woman I didn't recognize, wearing hip-hugger jeans and pink polo shirts. There must be a new stylist in town. Not that I'd consider switching. Nancy knew how to tame my lion's mane, a skill I'd yet to master.

Nancy waved. "Hi, Jen! When's that new book coming out?"

Somehow, the question didn't sting as much now that I had an answer. "April."

She flipped her short, pink-striped brown hair. "Great! I can't wait to read it."

The two women settled into a booth on the back wall.

I turned to Angus. "How are you going to handle your lunch rush with Marcus at the police station?"

He filled two water glasses from a nozzle on the soda machine. "I'll do the cooking, and I called in a server, but she can't be here for another hour. She has to wait for her babysitter. I should be okay, though. Tuesday lunch isn't too bad."

I should offer to help, but I had no restaurant experience other than as a customer. Still, how hard could it be? There were only two of them. I could handle it, and Angus was my friend. He'd do it for me. "How about I help you out until she gets here?"

"I don't think so, Jen. Have you ever waited tables before?"

"No, but I'm sure I can figure it out. Take their drink orders, then bring them their drinks, take their food orders, and deliver their food, right? Easy-peasy."

Angus pressed his lips together. "When you put it that way, yes. However, the job's not that simple." He settled his troubled gaze on mine. "Okay. You'll find aprons and pads in the storeroom in the back. And thank you."

Doubts hit me the instant he agreed. Could I really do this? Sure. I could handle two customers. "You're welcome."

After running Savannah over to the bookstore, I returned to the diner for my lunch shift. I was a waitress now. My mother would love that turn of events. Finally, I had a *real* job. Even if it was only for an hour or so. I should frame my first tip and give it to her for Christmas.

In the storeroom, I found myself surrounded by canned goods, condiments, and paper supplies on racks. A silver metal door in the left wall led to what I assumed was the cooler for meats and other perishables. In the corner of the right wall was a table with server supplies and apron-laden hooks on the wall above.

I wrapped an apron around my waist, grabbed an order pad and pen, and stuck them in the front pocket. When I returned to the dining room, I discovered three more tables had filled while I'd prepared myself.

Uh-oh.

My heart raced as panic slithered into my chest.

Calm down, Jen. You can do this.

Deep breath in, slow breath out.

Okay. I had to take it one step at a time. I'd eaten in a ton of restaurants. I knew the routine. First things first. Get the drink orders.

I approached the nearest table and introduced myself to a middle-aged man and two young women passing through town. I scribbled one Pepsi and two diets on my pad. So far, so good.

The next table had the four guys who worked at the hardware store. No introductions necessary. Four sweet teas. Excellent.

I moved on to table number three as two more couples came in and sat on opposite sides of the room. Sweat broke out on my forehead. I added two more Pepsis to my pad and acknowledged the newcomers.

I hustled to the drink station and poured the drinks, managing to arrange them on two trays. I checked the pad to see who would get what. *Crap!* I'd written them all on the same sheet.

No problem. I could separate them when I took the food orders.

Gripping the trays in cramping fingers, I tiptoed to the hardware-guys' table to drop off the sweet teas. They were ready to order, but I had to deliver the other drinks first. I made it back to the first table without incident, then realized I had no idea which of the drinks were diet and which were regular. I had to start all over.

Since I'd yet to bring him any food orders, Angus grabbed a pad and came out to help. I carefully separated the drinks on one tray, and Angus called out the new orders he'd taken. I poured them, too, and placed them on a second tray.

I crept toward the first table again, carefully balancing the two trays. About halfway there a voice called out, "Hey, Jen! We only get forty-five minutes for lunch."

When I turned my head, I kicked a chair leg, and dove face-first into the pool of Pepsi that resulted from the fall. Angus sent me to the back to clean up and dry off while he mopped up the mess. "Thanks for trying, Jen. Not everyone's cut out for this."

I wrung brown liquid out of my apron into the mop sink, fighting back the disappointment. I'd been fired from my first and only job.

When the real server arrived fifteen minutes early, everyone, including me, applauded. I'd never been so happy to see another person in my life, and I'd never take a restaurant worker for granted again.

CHAPTER TEN

The Riddleton Community Center was on the corner of Park and Main, directly across from my apartment complex. The white brick and glass building lent a touch of modernity to the town's otherwise 1940s ambience. I couldn't decide if I liked it or not, though. I appreciated having a place in town for people to gather, but if I was going to live in a quaint, small town, I wanted the town to remain quaint. If necessary, the twenty-first century was only a few miles away in Blackburn or Sutton.

One volunteer, wearing a red-checkered flannel shirt and jeans in a perfect imitation of a lumberjack, stood on a ladder in front of the window, which depicted Santa tossing meatballs to elves that held out plates mounded with spaghetti. Mrs. Claus waited to slather them with marinara sauce.

The scene was a tribute to the center's spaghetti dinner meet-and-greet held on the first Friday of every month. Though I lived across the street, I'd yet to attend, as I suspected, in my case, the evening would be more of a meet, greet, and "When's your book coming out, Jen?" occasion.

The lumberjack fumbled with a tangled string of Christmas lights seemingly destined for the center's awning to complement the flashing lights around the windows. If he could straighten them out. Probably a good thing I couldn't hear the words he grumbled under his breath.

People around here treated the decoration contest as if the town council judges were members of the US Olympic Committee, and they all competed for the gold. Last year, the lumberjack hooked up so many lights, he blew the transformer and knocked out electricity to the entire block for an hour. The absence of an extension cord attached to the inflated Santa oscillating precariously on the roof demonstrated he'd learned from his mistake. As far as I could tell. He wasn't done yet.

I strolled past the "Vote Here" signs to the double glass doors. Inside the spacious structure, a ten-foot Christmas tree covered with blue and silver garlands, flashing lights, and paper decorations, provided by the children's Saturday afternoon arts and crafts group, filled one back corner. A nativity scene occupied the other. The holly-berry garland with lights strung around the tops of the walls kept watch on the tables with wreaths attached to each end. I had no doubt the community center volunteers had set their sights on a contest victory. They'd have to get past Lacey, though. If she ever finished planning her decoration scheme.

I joined the short line to show my ID and receive my ballot.

Lula Parsons, in a knee-length, charcoal-gray skirt suit that augmented her pale-gray eyes, grabbed my sleeve on her way out. "Hey, Jen, I'm happy you're here."

"You, too." I was dying to ask if she'd voted for common-sense government from Veronica or donuts from Bob but respected her privacy. I took the circuitous route instead to encourage her to volunteer the information. Daniel would be proud. "Veronica's having what we hope will be a victory party at the bookstore tonight. Would you and George like to join us? It's nothing big, just a bunch of us hanging out, waiting for the results. The Dandy Diner's providing food and soft drinks. If you want anything harder, you'll have to bring your own."

She spread her cherry-red lips into a grin. "Well, thank you, dear. That sounds lovely. I'll mention it to George."

"We're starting at six, if you decide to come."

"I'm sure we will. George loves a good party."

I covered my surprise with a smile and a nod. I didn't get that impression from Lula when she'd described him in the bookstore. "Terrific. I'll look forward to seeing you."

"Did you enjoy your visit to the church yesterday?"

The cane-wielding geezer ahead of me in line moved up, and I followed. "I did. I'd love to explore those tunnels one day. I'm thinking of using them in my next book."

Lula tugged her suit jacket back into place. "I'm not sure that's such a wise idea. Remember the kid who got lost."

"That's just a rumor, I'm sure. If nothing else, the rumrunners probably found him. Now, whether or not they allowed him to leave might be a different

101

story. They wouldn't have wanted him to reveal their secrets."

Lula paled and covered her mouth. "Oh, dear! You think they murdered that poor boy?"

Nice going, Jen.

"No, I'm sorry. I didn't mean to upset you. That's just my mystery-writer's mind talking. I'm sure, if a boy even got lost in those tunnels, he found his way out with no trouble. You know how these stories take on a life of their own."

"You're right, of course, I'm being silly. That story's one of the reasons I've never gone down there."

The geezer caned away, and it was my turn. "We should go together, then."

"I'll have to think about that." She gestured toward the table. "I'll let you go, so you can cast your vote. I hope to see you tonight."

"Me too."

I handed the poll worker my driver's license, and she swiped the magnetic strip through her machine. After a quick study of her computer screen, she handed it back, along with a paper ballot inserted into a privacy folder. I grabbed a Sharpie from the tray and strolled to the nearest vacant seat.

With only two names on the ballot, I took less than a minute to blacken my preferred oval and feed my ballot into the machine at the front of the room. I'd spent more time waiting in line than I had actually voting. It was worth it, though. I'd had my say.

I popped my "I Voted" sticker on my sweatshirt and stepped out into the clear blue, sunny sky. The temperature hovered in the mid-fifties, and the sidewalk Santa in front of the Goodwill wiped sweat off his brow, singing along with "White Christmas." I waved, and he rang his bell.

When I opened the door to Ravenous Readers, Savannah charged, performing her duties as our official greeter with gusto. She slid to a halt and sat on the line we'd taped on the carpet ten feet from the door. I'd spent two weeks training her to master that trick. It was time well spent, though, since she no longer frightened people away before they made it all the way into the shop.

The bookstore had no customers at the moment, however. I suspected it would likely stay that way until the police arrested someone for Travis's murder, which made no sense. The three of us weren't considered suspects as far as I knew, but humans weren't always logical. Our innate fear encouraged us to avoid even a hint of danger. Survival of the scaredest.

Charlie scrolled through his phone at the coffee bar, while Lacey leaned on the display case by the cash register, drawing in her sketchbook and chewing on her lower lip.

I propped my elbows on the counter beside her. "How's it going?"

"Not bad, I think." She turned the pad around to show me what she'd come up with for the window display.

On one side of the door, she'd drawn Santa seated in a wingback chair beside a lit fireplace, feet and stockings propped on an identically patterned ottoman, reading *'Twas the Night Before Christmas*. On the other side, Rudolph was hitched to a loaded sleigh, checking his wristwatch with an annoyed expression on his face.

"I love it! But, what about the door in between? We need something to connect the two."

"I considered snow with a small town in the distance."

I pursed my lips. "But Santa's still at the North Pole. How about his workshop instead? With elves lined up in front with their arms crossed, tapping their feet or something."

She broke into a grin. "That's perfect. I'll start on the drawing."

At least the downtime would be useful for something. "Did Veronica bring over the decorations for the party?"

Lacey pointed toward the back of the store. "She did. They're in the stockroom."

I straightened up. "Great. I'll work on those while you finish up."

I ambled back to the storeroom with Savannah bumping the backs of my legs. Although she no longer resembled a flop-eared baby bird as she did when the woman in Savannah gave her to me, she would always be my little girl. I couldn't imagine life without her anymore.

On the floor right inside the doorway, I found the banner and campaign posters Veronica had asked us to put up. The signs would be spaced around the walls, and the banner would hang from two hooks screwed into the ceiling for when we had particular sales going on. We hadn't used them yet, since we ordered inventory sparingly. One or two copies of each book at a time. Perhaps that would change when Charlie got our websites up and running.

Charlie helped me with the posters of a smiling Veronica touting her acting-mayor accomplishments—

the stoplight she'd had installed on the corner of Main and Pine and the newly filled potholes on Walnut. I'd just put the finishing touches on the "Ronnie for Riddleton" banner when Brittany called. I climbed down the ladder and swiped the screen. "Hey, Britt! Did you find anything?"

She chuckled. "I'm fine, thank you. How are you?"

I sent her a narrow-lidded glare, which she obviously couldn't see. "I just talked to you this morning. Gimme a break."

"I'm messing with you. And yes, I found a couple of things you might be interested in. I just sent you a photo of Mathews and Travis together in the church when Travis was a kid."

My phone pinged, and I opened the message. Father Mathews and altar-boy Travis stood side-by-side in their vestments. Mathews, grinning broadly, had one arm around Travis's shoulders. Travis wore a tight-lipped smile, appearing as if he'd rather be anywhere else.

"This is awesome, Britt. Travis doesn't seem very happy."

"It gets even better. Three weeks after this picture was taken, Mathews was transferred to a parish in Idaho. No explanation given."

Weird. "Maybe Travis was a troubled teen, and Mathews was helping him. That could be why Travis's life fell apart so unexpectedly when Mathews left."

"Possibly."

"Unfortunately, that theory doesn't do much to help me get Marcus off the hook. Havermayer's holding him in jail while she searches for proof he's the murderer. All because of some letters they found in Travis's apartment."

I gave her a brief rundown of what Angus had told me about the letters the detectives had found, officially making me a gossipmonger passing on third-hand information. But what else did I have? It wasn't like Havermayer would let me read them for myself.

Brittany sighed. "But the detectives never said anything about the actual contents, right?"

"Right. We don't know what they were discussing, only that Havermayer considered it questionable enough to keep Marcus in jail."

"At least they can only hold him for twenty-four hours without charging him."

"Yeah, but I don't believe for a minute Marcus had anything to do with Travis's death. The only way to get Havermayer off his tail is to find someone else for her to chase. I know her; she's not looking at any other suspects."

Brittany blew another sigh into my ear. "Just be careful. Please? She'd be just as happy to lock you up too."

"I'm always careful."

She barked a laugh. "Oh yeah? I have a newly reconstructed ankle and a limp left over from the last time you were *careful* that say otherwise. Bye, Jen."

"Bye." I swiped the red button to end the call, then lowered my head, hoping the wave of guilt would ebb. I hadn't exercised caution when I'd let Brittany come with me during my investigation into Chief Vick's murder. She'd trusted me, and I'd let her down. Again.

I could do nothing about what'd happened to Brittany, but I could make sure nothing happened to Marcus he didn't deserve. I needed more information about Hank

Mathews. If any possibility existed that he was involved in Travis's death, I needed proof even Havermayer couldn't ignore.

I glanced over at the coffee bar. "Hey, Charlie, you got a minute?"

CHAPTER ELEVEN

With Savannah tucked away at home, happily gnawing on a femur bone stuffed with peanut butter, I returned to the bookstore at five forty-five for Veronica's victory party. Fingers crossed on the victory part. Veronica had done actual work for Riddleton in only six months. Imagine what she could accomplish during a whole four-year term.

Bob had presented virtually no platform, and he'd refused an opportunity to debate the issues with Veronica. A lifelong Riddleton resident who baked incredible pastries, he was an overall nice guy. Someone you could run to in a crisis, and he'd always be there. Was that enough to make him a good mayor? Half the town seemed to think so.

The banner I'd hung earlier had succumbed to gravity on one side, so I went to the stockroom for the ladder. Lacey was gathering books to ensure the shelves were stocked for the party. Lightning might strike, and someone could want to buy something.

"Do you need some help?" I asked, grabbing the ladder.

"No, thanks. We haven't sold much the last couple of days."

"I'd say I hope the police get it together and find the killer soon, but since right now they have Marcus in mind, I'm not so sure. I'd rather they take their time and arrest the right person, no matter how much business it costs us."

Lacey carried her load onto the sales floor. "I know what you mean, but how sure are you that Marcus didn't do it?"

"A hundred percent. I can't imagine any possible reason he'd have to risk his kids ending up being raised by a parade of strangers. He's worked too hard to make a good life for them."

"But the truth is, Jen, you don't really know him. People do stupid things all the time."

I erected the ladder under the banner, searching for a way to put my gut feelings into words. "In a way, you're right. I don't really know him. But my instinct tells me he didn't do this. Even when he was a drug dealer, he never killed anyone."

"That you know of."

My abdominal muscles tightened. She was right. It wouldn't be the first time I'd ever misjudged someone. However, until I had a rock-solid reason to believe him guilty, I had to do whatever I could to help him.

Lacey shelved her last volume in the Art section abutting the front window. "Did you learn anything interesting at the church yesterday?"

"Maybe. I'm not sure yet. I need more information about Father Mathews. Charlie's supposed to be digging some up for me." I glanced around the store. "Where is he anyway?"

She chuckled. "He went home to change for the party."

"Uh-oh."

"Exactly."

I straightened the banner, and Lacey helped me carry the ladder back to the storeroom.

She wiped her hands on the back of her khakis. "If you don't mind, I'm going to run home and change, too."

"Not at all. I got this."

I strolled around the store, ensuring the chairs were straight and the tables clean. A fruitless endeavor. They couldn't be dirty with no customers. With luck, we'd have a couple tonight. Reasonable people had to see we had nothing to do with Travis's murder. The key word being "reasonable."

Angus had laid out the food on four tables on one side of the room near the Romance section. My stomach rumbled at the array of potato skins smothered with bacon and cheese, chicken tenders with three sauces, and a variety of sandwiches. Top that off with coleslaw, potato salad, and barbecue baked beans, and I wasn't sure I'd even make it to the dessert table. However, the brownies, chocolate chip cookies, and angel food cake almost ensured I would, no matter how stuffed my belly was.

Charlie rolled in at six exactly, wearing a black suit with a white dress shirt and a red, white, and blue tie. His short black hair was plastered to his scalp, resembling a nineteen-twenties pilot's helmet, and his brown eyes were showcased by thick, black eyeglass frames with no lenses. My face reflected in the toes of his black oxfords.

I shook my head. "What are you supposed to be?"

He tapped the handwritten "Vote for Me" sticker tacked to his lapel. "A politician, of course. Can't you tell?"

"Yup. I was just making sure you knew."

"Ha ha. Where is everybody?"

"Good question. Veronica and her campaign team will be here, I'm sure. I guess nobody else wanted to be the first to arrive."

Charlie jutted his chin toward the door. "Speak of the devil."

I turned around. Veronica burst through the door, husband and twins in tow, cellphone plastered to her ear. Local attorney Theodore—Ted to his friends—Winslow stood a head taller than his wife, despite the rounded shoulders from years spent hunched over a desk studying legal texts. Dad and the boys had dressed alike in dark-blue suits, white shirts, and light-blue ties. Although, Ted spent much less time pulling at his collar than his sons.

Veronica's pursed lips and lowered eyebrows started my pulse racing. Was she losing? A local election in a small town like Riddleton wouldn't make the TV news, so I had no idea how the votes had tallied so far. Unfortunately, no Steve Kornacki to break this race down for us, minute by minute.

Her face brightened as I approached, but I could tell it was only an act for my benefit. "How's it going?"

She shook her head. "I just left the community center and it's close. Much closer than I'd hoped for. I'm only leading by a handful of votes."

"I'm sorry. The polls don't close for another hour, though. Don't lose faith just yet. Besides, you only need one more vote than he gets."

"True, but I was hoping for enough of a lead to avoid a recount."

The bells over the door jingled, and Lacey came in,

111

followed by a small group of Veronica's campaign workers. At least a few people in town weren't worried about a murderer stalking our bookstore. It would be nice to see someone without a direct connection to Veronica join us, though.

As if they'd read my mind, Lula Parsons arrived, with her husband George close on her heels. She was still wearing her charcoal-gray suit as if she'd come straight from work. Retiree George looked relaxed in black slacks and a light-green polo shirt. The overhead fluorescents reflected off the section of his scalp not covered by his ring of more-salt-than-pepper hair.

I guided them to the food table, where the campaign workers loaded plates as if they hadn't eaten since the last election. "I hope you guys are hungry. Angus outdid himself tonight."

Lula smiled and smoothed back her vanilla-blond bob. "I skipped lunch to vote, so I'm starved."

I handed them plates and plastic silverware, then took some for myself. A casual dinner would be the perfect opportunity to discuss Hank with Lula. I had a feeling, though, George was the kind of guy to dominate every conversation. With luck, I'd be wrong.

We carried our plates to a table near the Biography section. Perhaps I'd gain inspiration from some of the great minds displayed there.

We ate in silence for a few minutes while I waited for George to make his move. Nothing. He attacked his food with gusto, eyebrows pinched together over his nose, leaving the way clear for me to talk to Lula.

"I really enjoyed my tour of the church yesterday. I'd never seen the inside before. It's beautiful. A little spooky, but beautiful."

Lula beamed as if she'd built the place herself. "Thank you. I'm so lucky to be able to work there."

George's scowl deepened. "Humph."

Lula gave him a side-eye. "My husband isn't a fan, but he knew who I was when he married me."

"You spend more time at that church than you do at home." George dropped his sandwich onto the plate. "I made enough money for you to retire, too, you know. You need to spend more time taking care of me instead of that priest."

Lula stared at her plate.

I ignored George's outburst. "How long has Father Hank been with the parish, Lula?"

"Four years, this time around."

Excellent. She'd opened the door to questions about Mathews's abrupt departure. "This time around?"

"Yes. He left twenty years ago or so, then came back."

George tucked his food into his cheek like a chipmunk, and said, "He should've stayed gone, if you ask me. Pretty Boy's nothing but trouble."

"Pretty Boy?"

Lula chuckled. "When I was in high school, we girls called him 'Father Romeo' because he was so handsome. More than one of us had a crush on him." Her face pinked. "Not me, of course."

Of course. "I'll bet that made for some interesting confessions on Sunday."

She sat up straight in her seat. "I wouldn't know."

"Why did he leave?"

She pushed potato salad around her plate with her fork. "I'm not sure. I was a part-time housekeeper at the time, so I wasn't privy to much that went on."

Why do I find that hard to believe? "What did the rumor mill have to say?"

"Not much, actually. It was all very hush-hush."

No help. Time to switch tacks. "Did you know Travis Underwood?"

"The man who died? That was a terrible thing. So sad."

"Had you met him when he was younger? I think he was an altar boy."

She chewed on her lower lip. "I knew him in passing. He was actually my third cousin—my mother's second cousin's son—but we didn't interact much. I tried talking to him after he started getting into trouble, but he wasn't interested. I was too old. Almost thirty."

Almost thirty was too old? Where did that leave me? *Whatever.*

"What kind of trouble?"

"Oh, you know. The usual: drugs, vandalism, petty theft. I heard he even stole a car once, but I don't know if that's true or not."

I glanced at George, who was suddenly interested in our conversation again. "When did all this start?"

"If I remember correctly, right after Hank left. I guess he was keeping Travis in line. When he transferred, Travis went wild."

"That's a shame."

George swallowed another mouthful. "That kid was no good from the start. I'm surprised Hank kept him in line as long as he did."

Lula glared at him. "That's not true, George, and you know it. Why would you say such a thing?" She waved her fork. "And how would you know, anyway? You were too busy being a big shot in Blackburn to pay attention to anything going on at home."

He glared back at her. "I set you up pretty good, didn't I? I didn't hear you complaining when I bought you that big farm you never spend any time at."

Time to defuse the situation. "What made Hank come back?" I asked Lula.

Her full-toothed smile returned. "He told me he loved it here, so when the spot opened up again, he asked for a transfer."

George gathered his empty plate and took it to the trash can.

Suspecting what the answer would be, I asked, "Are you enjoying working with him?"

Lula's eyes glistened. "Oh, yes! He's a wonderful man. A bit of a slob, though."

"I guess we're all guilty of that at times. I've been known to leave my share of clutter in my wake."

She put down her fork. "Maybe, but he's a priest. For someone who's forsaken worldly possessions, he certainly can make a mess with what he has. Clothing everywhere, dirty dishes—he even left a steak knife under his mattress! I almost cut myself tucking in his sheets. I mean really, that's too much."

A steak knife or a murder weapon? "I see what you mean."

The front door opened, and Brittany and Olinski joined the party. He'd changed out of his uniform into khakis and a light-blue dress shirt, mostly hidden by his brown leather jacket. Brittany still wore her librarian suit: a knee-length plaid skirt and white silk blouse. She saw me and waved. Olinski nodded and made a beeline for the food table. Apparently, the trash compactor that served as his stomach needed a refill.

I turned back to Lula. "I've enjoyed our conversation, but I really should mingle."

She nodded. "I have too. We should do it again, sometime."

George returned as I rose from the table. "George, it was good to meet you, finally."

He grunted.

It would be difficult to tear myself away from his brilliant conversational skills, but I had to try. I gathered my trash, dumped it, and joined my best friend and ex-boyfriend at their table near the Writing section. "Hey, guys, what's up?"

"Not much," Brittany replied as Olinski attacked his roast beef sandwich.

I pointed my thumb at Olinski. "Don't you ever feed him?"

"Are you kidding? All he does is eat. If I ate like he did, I'd be the size of this building."

"He still thinks he's playing football, but that tummy's getting easier to see every day."

He gave us a closed-mouth smile to ensure nothing escaped before he could swallow. Finally, he did. "I'm glad you two are having fun. I'm a growing boy."

Brittany and I exchanged glances.

I poked Olinski in the ribs. "Yes, but in the wrong direction. You're supposed to be growing up, not out."

He winked at Brittany. "More of me to love."

She looked up to the heavens without moving her head.

I laughed. "I think I'll leave this discussion for the two of you."

A man entered and handed a slip of paper to Veronica. She glanced at it, crumpled it up, and threw it in the trash. Another preliminary vote count? It wasn't good news from the look of it. The polls didn't close for another fifteen minutes, though. Perhaps the latecomers would swing things Veronica's way.

Bob's Bakery hosted his victory party, but the store was out of view from where I sat. I could only imagine the merriment generated by the same news that caused Veronica's frown. However, I didn't hear any well-rounded women singing yet, so it must not be over.

Searching for a distraction, I turned to Olinski. "When are you going to release Marcus? You know he had nothing to do with Travis's death, right?"

His eyebrows arched. "Do I?"

"You should. He's been an upstanding citizen since he moved to Riddleton."

He scoffed. "An upstanding citizen who violated his probation by associating with a known felon."

"A known felon who sought him out, not the other way around."

"You sure? What do you know about it?"

I pressed my lips together, containing the angry dragon rising quickly toward my tongue. "I know Marcus."

"You mean, the Marcus he wants you to see. You don't know anything about Marcus the ex-con and what he's capable of."

"Perhaps not, but I can't imagine any version of Marcus would put his daughters at risk."

Olinski leaned back in his chair. "I'm sorry, Jen, but we don't have the luxury of making our decisions based on what we imagine someone might do. We have to go where the evidence takes us. Havermayer wants to hold him a while longer, and she has my full support."

I opened my mouth to let the dragon out, but Brittany laid a hand on each of our arms. "Okay, that's enough. Let's talk about something else."

Her attempt to maintain a peaceful conversation between Olinski and me was admirable, but I wasn't ready to let it go. "Lula told me she found a knife under Father Mathews's mattress. From what she described, it could be the murder weapon."

Olinski swallowed another mouthful. "Oh? What'd she say?"

"She said it was a steak knife, which fits Ingrid's description of the stab wounds."

He shrugged. "Possibly, but it could be left from a midnight snack, too."

I cocked an eyebrow. "And he hid it under his mattress?"

"Maybe he didn't want anyone to get hurt. Who knows? I'll talk to her, okay?"

There was no point in arguing with him, but hiding the knife made it *more* likely someone—like the person making Mathews's bed—would get hurt, not less. And where was the plate that held the snack that required a steak knife? Lula never mentioned finding it in her Hank's-a-slob anecdote. Nope. It made no sense.

At seven fifteen, the courier returned with another slip of paper in hand. A grin spread across Veronica's face as she read. A campaign worker handed her a phone, and Veronica listened for a minute, then returned the cell and faced the crowd.

"Ladies and gentlemen, may I have your attention please?"

The room fell silent as we all waited for the results. Veronica cleared her throat. "The final tally is in. We

118

won by twenty-three votes, and Mr. Underwood has called me to graciously concede. Thank you all for the hard work, dedication, and donations that led to our victory. I'm looking forward to serving the people of Riddleton for the next four years."

I joined the crowd in a standing ovation, then made my way to where Veronica was shaking hands with her campaign team. "Congratulations! I'm so happy for you."

She wrapped me in a hug. "Thank you. And thanks for all your help."

"I didn't do anything, but you're welcome."

Veronica released me and put her hands on my shoulders to look me in the eye. "You did more than you realize. You propped me up every time I got discouraged. You're a real friend."

My eyes filled with tears. Nobody but Brittany had ever said that to me before.

CHAPTER TWELVE

I opened my eyes to Savannah stretched across my chest, watching me with her wet, black nose an inch from my eye. I pushed her off, and she scooted back into position, giving me a doggy hug. "C'mon, little girl, you have to move." I sat up, and she slid down off the bed. When I wiped my face, my hand came away wet. I must've been dreaming. No idea about what, though. Whatever it was, my furry baby was there to make it all better.

I threw on my sweats and headed for the living room, where my Nikes hid under the coffee table. Savannah pranced by the door as I laced them up. She was house-trained now, so I had little fear of an accidental puddle, but still didn't want to push my luck. The sun had barely crested the horizon, so I donned a jacket too. No telling what kind of weather I'd encounter out there. It was Christmastime, after all.

When we reached the bottom of the steps, I found an upper-forties chill and a low-lying mist that would burn off when the sun rose a little higher in the sky. Not too bad for a Wednesday in the second week of December.

Savannah pranced her way around the block, reveling

in the cool weather and poking at the Santas and Rudolphs camped out on my neighbors' lawns.

I gave my girl fresh food and water, then turned my attention to the coffeemaker. The brew cycle hadn't finished yet, but I grabbed the pot and poured myself a cup. The aroma chased the cobwebs out of my brain. Before I could swallow my first sip, though, my phone rang. Who was crazy enough to call me at this hour of the morning?

Echolocation led me to the cell, which was under a couch cushion. A quick glance at the screen answered my question. My mother. Who else?

"Hi, Mom. How are you? Is Gary all right?"

"He's better, thanks. What do you think about rescheduling that cookout we were going to have the other day?"

"I don't see why not. When were you thinking?"

"Whenever works for you. I think Gary could use a distraction, and you know how he loves Savannah."

Right. Whenever worked for me, as long as it was when she had in mind. "It's a pretty day outside, why don't we try for this afternoon? I think we all could use a distraction."

"That sounds great."

I signed off, telling my mother I had to work on my book. But first, I called Eric, so he wouldn't think I'd forgotten him again. I did care about him, and he was good for me, as my mother liked to remind me every chance she got. Eric was a keeper. Steady, reliable, even cute. But something was missing in our relationship, and I couldn't quite figure out what.

"Hey, what're you up to?" I asked when he answered the phone.

121

"Putting together the paperwork to get an arrest warrant for Marcus."

"What? Why? You know he had nothing to do with Travis's murder."

"I wish I did. We found a blackmail note from Travis in Marcus's room yesterday. Apparently, Marcus was involved in the death of another inmate while he was in prison, and Travis covered up for him. He was demanding money to keep silent about it. We think Marcus killed him to make sure he didn't tell anyone."

"That's ridiculous. If Marcus had snuffed someone in prison, the administration would've known about it. There are cameras everywhere."

"Everywhere but the showers. And that's where the guy died. We contacted the warden at Broad River Correctional. They looked at Marcus, but couldn't prove anything. Travis was the only other person there. His eyewitness testimony could've put Marcus away for the rest of his life, but he vouched for him instead."

Marcus must've vouched for Travis too. "I refuse to accept the idea that Marcus murdered that man. Maybe it was self-defense."

"Maybe, but then why not just say that? Why insist he found the guy dead and knew nothing about how he got that way?"

"What if it was Travis, and he didn't want to rat him out?" I switched the phone to my other ear. "I don't know. What does Marcus say about it?"

"He's not talking. We have no choice, Jen. The circumstantial evidence is overwhelming. Put that together with the fight they had the night Travis died, and it's a solid case."

Maybe not. "Not necessarily."

"What do you mean?"

"Lula Parsons from St. Mary's told me she almost cut herself on a knife in Father Mathews's room yesterday that fits the description of the murder weapon. She found it stuffed under his mattress when she tried to make his bed."

"There are a lot of knives that fit the general description Ingrid came up with. And frankly, we're looking at her as an accomplice, so we can't necessarily trust what she found. She and Marcus are pretty tight. The stab wounds were precisely placed. Ingrid herself told us it looked like a doctor did it. Well, she's a doctor."

I clenched my empty fist by my side, fingernails digging half-moons into my palm. "There's no way Ingrid would point a finger directly at herself."

"Maybe not, but that doesn't mean she wasn't involved."

"You've been spending too much time with Havermayer."

"She's a good detective."

My hand cramped, and I shook it out. "Look, you can't close the book on this without looking into Father Mathews. He knew Travis when he was a kid. Brittany sent me a picture of the two of them together, and Travis seemed very uncomfortable. Then Mathews was transferred to Idaho out of nowhere, and Travis's personality did a one-eighty. He went from being an altar boy to being a hoodlum. It can't be a coincidence. There has to be some connection."

"I don't know, Jen."

"Just promise me you'll look into it. You can still arrest Marcus if you have to, as long as you're open to the possibility it wasn't him."

"I'll see what I can do, but Havermayer's made up her mind."

So, what else is new? "Thank you."

As I laid the phone down on the counter, I realized there wouldn't be much Eric could do. Havermayer had her sights set on Marcus, and tunnel vision was her middle name. What was the basis for her determination, though? Sure, the blackmail note was damning but certainly not proof of anything. And they found his fingerprints on the paper in Travis's pocket, and Marcus never mentioned it. Strange, but not necessarily nefarious. The only real evidence she had was the fight between Marcus and Travis the night Travis died.

It seemed I was the only person left solidly in Marcus's corner besides Ingrid. Eric told me they'd found the blackmail note when they'd searched Marcus's rooms. What if they had missed something that proved Marcus innocent? Only one way to find out. I had to see for myself.

Mary Washington lived in a craftsman-style two-story home on Riddleton Road between Walnut and Pine, right up the street from the First Baptist Church. Six brick steps led to a wraparound porch with a swing hanging in front of each bay window on either side of the solid oak front door, decorated with a green wreath holding a red bow. Widely spaced pillars wrapped with red garlands supported the roof jutting below the three four-paned windows that delineated the upper story. A double-windowed attic rested top center like a top hat with eyes that watched every move I made.

I trudged up the steps and pressed the illuminated button next to the door. The ensuing ding-dong reverberated through the house, momentarily drowning out the roasting chestnuts of the "Christmas Song." From deep within, I heard a faint, "I'm coming. Hold on now."

A minute later, the door eased open. An old black woman wearing ninety-five years' worth of wrinkles and sagging skin breathed heavily in the doorway. A gap-toothed smile split her face.

"Miss Jen! It's so good to see you." She stepped back. "Come in and rest awhile."

I stepped into the spotless living room. "Hi, Mrs. W., how've you been?" I followed the throw rugs protecting the shiny, deep-chocolate hardwood floor to the ancient but well-cared-for, beige leather couch. "I was so sorry to hear about Harry."

She pressed her lips together, then said, "He ain't suffering no more. I'm grateful for that." She started toward the kitchen. "Let me get you some tea."

"No, thank you. I don't need anything."

"Of course you do. I'll bring some cookies, too. I made them yesterday, but they should still be good. I always make sure there's cookies in the house for those sweet little girls."

No point in arguing. "Thank you."

I wandered around while I waited. Framed photographs covered every flat surface—ranging from the Washingtons' wedding pictures to what was most likely the last photo Mary and her late husband Harry took together before cancer claimed him. They had no children, but interspersed with the wedding pictures were dozens of kids in various stages of growing up. Nieces and nephews, perhaps. Regardless, this home was filled with love for sixty years or more.

Mrs. W. shuffled in, carrying a tray holding a pitcher of sweet tea, two glasses, and a plate of chocolate chip cookies. I rushed to take it from her.

"Thank you, dear," she said as I set the tray on the coffee table and poured tea for each of us. "You're sweet."

We settled on the couch and sipped our drinks. I sampled a cookie, which sent my taste buds to Nirvana. "This is delicious. Marcus has some lucky little girls."

She smiled. "Do you know when Marcus is coming home, Miss Jen? The police went through all his stuff yesterday. Made a big old mess. I fixed it, though."

I shook my head. "You're a very kind woman, Mrs. W., but I don't know when they're going to let him go. That's kind of why I'm here."

"What do you mean?"

I leaned toward her. "With your permission, I'd like to look through Marcus's and the girls' rooms to see if I can find something the police missed that might help him."

"I know you want to help, but I don't think I should let you look through his things without asking him first. The police gave me that paper and said I had to." She gestured toward the warrant lying on the table.

I finished my cookie, buying time to come up with a response that might change her mind. *Come on, Daniel, don't fail me now.*

"I understand, and normally I'd agree with you, but Marcus needs help right now. They're going to arrest him for something I know he didn't do. You don't believe he killed that man, do you?"

She laid her hand on her ample bosom. "Oh, no. He would never do that."

"Then please let me try to help him. I probably won't find anything. The police are pretty thorough. But I think it's worth the chance, don't you?"

She nodded and gestured toward the stairs leading to the bedrooms. "Their rooms are on the right, and I hope you find something. Those little girls need their daddy."

"Thank you."

A long, narrow staircase led to the second floor. At the bottom, a stair lift chair rested, waiting for Mrs. W. to require a ride. I kept to the decorative runner in the middle.

Larissa and Latoya, Marcus's daughters, slept in the room directly across from the staircase, as indicated by the twin four-poster beds and overflowing toy box. Marcus's room was to the right. I tried that one first.

The chamber had a distinctive male flavor to it: utilitarian brown furniture, plain beige curtains, and the lingering smell of aftershave. It was also spotless. Mrs. W. was a wizard at cleaning up the aftermath of a police search. I'd have to hire her the next time the cops turned the bookstore upside down. Although I fervently hoped there'd never be a next time. Twice was more than enough for me.

I went through the dresser drawers, checking underneath for secret messages. No luck. The closet had no hidden trapdoors and no damaging or exculpatory papers taped to the shelf. I checked for loose carpeting near the walls and even removed the cover to the vent near the ceiling. Nothing there. I searched everywhere I assumed the investigators had covered, plus any place else I could think of. I swallowed my disappointment and moved across the hall.

Repeating the entire process in the girls' room achieved the same results. I flopped down on one of the beds and leaned against the bedpost, "Does Your Chewing Gum Lose its Flavor..." running on a loop through my head.

Terrific. That earworm wouldn't go away any time soon. However, something about the bedposts gnawed at me. Something I saw on a TV show once. In that episode, the tops of the bedposts came off, and a note was hidden inside one of them. I might as well try it. What did I have to lose?

I twisted and pulled on the tops of all four bedposts of the bed nearest the door. They were stuck fast, almost as if the post was one solid piece of wood, although the seam between the top and the post was obvious.

Next up? The bed by the window. The three accessible posts were the same as the ones on the other bed. The only thing between me and a wasted morning was the corner post by the window.

Clambering on the neatly made bed, I propped one knee on the pillow and the other leg against the wall. This was my last chance to find something to help Marcus stay out of prison. My last chance to set an innocent man free.

Deep breath in, slow breath out.

I grabbed the top of the post, twisted, and pulled. It came off easily, and I lost my balance, flipping backward off the bed. I hit the floor with a grunt and a flash of pain through my ribs. I lay there clutching the post top until the discomfort eased and my breathing slowed, then turned it over. In the hole, pressed against the side, was a scrap of paper.

An attempt to reach it with my pinky failed at the

second knuckle, so I trotted downstairs and asked Mrs. W. for a pair of tweezers. She found them in her manicure set, and I fished the scrap out of the hole on the fourth try.

In tiny block letters, written in pencil, were the words:

I KNOW YOU DIDN'T DO IT.
TRAVIS SET YOU UP.

I reread the message as I climbed the stairs to return the post top to the bed. Who wrote it? And what did it mean? I had to ask Marcus.

CHAPTER THIRTEEN

My hand shook as I read and reread the note. On the one hand, the cryptic message proved Marcus had no reason to kill Travis because he hadn't murdered anyone in prison. But Travis was obviously willing to lie about Marcus's involvement, giving Marcus a reason to want him dead. I suspected Marcus agreed or he wouldn't have hidden it. A headache blossomed behind my eyes as I stuffed the scrap of paper in my pocket and trudged down the stairs.

Mrs. W. had fallen asleep on the couch. I tiptoed to the coffee table, gathered our dirty dishes, and gently placed them in the sink. Caring for the girls and worrying about Marcus had worn her out. Being old enough to have lived through the Great Depression, five wars, and a fifth of the twenty-first century probably didn't help much, either. I had to get Marcus home soon.

I sauntered down Riddleton Road past the A-frame houses where the battle of the Christmas decorations was in full swing. Fat, happy Santas, snowmen, and nativity scenes graced every yard. Plus, lights, lights, and more lights. Multicolored, mono-colored, flashing, static lights wrapped around windows, doors, and roofs.

The electric company would be tap dancing when the January payments came in.

The note burdened my mind. It was evidence I should give to Eric. However, Havermayer would use it as the final proof she needed that Marcus murdered Travis. I didn't care how many notes I found. Nothing would convince me Marcus had killed Travis. I needed to talk to him.

I hung a left on Pine and then again on Main, past the town hall to the police station. The steps to the entrance seemed a mile long in my current mental state. I plodded up, wishing I had Mrs. W.'s stair chair. Shaking off the malaise, I opened the door and strolled past the headshots of former officers to the duty sergeant's desk. The atmosphere seemed much less gloomy than the last time I was here, which was the night I broke in to obtain proof Eric had nothing to do with evidence being missing from the property room.

When I told the duty sergeant I'd come to visit Marcus, he phoned Havermayer for approval. Apparently, she was so determined to keep him under wraps, she screened his visitors. Regardless, a few minutes later, Zach escorted me to the visitor's booth. I tried to speak to him, but he marched ahead, stone-faced, as if we'd never met before.

I wanted to put the little twerp over my knee, but honestly, he was his father's son. Tobias Vick had been a cold, disagreeable man that few people outside his immediate family had mourned deeply when he was murdered. I couldn't blame Zach for his upbringing.

It took a few minutes for them to bring Marcus up from the holding cells, and I hardly recognized the man that occupied the seat across from me on the other side of the Plexiglass barrier. His face was puffy, as if he'd had a fight, and a two-day beard growth eclipsed his normally pencil-thin mustache.

Zach removed the handcuffs, slid the window open so we could talk, then moved a discreet distance away.

"Thanks, Zach."

He leaned against the wall and pulled out his phone. I turned back to Marcus, who rubbed his wrists. I touched his hand. "How are you?"

"Okay, considering I don't belong in here." Bitterness dripped off his words.

"I know you don't. What are they telling you?"

He swiped a hand over his face. "They're telling me I killed Travis because he was blackmailing me over something that happened ten years ago, and I'm going to prison for the rest of my life."

"What did he have on you?"

"I walked into the shower room one day and found Travis standing over a guy dead on the floor. A guard came in a minute later, and Travis told him we'd come in together and found him like that. I didn't disagree. He was my friend."

"But something went wrong."

"Travis started telling people I did it, and he'd saved my butt. The word traveled fast and eventually the warden got wind of it. They brought me in for questioning, but all they had was rumors, so they couldn't do nothing to me."

"Then, Travis got out and needed money, so he blackmailed you, saying he'd tell them you did it, if you didn't pay."

"Right. And I can't prove that's not the way it happened. I also can't prove I didn't murder Travis. I'm screwed."

"No, you're not. You still have me. I won't let you

go to prison for something you didn't do. I promise you that."

He shook his head. "No, Jen. There's nothing you can do for me. You'll only get yourself in trouble."

I'll take my chances. "What happens now?"

He studied his fingernails. "Now, I get arrested and transferred to Sutton County Detention."

Sutton County was a real jail, not just a holding cell. He'd have to deal with other inmates. "Why can't you stay here?"

"They'd have to transport me back and forth for court. Besides, my lawyer's office is there. It'll be easier for him to talk to me."

"Who's representing you?"

"Ted Winslow, but I don't know how I'm gonna pay him. I gave him all my savings to get him to sign on for the arraignment. I don't know what I'm gonna do for the trial, but I don't want no public defender. Not for no murder case."

Fear radiated from his eyes. I had to help him. "I don't blame you. Let me see what I can do. If things work out right, you won't need him for anything but the arraignment."

Zach looked up from his phone. "All right, Jones. Wrap it up."

Marcus nodded.

I took his hand. "Is there anything you need? Cigarettes maybe?"

He chuckled. "You know I don't smoke."

"No, but everyone else in Sutton County probably does. You could trade them for stuff you *do* need."

"You watch too much TV. I can deal. It's not my first time, you know."

"I know. Take care of yourself. I'm going to get you out, just give me some time. All you have to do is keep it together until I do."

He stood and held his hands toward Zach, who handcuffed and led him away.

I stepped out into the sunshine and inhaled deeply. I'd never been in jail, but I somehow felt like I'd just gotten out after serving ten years. I could only imagine how Marcus must feel. The flashbacks he must have. Flashbacks of a life he thought he'd left behind for good. I had to help him. Although it would be easier if he hadn't fought with Travis the night he died.

When I hit the bottom of the steps and turned toward the town hall, I realized that, even though I had no idea how to get him out of jail, I might help with his attorney's fees. At least I could ensure he had competent representation during his trial. Maybe even his appeals if the jury somehow convicted him.

I sprinted up the steps and entered the town-hall building. Veronica's old office was empty on my immediate right, her new one dead ahead at the end of the hall. I stood in the doorway and waited for her to get off the phone.

She noticed me, held up a finger, and then gestured toward a chair in front of her desk. I scrolled through my phone as she completed her mayoral duties. Nothing interesting, which was fine with me. I had enough interesting things to worry about.

She ended her call and smiled. "Hi, Jen. What can I do for you?"

"I just came from visiting Marcus."

Eyebrows lowered in concern, she asked, "How's he doing?"

"He's all right. They're getting ready to transfer him to Sutton County."

"I'm sorry to hear that. I guess that means he's been charged."

I nodded. "He told me your husband is representing him, but he's not sure how he can pay him."

She leaned back in her chair. "I try to stay out of my husband's business."

"I understand. I don't know him very well, or I'd ask him myself, but I wonder if you could see if he'd consider representing Marcus pro bono. Marcus can't afford to pay him any more than he already has. I don't believe he had anything to do with Travis's death, and I don't want to see him convicted because he had a bad lawyer."

"I'll ask, but I don't know what he'll say."

"If he can't do it for free, maybe he'll consider a reduced rate? I'm willing to help with the payments. If Marcus goes to prison, his children will end up in the system. Those little girls don't deserve that."

"I agree. Let me see what I can do." Her phone buzzed again. "Is there anything else you need from me?"

I stood and shook my head. "Thank you for trying."

She smiled again and picked up the handset.

As I left the town hall, my brain boomeranged between how to help Marcus to whether to tell Eric about the note I'd found in Marcus's daughter's bedpost. I couldn't even discuss it with Marcus because Zach had standing right there. He'd made a good show of being otherwise engaged, but I was sure he'd listened to every word. Either way, I couldn't take the chance because the note was as incriminating as it was exculpatory, depending on how you wanted to look at it.

I decided Savannah needed a walk to clear her head. She'd had a lot on her mind lately, and a little fresh air would do her good. She made her agreement obvious when I came in, and she pulled her leash off the doorknob.

We headed back out, and within a few minutes, I recognized that the residents of Park Street had gotten together and planned their community decoration scheme. Rather than competing against each other, they aimed to win as a group.

Each house had its own theme. On one side of the street, Santa and his North Pole workshop—complete with elves and tools and wall-to-wall toys—led to a Christmas village, and Santa in a flying sleigh carried gifts from one display to the other. I had no idea how they'd rigged that up, but it was impressive, without a doubt.

The other side of the street picked up the religious aspect of the holiday. The first house showed the wise men carrying their gifts, accompanied by children, angels, and camels. In the next yard was a lifelike nativity scene, complete with animals. The last lawn had angels leading a grownup Jesus to a church with an illuminated cross for a spire. The combined sides of the street covered all the bases.

We passed through the wrought-iron gates of Riddleton Park into a winter wonderland. Fake snow covered the ground, and a dozen motorized children—bundled up for cold weather—skated the artificial ice path that weaved among the trees. A workshop filled one end of the park, and elves in rolled-up sleeves built toys while a coatless Santa supervised, thumbs hooked in his suspenders. I kept Savannah on her leash to ensure she didn't tinkle on Santa's shoe.

One trip around the mile-long track that encircled the park brought us back to the entrance. I turned right on Second Street to make the loop down Walnut to the bookstore, but when we hit Pine, I took a detour to the library instead. Brittany might have information on Father Mathews.

I crunched the remains of pine cones under my feet, dropped by the tree behind the listing picnic table in the empty library parking lot. Savannah picked her way around them since her foot pads didn't offer as much protection against sharp edges as my Nikes. Her head was up, though, so how had she missed them all?

We trotted up the stairs into the building and negotiated the dim hallway that led to the brightly lit reading room. Brittany had hung Santa wreaths around the walls, and a six-foot tree behind the counter was decorated with lights, silver garlands, and slips of paper with the names of the children to receive the donated wrapped gifts underneath.

Brittany hid in a back corner, pushing her trolley along the wall, shelving books. I released Savannah's leash so she wouldn't dislocate my shoulder trying to reach her favorite person. My German shepherd charged the cart, then slid to a stop and dropped to her haunches when Brittany held her hand out to stop her. Another miracle created by hours of training.

After a thorough neck scratch and an exchange of kisses, Brittany turned my way. "What are you two up to today?"

I filled her in on my Tour de Riddleton and my conversation with Marcus.

Brittany shook her head. "I can't believe he's implicated in Travis's death. And the death of another

137

inmate while he was in prison. He's worked so hard to turn his life around."

"I don't care what the evidence says. There's no way he killed those guys. I'm at a loss as to how to help him, though. The circumstantial evidence is overwhelming. His only hope is if I can find someone else to point a finger at. And convince Havermayer to follow the lead."

"What do you have so far?"

I blew out a hard breath. "A deep suspicion of Father Mathews and a slim hope it could still be a robbery gone insane. But the police have already ruled that one out."

"I might be able to help with the Father Mathews aspect."

Brittany walked back to the checkout counter, with Savannah bumping her nose against the backs of Brittany's legs. She pulled out a treat bag and handed one to the dog to keep her busy for a minute. Then she gave me a printed copy of an article from the *Idaho Statesman* from four years ago. The headline read: *Local Priest Accused of Affair with Parishioner*.

The local priest was Father Mathews, but there were no details about the parishioner. "Were there any follow-up articles? And is there that little real news in Idaho?"

"Apparently. However, I did some more digging and discovered Father Mathews was transferred back to Riddleton only a few weeks later."

"I guess Father Romeo strikes again."

She cocked her head. "What do you mean?"

"Lula told me all her high-school girlfriends had crushes on Father Mathews. They called him Father Romeo."

"Funny. Sounds like he might've had a similar problem here in Riddleton. He did leave rather suddenly, didn't he?"

I nodded.

"What if he was involved with a relative of Travis's and he objected? Maybe they argued about it and Father Mathews killed him."

If there was such a person, Brittany might've found the smoking gun we needed to take the heat off Marcus. Well, the smoking priest, anyway.

CHAPTER FOURTEEN

Ravenous Readers had two customers when Savannah led me through the front door: Veronica Winslow, who'd stopped by on her way home from work to find a new bedtime story for her boys, and Lula Parsons. Inviting her to Veronica's victory party had paid off with a new regular customer. That worked for me. We needed all the help we could get.

Charlie packed up some cookies for Veronica to serve for dessert. Savannah trotted over for crumb collection duty, but Charlie wasn't a three-year-old-boy, so she lay with her head on her paws, hoping for a sympathy cookie instead. She had no luck with that one, either. Poor baby would have to settle for the remains of whatever my mother was making for dinner.

I helped Charlie break down the coffee bar since it was five forty-five already. Where had the day gone? In retrospect, I'd actually been busy. I'd done little writing, but I'd gathered some information at least. I was now pretty sure Marcus was innocent of the crime Travis had accused him of, but he'd been arrested for murdering his accuser and transferred to the Sutton County

Detention Center. Some might consider that a fair trade. I considered it a travesty.

Veronica came over to collect her cookies. "Hi, Jen. I spoke with Ted about what we discussed in my office. He said he'd represent Marcus pro bono through the arraignment, but he's not sure what he can do if it goes to trial. We're going to talk more tonight, after the kids go to bed. I'll let you know what we come up with."

"Thank you." I squeezed her arm. "You're a good friend."

"Don't worry. One way or the other, Marcus will have a good attorney when the time comes. You have my word."

Veronica's word was good enough for me. She'd proved herself many times since she'd become the mayor. However, if I did my job right, Marcus wouldn't need Ted's services. "I appreciate that."

"What was that all about?" Charlie asked when she left.

"Her husband is representing Marcus, and she's going to ask him to do it pro bono if he can. Or at least reduce his rates."

"I can't imagine he'd say no to reducing his rates to get a high-profile case like this one."

"I hope you're right. Since we're on the subject of getting paid, how are those new websites coming along?"

"Pretty good," he said, carrying the coffee urn to the utility room to dump it.

I followed with the utensils from the pastry case.

He scrubbed the urn with a soapy sponge on a stick. "I revamped the store site so people can make purchases online. The inventory was already listed, so all I had to do was add 'select' buttons to each item and create the shopping carts. We'll receive an email alert with each purchase."

"How long will we have to get the orders out?"

"I thought two days to pack and ship would be reasonable, but I wanted to discuss it with you first before we went live."

"That sounds doable. Between the three of us, we should be able to handle it. We can always adjust later if necessary."

"That's what I thought. As soon as I'm done with our site, I'll open our Amazon and eBay seller accounts. Opening the accounts will be easy, but listing the inventory will be time-consuming. Although, there might be a way to upload the inventory directly from our site. I'll have to look into it."

"That would be nice. If not, we can do them one at a time and all pitch in as time allows. Can more than one person add inventory at the same time?"

"I don't know. I'll see what I can find out. If push comes to shove, we can try it. If it works, it works, and if it doesn't, we'll just try something else."

"Sounds like a plan."

Charlie finished the dishes and left them on the rack to air-dry overnight.

I went up front to see if Lacey needed help with anything. She was serving Lula, who'd made two selections each from the Mystery and Romance sections.

"Find anything good?" I asked Lula, propping my elbows on the counter beside her.

"Everything here is good," she said, brushing back her vanilla-blond hair. "At least everything I've purchased so far. Today I wanted something to keep me busy while George is out of town. And restock my rainy-day pile."

"Oh? Where's he off to?"

"No place exciting. Just some family thing. He'll be back tomorrow night."

Four books for one day? She must be valedictorian of the Evelyn Wood Speed Reading program.

"In fact," Lula continued, "I was going to ask if you ladies would like to join me for dinner tonight. I almost never get to just relax with friends."

Friends? I'd only spoken to her a couple of times, and, as far as I knew, Lacey'd only met her last night at Veronica's party. She was clearly lonely.

"I'm sorry. I wish I could, but I'm having dinner at my mother's tonight. Perhaps some other time?"

She looked hopefully toward Lacey.

Lacey shook her head. "I'm sorry, too. My family's expecting me. And I'm bringing dinner, so if I don't show, they don't eat."

Lula's mouth drooped, and she quickly covered it with a smile. "I understand. I'll give you more notice next time."

Lacey smiled. "That would be better for me. You know how kids can be."

The faraway look in Lula's eyes revealed her unspoken answer to that statement.

I followed Lula to the door, to lock it behind her.

She rested her hand on the doorknob. "I was hoping to have a chance to speak to you, Jen. I think I have an idea who might've stabbed that man they found behind your store. I tried to tell the police about it, but they told me they already had their perpetrator, and they were certain he was guilty. My suspicions didn't hold up against that."

What should I do? My mother was expecting us, and Gary needed to spend time with Savannah to keep his spirits up. But Lula might have answers to the question of who killed Travis Underwood. She also might have answers to my questions about Hank's relationship with Travis. And it seemed like she needed a friend right now. George didn't strike me as the type to encourage her friendships with others. Having dinner with her tonight was the least I could do. Besides, I could use another friend too.

"All right, Lula. I'll call my Mom and reschedule. I have to take Savannah home, so can you meet me at the diner in about half an hour?"

Her face brightened. "Wonderful! I'll get us a table and start reading while I wait. Thank you so much." She left before I could change my mind.

Now I had to call my mother. My stomach churned. She would be angry. Especially if I told her the real reason for the cancelation. Forget angry; she'd be furious about my getting involved in another murder investigation. I had to come up with a better excuse. Well, a different one, anyway.

I chewed on it all the way home. I could tell her I didn't feel well, but if someone told her I was at the diner, she'd know I'd lied. I couldn't say I had to work, because the bookstore closed at six, and I couldn't claim a writing emergency, either, because this book had no deadline. The only viable option left was to tell her Savannah was sick. If someone noticed me at the diner, I could say I stepped out to get something to eat and ran into Lula.

Oh, what a tangled web we weave…

With my fingers crossed, I made the call. Mom's anger quickly dissolved into concern when she learned Savannah didn't feel well. My guilt level rose with equal speed. I hated lying to my mother, but I had to know what Lula wanted to tell me about a potential new suspect. Marcus's situation had zoomed past difficult to desperate.

I still had a few minutes before I had to meet Lula, so I called Eric to tell him about the Idaho article Brittany had discovered and the note I'd found in the girls' room.

"You should've brought us that note right away, Jen." He used his irritated voice.

"I know. I'm sorry. It's not like I waited months, though. I only found it this morning, and I did the right thing in the end. Doesn't that count for something?"

"Of course it does. I appreciate you bringing it to my attention. I just wish it hadn't been such a challenge for you."

Challenge? My heart pounded into my breastbone. "What difference would it have made anyway? You'd already made up your minds Marcus murdered Travis. You arrested and transferred him to Sutton County without knowing anything about this note. I think you're angry that I found it and your people didn't."

He inhaled loudly enough for me to hear. "I'm disappointed that our guys missed it, sure, but the issue is you withheld it from me. Don't try to change the subject."

"Well, try this on for a change of subject." I hung up on him.

Clearly, I had a long way to go if I was going to grow up by Sunday.

Lula had secured the table under the Marlboro Man, who currently had an elf hat covering his usual cowboy hat. Wednesday night was the busiest dinnertime of the work week, and the diner was filled with couples on "Hump Day" dates. Rather than being one of that crowd, I'd just hung up on my boyfriend and joined a middle-aged woman whose husband was out of town. And canceled a date with my mother to do it. What did that say about me? Nothing I wanted to hear.

Tonight's special was meatloaf, and we both chose that with mashed potatoes and peas. It was only a hamburger in another form, right? Ditto the mashed potatoes. I'd eat the peas only to satisfy my vegetable needs for the week. Maybe if I ate them slowly enough, they'd be good for the whole month.

We chit-chatted while we waited for our food, and Lula told me about the farm she and George lived on outside of town. "Do you like horses?" she asked.

"I don't know. I've never been around them. I saw a pony once at a friend's birthday party, but I didn't ride it."

Lula sipped her tea. "Why not?"

"It looked at me funny."

She covered her mouth to keep her drink inside long enough to swallow. "Well, we'll have to do something about that. I'm off Friday afternoon. Why don't you come out to the farm? I have a mare gentle enough for my three-year-old niece to ride. And she won't give you any dirty looks."

The horse or the niece? I shot Lula a mock glare, but

honestly, I had asked for it. However, I had no interest in riding a rocking horse, let alone a real one. But could I turn my back on someone who clearly needed a friend? Besides, I liked Lula. Maybe we could be pals. "Sure. Why not? What's the worst that might happen?" I'd make my fourth trip to the hospital in a little over a year.

I gave her my number so she could text me the address.

The crowded restaurant and Angus's continuing short-handed status let me assume it would be a while before our dinner arrived. Might as well get down to business. I took a swallow of my Mountain Dew. "How long have you worked at St. Mary's, Lula?"

"All my life, just about. I started after high school as a part-time housekeeper at the rectory and worked my way up from there."

"Have you always worked for Father Hank?" There's nothing like a little feigned ignorance to coax information out of someone.

"No, he left for a while and came back when Father Preston retired four years ago."

I pretended she wasn't telling me things I already knew to keep the conversation going. "So, he came back because there was an opening?"

"Right. He told me he missed it here, and the weather in Idaho was terrible in comparison. He jumped on the chance to return to Riddleton."

"I heard he had some trouble out there in Idaho."

"Trouble? He's never mentioned anything about it."

No surprise, of course. "I saw a newspaper article that said he'd been accused of having an affair with a parishioner."

She shook her head. "That can't be true. Hank would

147

never do such a thing. He's a good man, and an excellent priest."

"That's what the paper said. And right after that, Hank was transferred back here."

"Well, it has to be a coincidence. He told me he'd been trying to get back here for years. Father Hank would *never* break his vows!" She crossed her arms and glared at me.

I raised my hands in surrender. "Okay. I'm sorry if I upset you. That wasn't my intention. I was just wondering if you knew anything about it."

"Nothing to know," she said, her eyes throwing darts at me.

Time to change the subject before her head spun around and pea soup spewed out of her mouth. I doubted St. Mary's had an exorcist on call. "What did you want to talk to me about? You said you knew something about Travis's death?"

She stared at a point above my head, pressing her lips together. "Well, I don't know about that, but I did see a teenaged boy with a knife in here the day that man was killed."

My eyebrows shot up. "A teenager with a knife? Did you know him?"

"I've seen him around, and someone told me he's been arrested twice for attempted robbery. Both times using a knife."

"Attempted robbery? Sounds like he wasn't very good at it."

She smiled. "No, probably not."

"What makes you think he's the one who killed Travis? The police ruled out robbery right away, although I'm not sure why."

"I was waiting for my to-go order, and I heard him talking to his friend about going after a new guy in town that night. He said the guy wasn't allowed to carry any weapons because he was on parole, and it should be an easy score."

Angus brought over our dinner plates and set them on the table. "Sorry it took so long, ladies, we're still short-handed."

I patted his arm. "No problem. I understand."

Lula looked up. "Angus, do you remember that kid sitting at the counter Friday night when I came to pick up my food?"

"Which one?"

"The one talking to his friend about the new guy in town. The one with the knife."

Angus's eyes widened. "I remember him blustering about something. I didn't pay much attention at the time. But I had no idea he had a knife."

"I saw it on his belt when he reached for a napkin. I didn't take what he said seriously, either. In fact, I'd forgotten all about him until this morning. But now I think he might've had something to do with that man's murder."

"You really think so?"

"It makes sense, don't you think?"

Angus nodded. "Now that you mention it, you might be right."

Finally, a direction to point Eric in that didn't lead to Marcus. Too bad I'd just made him angry. Perhaps I should've ordered the crow instead of the meatloaf.

CHAPTER FIFTEEN

"Have Yourself a Merry Little Christmas" crooned its way into my consciousness Thursday morning. Savannah snuggled against my leg, and I scratched her behind the ears. She lifted her head, then laid it back down again. "Hey, sleepyhead, it's time to get up."

She blinked at me, chin nestled between her forelegs.

I lifted her snout and let it go. It fell back to the bed. She was fine when we went to sleep. "What's wrong with you, little girl? Did you drink too much last night while I was out? Come on, let's go for a walk. It's a perfect hangover cure."

I grabbed my sweats and threw them on, watching her response. She stood and slid off the side of the bed. Balanced on unsteady legs, she watched me tie my shoes. I gave her a two-handed back scratch, which ended at the base of her tail. She loved it, as always, but when I stopped, she didn't immediately swing her butt around for round two.

Huh. I'd have to see what she did outside.

Savannah walked to the door and sat while I leashed her up. She made no effort to play with the leash or duck away from my hand. Overnight, my dog had aged

150

ten years. My stomach sank as we minced down the steps one at a time to the street.

She squatted by the oak tree with no problems or complaints. Okay, that eliminated a urinary tract infection. One down, four-hundred and ninety-nine possibilities to go. Perhaps she ate something that upset her tummy. I tried to remember any trail treats she'd picked up while outside yesterday. Nothing came to mind. In fact, she'd been particularly discriminating, turning up her nose at anything that didn't have meat. I'd taken that as a sign she was well-fed. Perhaps I'd let my ego run away with me, and she'd been getting sick instead.

Or someone fed her something toxic. I'd received a note threatening her during the last investigation. What if the same was happening here, only the person went directly to action instead of warning me first? Had somebody poisoned Savannah to frighten me away from looking into Travis's murder? But how could they get to her without my knowledge? She was always with me or someone I trusted.

Was karma paying me back for lying to my mother last night? I'd said Savannah was sick, so now she really was. Either way, this was all my fault.

She plodded down the sidewalk to the corner, making no attempt to eliminate anything else, and didn't object when I turned her back toward the apartment. She hated to turn around. Like a car from the 1800s, she had no reverse, which was why, under normal conditions, I had to walk her all the way around the block to get her home.

We trudged up the steps, and Savannah sat while I unleashed her. I filled her food and water bowls, but she only sniffed them, then climbed on the couch to lie down. Regular kibble wasn't tempting enough. What else did I have?

Cheese. She'd take my fingers off for a piece of cheese. If she wouldn't eat that, we were in trouble.

I grabbed a slice out of the refrigerator and carried it to where she lay curled in a ball with her nose tucked under her hind leg. I tore off a corner and held it near her nostrils. She moved her head away.

Swallowing back the panic creeping into my throat, I felt her all over, looking for anything amiss. I found nothing, and she didn't react until I reached her belly. When I touched a lump under her skin that wasn't there yesterday, she whined.

I shushed her and hugged her head, on the verge of tears. A deep breath forced them back. "It's okay, baby. We're going to see Dr. Felton right now. I know he's not your favorite person, but he'll make you all better. I promise."

Savannah nuzzled my neck, then rested her chin on my shoulder. I kissed her between the eyes and searched for my phone, finding it stuffed in my shoe under the coffee table. When I pressed the icon beside Riddleton Veterinary, a recorded message responded on the second ring.

Damn! They didn't open until eight. It was now seven thirty, which left me half an hour to kill. Actually, twenty-five minutes since I intended to be standing by the door when they unlocked it.

The Riddleton Veterinary Clinic was in a refurbished A-frame on the corner of Oak and Second, next door to the Snip & Clip. When I pulled into the parking lot at seven fifty-five, a car and a pickup truck filled the spots on either side of the door. I slid in next to the pickup, which had a Harlequin Dane towering in the back. The black patches on its immense white coat reminded me of a Dalmatian whose mother had been exposed to radioactive fallout while pregnant. It wagged its whip-like tail when I stepped onto the asphalt.

I helped Savannah out of the car, where she'd curled on the back seat, and walked her to the door. She carried her head down, tail between her legs. The vet tech unlocked the door and held it open for us. We followed her to the counter to check in, the man with the Dane close behind. Savannah paid no attention.

The office decorations included educational posters about heartworms, fleas, and allergies. The lone offering to the Christmas decoration contest was a small artificial tree in the corner covered in dog and cat treats suspended on strings. Savannah paid no attention to that either. That's when I knew for sure we were in trouble.

The tech finished checking in the Dane and the kitty carried by the woman in the car, and gestured for me to follow her. She led us to the floor scale. Savannah stepped onto it and sat. She weighed seventy pounds— better than before, but still not enough to cover her visible ribs. I didn't know how much more I could feed her without going broke. It didn't matter, though. I'd do anything necessary.

We'd waited in the exam room for about five minutes when Dr. Quincy Felton came in holding a clipboard. My heart skipped a beat. Six feet tall and slender, he had collar-length brown hair and a mustache to match. Though in his late thirties, he'd yet to develop the standard-issue pot belly of a southern man. He'd make someone a great catch one day. Assuming he hadn't been caught already.

He squatted in front of Savannah and scratched her under the chin. "Hey, girl. What's bothering you today?"

I filled him in on her symptoms and asked, "Do you think someone could've given her something toxic? Like poison of some kind?"

He felt around on her belly while he listened to her tummy with a stethoscope. Savannah whined again when he found the lump. He looked up at me. "No, I think maybe she swallowed something she shouldn't have. I'm going to take an X-ray and see what we're dealing with."

Dr. Felton took Savannah's leash and led her into the back.

I paced the six-by-six cell until they returned. Savannah greeted me as if we'd been apart for years, then sat on my feet, leaning against my shins.

Dr. Felton tapped buttons on his tablet and showed me the X-ray he'd taken. It looked like she had three giant worms stacked on top of each other in her gut. A picture straight out of a science-fiction movie.

He pointed to an area partially hidden by her hip bone. "You see this distension here?"

No. I angled my head for a better view. No help. "Not really."

"It's hard to see, but it looks like she ate something. Are you missing any socks? Underwear maybe?"

"I don't know. I'll have to check."

"Well, if you are, I think we found it."

"How do we help her?"

"It's traveled a good way through the bowel. I think

154

she'll be able to pass it. She's already pushed it through the sticky spots, so it should come out on its own. Luckily, she's a big girl. If she were smaller, she might be in trouble already."

I stroked her head with a shaky hand. "What if it doesn't come out?"

"If she doesn't pass it by tomorrow, we'll have to operate, or she might die. I'm sorry, Jen. I wish I had better news."

Die? No way. Tears threatened to overrun my eyelids. "Um... exactly how do I help her pass it?"

"For starters, try some Dulcolax. The pills would be best in this case. Then keep an eye on her. She should poop it out, but if it gets stuck where you can see it, you can pull gently and slowly. With luck, you'll have your sock back this evening."

No thanks. She could keep it as a souvenir. "What if it doesn't come out?"

He pressed his lips together and gave Savannah an ear scratch. "If it's not out by morning, bring her in and we'll remove it surgically. If we don't, it could cut off blood flow to her bowel and cause an infection or worse."

"Worse?"

"The affected portion of the bowel could die and release toxins into her system. We definitely don't want that."

"Have you done many of these kinds of surgeries?"

"A few. Mostly on smaller dogs. They have a harder time passing things like this. I honestly don't think surgery will be necessary, but if it is, don't worry. I'll take care of her." He made a snip, snip motion as if his fingers were scissors. "I'm pretty handy with a scalpel. And I spent two years in medical school before I

155

switched, so if you decide to swallow a sock, I can take care of you too."

I tried to return his grin, but couldn't manage it. "Thank you. I think."

Three hundred dollars later, I loaded my little girl back into the car and took her home. I should've asked how much the surgery would be, but it didn't matter. If she needed it, I'd pay.

I settled Savannah on the couch with her favorite stuffed monkey for company, then tapped Eric's academy picture on my phone. He picked up on the fourth ring.

"Hello, Jen. What do you need?"

"What kind of greeting is that?"

"Well, considering you hung up on me the last time we spoke, you're lucky I answered at all. So, unless you called to apologize, I really don't have a lot to say to you right now."

I knew I'd forgotten something. "I'm sorry I hung up on you. I shouldn't have done that."

After a moment of silence, he said, "If you mean it, apology accepted."

"What do you mean 'if I mean it'? I wouldn't have said it if I didn't mean it."

"Glad to hear it." He sighed. "So, how are you?"

"Not so good. Savannah ate something while I was out last night and now it's stuck in her colon. If she doesn't poop it out by tomorrow, she'll need surgery."

The ice melted. "Oh, Jen, I'm so sorry. Any idea what it is?"

"Most likely a sock but it could be anything. I have to go get her some Dulcolax."

He chuckled. "Sounds like you have a fun day planned."

Tears welled in my eyes, and stress produced a

156

whinier voice than I'd intended. "It's not funny, Eric. She could die."

"I'm sorry. Would you like me to bring you the medicine?"

"No, you're working. She's sleeping at the moment, so I'll go out in a bit."

"All right. Let me know if you change your mind."

"I will. Thanks." I glanced over at Savannah. Still sleeping. I fought the urge to wake her up to make sure. No, she should rest. Better to just change the subject. "I had dinner with Lula Parsons last night."

"From the church? How did that happen?"

"Her husband's out of town and she was lonely. She told me she saw a kid with a knife in the diner the night Travis was killed. A kid with a record for armed robbery, and he was talking about the new guy in town."

"We ruled out robbery, remember?"

"Maybe that was premature."

He sighed. "I don't think so, but I guess we can look into it. What's his name?"

"She didn't know. I'll ask her about it again."

"Never mind. We'll check it out."

Relief flooded into my chest. Maybe they could clear Marcus after all. "Thanks. Oh, one other thing."

"What?"

"Did you know the vet went to medical school for two years before he became a vet?"

"No. What difference does that make?"

I had to spell it out for him. "According to the movie, gross anatomy is a first-year class. And he has access to ketamine. Doesn't that cover whatever Ingrid found so suspicious?"

"Hmmm. It might. I'll have to ask Ingrid. But what motive would he have to murder Travis Underwood?"

"I have no idea. Isn't that *your* job?"

"Very funny. I'll talk to you later."

He was still too angry to appreciate my lame attempt at a joke. "Bye."

I left my baby stretched out on the couch and went to the store for her medicine. As I checked out, it occurred to me I wouldn't be able to leave Savannah alone again after I gave it to her. Eric wasn't the only one I owed an apology to. I'd mistreated Lula at dinner last night. I needed to apologize to her too.

When I parked my car at St. Mary's, the imposing structure stared down at me. I shivered. What was it about the place that gave me the willies?

Shaking it off, I entered the nave and trotted up the stairs to Lula's office.

She was on the phone when I tapped on the doorframe. She waved me in and I wandered over to her desk. I picked up the photo of the much younger George in his military uniform. He was actually smiling. I hadn't ever seen him smile, although I'd only met him once. Maybe he was having a bad day. When she replaced the receiver, I put the picture down and sat.

"Hi, Jen. What can I do for you?"

"I just wanted to apologize for coming at you the way I did last night. I get caught up in these investigations and forget myself sometimes."

The phone rang again, and she picked up for a brief conversation, then dropped the handset back into the charger. "I'm sorry. Hank's in Blackburn, sitting with a parishioner in the hospital. I'm the only one here, and the phone's been ringing all morning."

"No problem. I understand."

"Thank you. And thanks for the apology, but it wasn't necessary. Friends speak frankly to one another, right?"

"Right. Hey, did you happen to remember anything else about that kid you saw in the diner on Friday?"

"Not really, but I'm going to try to find out his name for you. If I get a chance I'll make some calls. Somebody has to know who he is."

"I appreciate that. Anyway, I'll get out of here so you can get some work done."

"Thanks for stopping by."

I tripped down the stairs, eager to get home and give Savannah her pills. When I reached the bottom, I glanced back toward the kitchen where the entrance to the tunnels was, and an invisible string pulled me in that direction. One more quick peek wouldn't hurt anything, would it?

I scooted down the aisle into the room. On the wall opposite was the door to the rectory. Hank's living space. Could there be more clues in there?

The doorknob turned in my hand, and the door opened a crack. I glanced back over my shoulder to ensure I was still alone. Yup. I pulled the door open and ducked through, quickly pulling it closed behind me.

CHAPTER SIXTEEN

I found myself in a small dining room containing a square oak table decorated with a bowl of fresh fruit and surrounded by four ladder-back chairs. Religious-themed pictures dotted all the walls, except the one with a two-door buffet holding various-sized plates and glasses behind glass doors. How often did Hank have company for dinner? And who did the cooking? I pictured the tall, thin priest in the kitchen, shirtsleeves rolled up, wearing an apron, and clapped a hand over my mouth so I wouldn't laugh out loud.

The dining room opened into a sparsely furnished living room. A small couch, two matching chairs, a television, and two bookcases containing religious tomes covered it. On one of the bookshelves rested a silver tray holding a glass decanter containing an amber liquid and two glasses. At least Hank wasn't a teetotaler.

A short hallway with three doors—one on each side and one at the end—branched off the living room. I listened to ensure nobody moved around behind any of them. Nothing.

Going down the hall, I hesitated in front of the door

on the right. Still nothing, so I turned the doorknob, and the hinges creaked as the door swung open. I froze.

After a minute with no response, I stepped into the room. A neatly made twin bed, with a crucifix on the wall above, jutted into the center from the left. A curtained window took up most of the opposite wall, and to the right, an empty wardrobe stood open, along with a chest of drawers. A thin layer of dust on the nightstand told me the room had no occupants. A guest room with no guests.

I closed the door, the squeal crashing into my eardrums, and turned around. I hoped Hank found a can of WD40 in his Christmas stocking this year.

The door across the hall opened into an identical bedroom, minus the dust, plus a doorway leading into another room. Clutter of one kind or another covered every visible surface, and a pile of dirty—I assumed—clothes filled a corner by the window. Lula wasn't kidding about him being a slob.

I checked out the wardrobe. A black-and-white sea washed over me. Black pants and shirts hung on a rod, and white collars lined a small shelf on one side. On the bottom, shiny black shoes lined up like warriors in God's army.

Socks, underwear, and plain white T-shirts occupied the top drawer of the chest. The second drawer was dedicated to jeans and more adventurous T-shirts collected in various places. The third drawer: shorts, swim trunks, and polo shirts. Just like a regular guy. Who knew priests were people too? Probably everyone but me.

The nightstand drawer held a bookmarked Bible and a pair of glasses. Nothing else.

I carefully lifted the mattress on both sides to see if

the knife Lula found had a mate. Nope. Whatever Hank had to hide, it wasn't in this room.

In the adjoining room, I found a desk with a wooden chair behind it and a wingback in front that matched no other part of the decor. The walls were lined with bookcases. Papers and books covered the desk, and a laptop balanced on one corner. Except for the content of the material—most of the papers were notes for sermons and homilies, and the books were about religious themes or sermon preparation—the desk could've been mine. Nice to know I wasn't the only one in town who embraced chaos. In another life, we could've been soulmates.

The contents of the drawers seemed equally uninteresting until I discovered a small ring in the back of the bottom drawer full of blank legal pads. I removed the pads and stuck a pen into the loop. When I pulled the drawer up, the bottom came away, revealing several rubber-banded stacks of letters. Why on Earth had he hidden these?

I freed the largest stack. There was no return address on the letters. Hank had cleanly slit the envelope down the side, and I slid out a single sheet of paper covered in the smooth lines and curlicues of what had to be a woman's handwriting.

Dear Hank,

I was so excited when I received your letter telling me you were coming home. Your absence has left a hole in me that your correspondence could never have hoped to fill. I can't wait to see you again.

The past twenty years have done nothing to quell my love for you. It's as strong as it was the day you

162

left. Every day, I eagerly check my mailbox, hoping to find something from you. And soon I won't have to anymore because you'll be here.

You once told me our love could never be. Now I know you must have changed your mind, or you wouldn't be coming back to me. I'm counting the hours until I see you again.

Love Always—
You know who.
XXXOOO

Oh boy! Somebody had it bad for the priest. But who?

I opened the next letter in the group, hoping for a clue, but it was just more of the same. I considered reading the rest, but somehow it made me feel dirty, like I was eavesdropping on a couple of newlyweds. It could've had something to do with invading his privacy also. I replaced the letters in their respective envelopes and the rubber band around the stack.

The next pile was much smaller. I flipped through the correspondence from T. Underwood, which all had a Broad River Correctional Facility return address. Travis had stayed in touch with Hank. Funny how the priest had never mentioned that.

I slid the latest letter out of the envelope and unfolded it.

FATHER,
   I'M GETTING OUT SOON AND COMING HOME TO RIDDLETON. WE NEED TO TALK.
   TRAVIS

163

I took the letter and stuffed it into my back pocket. Something important had happened that Travis wanted to address now that he was out of prison. Possibly another motive for Hank to get rid of him. I had to show it to Eric.

As I replaced the false bottom of the drawer, footsteps came down the hall. My pulse raced and my hands shook. When the door to the priest's room opened, I squeezed under the desk, pulled the chair close, and held my breath.

Please don't come in here. Please don't come in here.

I pressed my fist against my mouth and released the air from my lungs, what seemed like one molecule at a time. Rustling sounds and footsteps came from the next room. Someone hummed tunelessly, the noise muffled by pounding in my ears. I strained to hear which direction the footsteps were traveling in. They seemed to move away from me.

Then the bedroom door closed, and silence fell. Could I risk coming out of my hiding place? What if Hank had closed the door so he could take a nap undisturbed? I didn't hear him settle on the bed, but my hammering heart could've drowned it out. Either way, I had to get home to Savannah. I'd been gone almost an hour.

Slowly, I pushed the chair away from the desk and peeked. No sign of anyone. I eased out and rested my weight on the seat, listening. Nothing.

Creeping toward the wall, I flattened myself beside the doorway, took a deep breath, then peered around the corner.

The room was empty. I blew out hard. Now I had to get out without anyone seeing me.

I crept down the hall, through the living room, and

into the dining room. Pressing my ear against the door to the kitchen, I listened for any movement. Instead of activity, though, I heard the humming again. Tuneless, sporadic, and generally annoying vocal pandemonium ricocheted off my eardrums.

Don't quit your day job, Padre.

Finally, it stopped, and he moved away from the door I leaned on. I could hear nothing else until he hit the staircase. The wooden planks didn't absorb the sound like the carpeted floor. I risked opening the kitchen door a crack. Across the nave, I could see the priest's lower legs laboring up the stairs. A minute more, and I'd be safe.

As soon as the voices echoed from Lula's office, I bolted for the double doors. Closing one slowly behind me, I ran for my car, jumped in, and tore out of there.

My hands shook so much I had difficulty holding the steering wheel. Luckily, home was only a couple of blocks away. I wiped my sweaty palms on my jeans one at a time, waiting for the adrenaline to dissipate while my mind raced.

Was Father Romeo having an affair? It wouldn't be the first time a priest had ever broken his vows, but Lula insisted it could never happen. And what about Travis? What did he want to talk to Hank about? If only I had Hank's response to that letter. Perhaps the police had found it in Travis's apartment. Even if they had, they'd never let me see it.

I slipped my Dodge into a parking spot in front of my building, grabbed the bag with Savannah's medicine, and sprinted up the stairs, my heart still galloping. It took two tries to get my key in the lock. Savannah's lack of response sent another surge of adrenaline into my chest. Had she taken a turn for the worse? I shouldn't have stayed out so long. My baby needed me, and I'd let her down. Good thing I had no children.

When I finally entered the apartment, my girl remained curled up on the couch. She lifted her head at my appearance and thumped her tail twice. I sat beside her, stroking her head. Then I opened the bag and removed the Dulcolax. She automatically perked up at the prospect of food, though I knew she'd never eat, even if offered a sirloin steak.

Wrapping the pill in cheese might help the swallowing process, but somehow I doubted she'd take it. It was worth a try, however. I returned to the couch with the Dulcolax cheese ball and held it in front of her nose. Savannah sniffed, opened her mouth, then changed her mind. I'd have to do it the hard way.

I separated the pill from the treat. Catching her by surprise, I pulled down her jaw and dropped the tablet into her throat, then clamped her mouth shut and rubbed her throat until she swallowed. When she didn't spit it back out, I considered the operation a success. Now all I could do was wait.

My laptop summoned me, and I settled at the desk. Writing would be a terrific way to occupy my mind while I waited for Savannah to do her thing. If I could concentrate. I watched the steady rise and fall of her ribs as she slept. The package said it would take six to twelve hours. Since she was moving a piece of fabric rather than hard, dry stool, I hoped for a quicker response. Either way, I'd be right here with her for the duration.

As I waited for my latest chapter to appear on the screen, I contemplated what I'd learned today. Father

Mathews might've had a years-long affair with a woman from Riddleton, and the town vet, Dr. Felton, had gone to medical school for two years before changing over. He had access to ketamine, and by his own admission, he was adept with a scalpel. What about other kinds of knives?

Snip, snip.

What motive could he have to kill Travis Underwood, though? Did they even know each other? Travis had grown up in Riddleton, while Felton had moved here from Blackburn after veterinary school. What else did I know about him? Not much.

I typed Quincy Felton DVM into the search bar. His smiling face and a photo of the clinic popped up. Below that: links to an emergency animal clinic in Quincy, Massachusetts, and a Department of Motor Vehicles field office in Quincy, California. No help there.

I handed off the task to my search-and-rescue librarian, Brittany.

Icon pressed, she answered on the second ring.

"Hey, Jen. What's up?"

I ran through the highlights of my day so far and set her to work digging into Quincy Felton's background and the letters from the anonymous woman Father Mathews might have been involved with.

"How is Savannah doing now? Any luck yet?"

"Not yet. She's still sleeping."

"Let me know how it goes. Is there anything I can do?"

I wish. "No, thank you. It's just a waiting game now. If you can find that info for me, it might help me get Marcus out of jail, though."

"Your wish is my command, Aladdin."

"Thank you, Genie, but that means I get two more wishes, right?"

I sensed her eyes roll before the call disconnected.

The more I watched the flashing cursor on my laptop screen, the more I thought about those tunnels under the church. Maybe I should forget the cheerleader thing altogether. I could move that to book four, should there ever be such a thing.

In this one, Daniel could pledge a fraternity, and one of the hazing exercises would be a trip to the tunnels in the middle of the night. Darkness, disorientation, and an excess of alcohol gets one pledge lost, and he turns up dead. Daniel would be the last to see him before they got separated, and he immediately becomes the prime suspect. Dana and Daniel investigate and discover the fraternity has been running drugs through the tunnels the way the rumrunners ran booze in the twenties. The drunk boy found the stash, and they killed him to keep him quiet. All I needed was a pool of suspects and the red herrings to go with them.

Yup. That was the ticket. Book three would be great.

I played with the story until I heard Savannah get off the couch. She went to the door, and I jumped up to follow. Two hours had passed since I gave her the pill. Maybe that would be enough. Dr. Felton had said the object was close to the bowel's end. After snapping on her leash, I followed her down the stairs with my fingers crossed all the way.

Savannah did her usual tinkle by the tree, then pulled me around the corner to the grass strip in front of the houses on Oak Street. She turned in a circle and hunched, but nothing came out. Sniffing down a few more feet, she circled and hunched again. Still nothing.

168

We followed the pattern down the street, almost to Riddleton Road beside St. Mary's. Perfect place to stop. We needed a miracle.

She hunched again, but this time when she stood up, I could see a tiny scrap of something poking out of her booty. Pay dirt!

I pulled out a plastic bag and turned it inside out around my hand. When I reached for the fabric, Savannah danced away. "Come on, little girl, let me get to it."

She circled around, wrapping me up in her leash like a maypole.

Spinning free, I tied the lead to St. Mary's fence and snagged the end of the offending object, pulling gently. I'd retrieved about three inches when she spun around again, yanking the rest of it out.

I held my breath and lifted the yuck-covered cloth up to eye level to figure out what it was. The barely discernible pattern proved it was no sock. It was the see-through lace, no-show thong Scott had given me for my twenty-fifth birthday, which I'd always considered more a present for him than me. No wonder it didn't show up properly on the X-ray. There wasn't enough fabric to see. Not that fabric was visible on an X-ray, anyway.

Where did she find the thing? I hadn't seen it in years. Of course, I hadn't looked for it, either.

I wrapped it up in the bag, so I'd never have to see it again. Then I hugged my good girl around the neck and took her home for lunch. I'd bet anything she was starving.

CHAPTER SEVENTEEN

I checked the kibble in Savannah's bowl and gave her fresh water. She wolfed down the food, and drank half the water. My belly reminded me I hadn't yet fed myself today, either. I needed to do something about that, but, as usual, my cupboards were bare. I found an old box of strawberry Pop-Tarts that expired two years ago in the back of the cabinet. Too bad Savannah wasn't still teething. The rectangular slabs would've been perfect for massaging the gums around her molars.

After tossing them in the trash can, I threw on my jacket for a trip to the diner. Savannah didn't budge, so I let her catch up on her sleep.

I waved to Sidewalk Santa as I passed the "Jingle Bells"-blaring Goodwill and ducked into the diner. Angus worked the grill for the three customers that constituted his Thursday post-rush lunch.

"You need some help?" I asked when he turned my way.

"No, I'm good, thanks." He flipped a burger and dropped a slice of cheese on top. "Help yourself to something to drink if you want."

"Thanks." That limited my choice of drinks for today. I had no idea how to make a milkshake.

I scooped some ice into a glass and pressed it against the lever under the Mountain Dew logo. As I took my first sip, Ingrid came in wearing civilian clothes—jeans and a pullover sweater bearing a decorated Christmas tree—and settled at the counter, staring at her close-clipped fingernails.

I grabbed a towel and wiped the Formica in front of her. "Good afternoon, ma'am. Can I bring you something to drink?"

She looked up and lifted one eyebrow. "Has the book business packed it in, luv?"

Yes. Well, maybe. "No, I just happened to be back here and thought you might be thirsty. Angus is a little busy at the moment."

"Oh. I'll have whatever you're having then."

"Coming right up." I poured another Dew and came around to sit beside her. "You okay? No patients this afternoon?"

Ingrid frowned, stripping the paper off her straw. "I'm as well as can be expected. I just had a visit with Marcus."

"Oh. How's he doing? Any good news?"

"He's all right. A bit frustrated, which is understandable. He's being arraigned for Travis's murder tomorrow morning."

I screamed inside. How could anyone believe Marcus Jones killed Travis Underwood? Just because they'd had a fight over Travis blackmailing him. For money. Marcus had no money. Travis had to know that. What did he really want?

On the outside, I held it together for Ingrid's sake.

"I'm sorry to hear that. I'm doing everything I can to convince the detectives he didn't do it, but they won't listen to me. I even gave them a couple of alternate suspects. They're determined to pin it on Marcus."

Her face twisted into a grimace. "Not only Marcus."

"What do you mean?"

She ran a hand through her short, loose curls. "They think I might be involved too."

"How so?"

"They think I helped Marcus because the stab wounds were so precisely placed."

What? "You're the one who pointed out the unusual stab wounds. That's ridiculous."

She sipped her drink. "I agree, but they're sending the body to Sutton for another autopsy. They suspect I fudged the original to throw suspicion away from Marcus. If the pathologist there finds even one thing I missed or got wrong, it could destroy my reputation."

Leave it to Havermayer to cast suspicion on someone with little or no evidence. The connection was razor-thin, but she made it nonetheless. "I'm so sorry, Ingrid. It isn't fair."

"No, but I suppose I should've recused myself in the first place because of our relationship. I did my job, but it might not look that way. I shouldn't have taken that chance."

"Maybe, but at the time you had no idea Marcus would end up being the prime suspect. And neither did anyone else. You had no reason to recuse yourself." I laid a reassuring hand on her forearm. "Don't beat yourself up about it. You did nothing wrong."

She gave me a half-smile. "I guess you're right. At least the defense can't use it against me. I had no reason to want him to be a suspect. Quite the opposite, in fact."

"That's true. It has to be the prosecutor who's nervous about your results. I'm sure the guy in Sutton will find exactly what you did. You have nothing to worry about."

"Thank you. I feel a bit better now. You're a good friend."

Tell that to all my other friends. "I'm glad you think so. Sometimes I'm not so sure."

She patted my hand.

Angus delivered his orders to the dining room, then brought me a refill and Ingrid a cup of tea. "What are you two so serious about?"

Ingrid filled him in.

He shook his head. "I wouldn't worry about it, if I were you. You're an excellent pathologist. I'm sure I found everything there was to find. How about I fix you something to eat? Things always look better on a full stomach."

"No, thank you, Angus. This tea will hit the spot," she said.

I opened my mouth, and Angus put his hand up. "Don't worry. I know what you want. I'll be right back."

Before I could reply, my phone rang, and Brittany's face filled the screen. I swiped.

"Hi, Britt."

"Hey, how's Savannah doing?"

"The medicine worked. She sprayed like a fire hose."

Ingrid glanced at me, her questioning eyebrows squeezed together.

I put my hand over the microphone. "Savannah was sick this morning. I'll tell you about it in a minute."

She nodded, and I turned my attention back to Brittany.

"Sorry. Ingrid heard me talking about Savannah and medicine."

"Oh. Where are you?"

"At the diner. I came to get something to eat while the mutt slept off her trauma."

"The mutt? She's a pure-bred German shepherd, remember?"

I remembered and had the food bills to prove it. "Well, when she does stupid stuff like this, she's a mutt."

"I hear you. What did she eat?"

Oh, boy. I didn't want to have this conversation in public. My face heated. I turned my back to Ingrid and whispered, "You remember that thong Scott bought me for my birthday?"

"That ugly lace thing?"

"That's the one."

Brittany guffawed into the phone. "Good for her. That monstrosity needed to be destroyed."

"No kidding." Time for a subject change. "Have you had a chance to look into that stuff we talked about this morning?"

"I did, but I really couldn't find much. Quincy Felton enrolled in the Medical University of South Carolina eight years ago, but never graduated. I couldn't get a clear picture of why, though. One year he was there, the next he wasn't. Of course, school records aren't posted for the general public, so short of hacking into their system, there's no way to know if he flunked out or just quit."

Hmmm. Hacking into the system sounded like a job

for Charlie. "Hold on a second." I turned to Ingrid. "You went to MUSC right?"

She nodded.

"When were you there?"

"I graduated five years ago. Why?"

"Did you know Quincy Felton? He would've been a year behind you."

She frowned. "The vet? No, I don't think so. But I spent all my time buried in books, so I didn't know too many people who weren't in my study group."

"Never mind, Britt. Ingrid doesn't know anything either. How about the letters? Any luck with who might've written them?"

"No, but I'm still working on that, although I don't know how much progress I'll make. Letters aren't like emails. There's no way to trace them back to who sent them. Especially with no return address on the envelope."

"I should've kept one. There might've been a clue I didn't notice."

Brittany laughed. "Still looking for that jail cell with your name on it, I see."

"No, only trying to get Marcus out of his."

"I get it. I'll keep trying."

"I appreciate it. I might have to put Charlie to work on it too. Between the three of us, we'll figure out what's going on. We have to. Marcus is being arraigned for Travis's murder tomorrow. If we don't discover who really killed him and why, he's going to be in big trouble."

"All right. I'll get back to work."

"Thanks." I hung up.

Angus brought my cheeseburger and fries, and I dug

in while Ingrid sipped her tea, lost in thought. I understood her frustration. Marcus was supposed to be innocent until proven guilty, and all the evidence was circumstantial. Would it be enough to convict him? Unless another viable suspect turned up, the answer would likely be "yes." I'd found circumstantial evidence against Hank, but it wasn't enough. If a jury had to choose between a priest and an ex-con, it would be easy. No choice, really.

Ingrid broke into my reverie. "What happened to Savannah?"

I gave her the play-by-play of the silly girl's exploits ending with: "If she had to eat something of mine, it might as well be something I hated, right?"

"Maybe so, but you got really lucky this time. It could've been much worse."

No doubt. It could've been surgery-or-death worse. "I know, but this is the first time she's shown any interest in my underwear. I'll have to make sure it's all off the floor from now on. Although, I haven't worn those things since my ex-boyfriend Scott left two years ago. I thought I threw them away when I moved. Guess I packed them in the junk-to-be-dealt-with-later box and left it in the back of the closet. I saw her sniffing around it the other day but didn't think anything of it."

"Don't blame yourself. It was an accident." She nudged my elbow. "You know, I never pegged you as the thong type."

"You got that right. It's just another example of how little my ex-boyfriend knew me. I'm pretty sure he bought it for himself."

"Good thing you're shut of him, then."

"No kidding." My phone rang. It was Eric. "Speaking of boyfriends…"

Ingrid dropped a five-dollar bill on the counter, then stood up to leave. "See you at the arraignment tomorrow?"

"You bet." I swiped the screen. "Hey, babe, what's up?"

He laughed. "You haven't called me that in ages. Savannah must be feeling better."

"She is. We got lucky and she passed a pair of my underwear." He didn't need the details. "I came down to the diner for lunch, and I'm on my way home to check on her now."

Angus met me at the register, and I paid my bill.

"What are you up to?" I asked Eric.

"Not much at the moment. Since we transferred Marcus, the case is in the hands of the DA now."

I pressed my lips together. There was no reason to start another fight with Eric on the subject. It hadn't been his decision. "And the district attorney is convinced Marcus is guilty?"

"He is. The circumstantial evidence is overwhelming, Jen."

But still circumstantial. The only real evidence they had was the fight. "What about Father Mathews and the kid with the knife? Aren't you even going to check into the possibility it might be someone else?"

He sighed. "It's not my call. I told Havermayer what you said, and she told me to let it go. You were just grasping at straws."

Grasping at straws? No. Determined to keep an innocent man out of prison. So much for not wanting to fight. "Is that what you think?"

"Of course not, but Havermayer's in charge. I have to do what she says."

Maybe Eric wasn't the man I thought he was. "How about doing what's right? You know there's no way Marcus did this."

"Do I? All the evidence points to him. He had means, motive, and opportunity. The trifecta. How do I justify looking elsewhere?"

I fumed, desperate for a response to prove him wrong. Nothing came to mind. The only proof I had of Marcus's innocence was my firm belief, and that was no proof at all.

"Look, Jen, why don't we have a nice dinner tonight and talk about anything other than this case? We've spent hardly any time together the past few days. I miss you."

"I wish I could, but I promised my mother I'd have dinner with them tonight. Gary needs a dose of Savannah to help perk him up."

"Is Savannah up to that?"

"All he really wants is for her to lie on the couch with him and watch TV. She's always up to that."

He sighed. "I think we need to spend some constructive time together. Just hanging out, talking about anything other than the latest murder investigation."

"Why don't you come too? Mom would love to see you. She thinks you're good for me."

Eric chuckled. "Okay, but what do you think?"

Oh, crap. I'd opened myself up for that one. What did I think? I wished I knew. I stuck with the essential truth. "I think you're a great guy, and I'm lucky to have you."

He laughed. "All right. What time is dinner?"

"Whenever we get there. You want me to pick you up?"

"Yeah, pick me up at the station."

CHAPTER EIGHTEEN

Eric and Havermayer were deep in discussion at the foot of the steps when I stopped to collect him. I had no idea what they were talking about, but I knew it wasn't alternate suspects to Marcus in the death of Travis Underwood. And I prayed it wasn't an invitation for her to join us for dinner. Nah. He'd never do that. Would he?

Savannah bounced around the back seat, wanting either to get out or get moving. I voted for get moving. We were all at Havermayer's mercy, however. The winter sun sat low on the horizon, and the temperature dropped in lockstep. Eric had better hurry, or I'd get chilly. And for me, chilly was synonymous with grumpy.

Havermayer finally ended her diatribe, and Eric hopped into the passenger seat.

"What was that all about?" I asked as he buckled himself in.

"Nothing really. She wants me to focus on the evidence at hand during our investigations instead of listening to outside forces."

Outside forces? A creative way of telling my boyfriend

to ignore me, no matter how relevant what I had to say might be. "In other words, me."

Eric stretched his legs and pulled at his seatbelt. "Not necessarily. She doesn't want me to pay attention to anyone who tries to tell me how to do my job. Unless it's her. She wants me to believe in myself and trust my instincts. What's wrong with that?"

I pulled away from the curb. "Nothing. You have good instincts. They don't always agree with hers, though, and she doesn't appreciate that. What did you say?"

"Not much. I just listened. She's trying to make me a better detective."

"You mean another drone with tunnel vision like her."

He scowled. "That's not fair, Jen. She's good at her job, whether you want to admit it or not. She doesn't see things the way you do. That doesn't make her wrong."

She wouldn't admit it even if she was. "She refuses to look. The problem with cops, as I see it, is they decide who committed the crime, then set about finding evidence to prove their theory, rather than follow the evidence to wherever it leads."

"I'm a cop."

"Yeah, but you'll at least listen to alternative theories. Havermayer won't. She sticks to her beliefs even in the face of all evidence proving her wrong."

Eric shook his head. "That's not true. But there has to be actual evidence to prove her wrong. Not theories and speculation. You can't just tell her someone else did it without proof to back it up."

I tightened my grip on the steering wheel. "Maybe,

but you can't find proof you don't look for. That's all I'm saying."

"I agree, but how's this for an idea? How about we don't talk shop anymore tonight? I vote we just have a nice dinner with your parents and relax for a change. What do you think?"

In other words, I was right. "I can handle that."

We rode the rest of the way in silence. It seemed we had little to talk about other than the latest crime wave. That didn't bode well for us. But how was I supposed to forget that Marcus was being arraigned tomorrow, and I believed him innocent? *How do I put that out of my mind and chat about the weather and my new book and what movies I've seen lately?* I had to find a way, though, or my relationship with Eric was doomed.

Savannah's tail whipped between the back and front seats, and she whined as soon as Mom's house came into view. She loved to visit Grandma and Grandpa. As the grandparents' handbook required, they spoiled her with treats and affection. And she responded by bolting to the house when I let her out of the car. I hustled to contain her before she scratched the paint off the door, trying to get in. Repainting it wasn't something I'd be good at.

My mother greeted Eric and Savannah with hugs and kisses, then put her arm through Eric's and led him into the living room. I stood on the porch with my mouth open until Mom turned around and said, "Are you coming?"

Okey-dokey. Guess I knew where I stood in the family pecking order. Somewhere between the dog and the garbage can. At least she didn't close the door on me.

That counted for something, right? I shook my head and stepped into the house.

The deepening darkness and lowering temperature had put the kibosh on grilling outdoors, so my mother had fried some chicken instead. Eric's favorite. She must've decided after I called to let her know he was coming. I didn't know where he stood on mashed potatoes, corn on the cob, and sweet potato pie but suspected they were on his happy list too.

Gary sat on the couch with his feet on the matching ottoman, watching a movie on TCM. I couldn't tell which one, but it was black and white, so I'd probably seen it before. His clothing hung on his skeletal frame, and his face was so thin it looked like someone had stretched latex over a skull to make a Halloween mask. Savannah lay beside him with her head in his lap, as if she knew he was too fragile to carry her full weight.

That's my girl.

I blinked back tears, while every ounce of the animosity I'd felt for him over the years drained away. He didn't deserve that kind of devastation. No matter what he'd done in the past.

I sat on the other side of Savannah. "Hi, Gary. How are you?"

He stared at the TV, jaw working. "You used to call me 'Daddy' when you were little. Do you remember that?"

"Yes." I never wanted to, though. My mother made me, and I stopped as soon as I was old enough to get away with it. Nobody would ever replace my father. Especially not wicked-stepfather Gary.

He ran his tongue over cracked, dry lips. "I liked that, you know."

183

Too bad he never showed it. He'd revealed more emotion in the last five minutes than I'd seen in the twelve years I'd lived with him. "Would you like something to drink?"

He lifted a finger toward the end table, where a glass filled with thick, brown liquid sat untouched. Some high-calorie, vitamin-laden supplement, I'd bet. I considered offering to help him but suspected his ego would respond angrily. I couldn't undo the damage his cancer had caused, but I could allow him his dignity.

Eric and Mom nattered away in the kitchen like old friends, and I felt a twinge of jealousy. Neither of them was as comfortable with me as with the other. I tucked that thought away for later deliberation. I couldn't deal with it right now.

I wandered in to check on the dinner's status. "Hey guys, need some help?"

Mom added milk to the mashed potatoes and fired up the mixer again. Eric sat on a stool at the island, eyeing the sweet potato pie. He caught me watching him and waggled his eyebrows. Fork in hand, he made as if to scoop up a bite. "Think she'd mind?"

"I think you'd find your fingers tangled up in those beaters."

Eric laughed. "Probably, but it'd be worth it."

"True. Besides, you don't work for a living anymore." I poked him with my elbow.

He grabbed my arm and pulled me to him. "I'd rather have a bite of you, anyway."

"Oh brother."

Arms wrapped around my waist, he said, "What? I'm serious."

"My mother's right over there."

"She doesn't care, and she isn't paying any attention to us. And she likes me, remember?"

More than she liked me, apparently.

I pecked him on the cheek and pulled away. "It's still embarrassing."

"You're embarrassed to be with me, you mean." He crossed his arms.

I took a deep breath and let it out. "That's not what I said. I'm proud to be with you. That doesn't mean I want to make out with you in front of my mother."

He gave me a sidelong glance. "No problem. We can save it 'til after the wedding."

Wedding? Who said anything about a wedding?

My pulse skyrocketed, and my hands broke into a sweat. I struggled to breathe, and it felt like an elephant sat on my chest. I was having a panic attack. I thumped onto the stool on the opposite side of the island from him.

Deep breath in, slow breath out.

He didn't mean it. It was a joke, so why was I reacting this way? We'd been dating for almost six months. The prospect of marriage shouldn't have brought on an episode like this.

Calm down, Jen.

"Are you okay?" Eric asked, concern muddying his emerald-green eyes. "You're beet red and sweaty."

I inhaled and released a few more times until my pulse slowed. "I'm fine. I have no idea why that happened."

He gave me a half-grin. "I guess the prospect of marrying me didn't go over so well. I'm sorry I brought it up. It wasn't a proposal, you know."

"I know."

He pressed his lips together, stood, and went into the living room with Gary.

As soon as the swinging door closed behind him, my breaths came easier. Now I only had to figure out how to fix the damage I'd done to our relationship.

My mother finished mixing the potatoes and handed me a beater, like she used to when I was a kid. "Are you two okay?"

I licked buttery whipped potatoes out from between the prongs. "We're fine. I just messed up again, that's all. So what else is new?"

She leaned on the counter and studied me. "Why do you think you keep doing that?"

"I don't know, and I really don't want to talk about it, if you don't mind."

Mom shrugged. "Suit yourself. But I suggest you figure it out soon or you're going to lose him. Don't let a good one get away. They don't come along every day." A wistful look came into her brown eyes.

"You mean like Dad?"

She nodded, wiped her hands on her apron, and picked up the potatoes and corn to carry into the dining room. I grabbed the chicken and followed.

Eric helped Gary to the head of the table. Savannah flopped on the floor between my chair and Gary's, hoping one or both of us would have a sloppy night. My mother filled our glasses with sweet tea and settled into the seat opposite her husband.

We passed the platters around the table and loaded up our plates. The savory aroma of chicken blended with the buttery potatoes and corn started a waterfall in my mouth. Nothing like a home-cooked meal to make everything all better. For a little while, anyway.

I bit into a drumstick and moaned as the crunchy coating and tender meat blended in my mouth. A forkful of potatoes went down next, then I attacked the corn on the cob as if it were a mortal enemy. The poor kernels didn't stand a chance.

Eric stuffed a large bite of chicken into his cheek and said, "Jen, you have to get the recipe for this chicken."

I chuckled. Clearly, he didn't know me at all. "Unless you have a death wish, it's probably not a good idea."

"Why?"

"Because the only part of the chicken I can do anything with is the egg. And even then it ends up scrambled whether I want it that way or not."

He pressed his lips together. "So what you're saying is I'm destined for a lifetime of scrambled eggs and takeout?"

A lifetime? What'd gotten into him tonight? "Something like that." I filled my mouth with food so he couldn't ask me more questions.

When we were done, I helped Mom with the dishes while Eric entertained Gary in the living room. It seemed my stepfather liked Eric too. This relationship had better work out; otherwise, I risked losing my entire family in the divorce. If only Eric would slow down a little. Give me some time to figure out what I wanted. I'd tried every way I knew to make him understand how I felt about things. Nothing seemed to get through.

Savannah spent the rest of the evening with her head in Gary's lap, and I was tempted to leave her with them for a couple of days. He seemed so much happier and healthier when she was around. But that would be an added responsibility for my mother to deal with. She had her hands full already caring for Gary.

187

My phone rang, and I checked the screen. Lula Parsons. What did she want?

I swiped and wandered out to the porch for some privacy.

"Hey, Lula! What's up?"

"I hope I didn't catch you at a bad time."

"No, not at all."

"I'm glad. I just wanted to see what time you were planning on coming out tomorrow."

"Tomorrow?"

"To see the horses. We talked about it at dinner the other night."

I'd forgotten. "Oh, yeah. What time's good for you?"

"I have to work in the morning, but I get off at noon. What do you think about having lunch, then you can follow me out to the farm? It can be tricky to find if you don't know your way around."

Sure, why not? I'd need a diversion after the arraignment. A broken leg would be distracting enough. "That sounds fine. I'll see you at the church at twelve."

I pressed the button and went back into the house.

"Who was that?" my mother asked.

"A friend reminding me we're supposed to meet up tomorrow to go horseback riding."

"Horseback riding? You?" She cackled. "When did you become so adventurous?"

"I didn't, but she insisted. She claims she has a horse so gentle her three-year-old niece can ride it. I couldn't come up with a reasonable argument."

Eric shook his head. "What time are you going? I need to know when to pick you up at the hospital."

"Very funny."

"Given your history, I'm willing to bet good money on it."

"Well, lucky for you, I don't have any good money. Otherwise, you'd be handing yours over to me tomorrow night."

"We'll see."

I left Savannah at my mom's since, between Marcus's arraignment and riding I'd be gone all day tomorrow, anyway, plus my mom insisted. Why should she be alone when she could bring comfort to Gary instead? And watch her favorite movies.

Eric and I rode home in a silence I didn't want to break for fear he'd bring up the subject of marriage again. Even in jest, it made me nervous. Something about the "M" word set my teeth on edge and always had. I didn't know why. The closest I could get to a guess would be my observations of my mother's marriage to Gary. I'd rather be alone than miserable for the rest of my life. At least I enjoyed my own company. Most of the time.

I pulled up beside Eric's car parked in front of the station and turned sideways toward him. "Thanks for coming tonight. Gary really enjoyed spending time with you."

"I feel bad for him. His treatment's really taking a toll."

"I know. I was shocked when I saw him. My mother made it seem like he was doing great."

I couldn't see Eric's facial expression, but his concern was palpable in the dark.

"He's still fighting. That's the important thing." He shifted in his seat and took my hand. "Are you still fighting, Jen? For us, I mean."

"Of course, why would you ask that?"

He traced the lines in my palm with his forefinger. "It doesn't feel like it very often. Sometimes, I think I'm the only one in this relationship."

"I don't mean to make you feel that way. There's just so much going on right now. I'm doing my best to juggle it all, but you know I've never been very good at that."

"I do, which is why I have to wonder why I'm always the last thing you consider. I can help you with everything else, but you won't let me. I love you. Let me help you."

I squeezed his hand. "I love you too, but sometimes I feel like we're at odds over everything. You can't help me if you don't believe in what I'm doing. All you do is try to talk me out of it. That's no help."

He lowered his eyebrows. "I'm worried for your safety. The things you want to do can be dangerous. Surely, you don't expect me to support your efforts to go up against a murderer."

"I expect you to support me in whatever I try to do. Just like I do you."

"Well, I can't do that. I won't help you get yourself killed or maimed or kidnapped. How could I live with myself if something happened to you, and I didn't try to stop it?"

I blew air out through pursed lips. "I don't know, but I have to be true to myself. Can't you see that?"

He released my hand. "I guess I need some time to think. Maybe we shouldn't see each other for a while. A break will give both of us a chance to decide what we really want."

"Is this a break or a breakup?"

"I'm not sure. I'm sorry." He opened the door and slid out of the car. "Good night, Jen."

I rested my forehead on the steering wheel. He'd been dropping hints about marriage all evening, and then he'd broken up with me. All this time, I'd thought I was the confused one. Guess I was wrong.

CHAPTER NINETEEN

The Sutton County Courthouse was a brick building with a stone facade. A half-dozen stone steps with a handrail up the middle led to the double-door entrance. I dropped my keys and phone into the bowl held by a Sutton County Sheriff's deputy and strolled through the metal detector. Another deputy on the other side handed them back to me.

The interior had clean, modern lines, and a wide staircase to the second floor encompassed most of the lobby center. Behind the stairs, a redhead scrolled her phone at the information desk, waiting for someone to ask her a question. I was happy to oblige.

"Excuse me," I said as I approached.

She laid her phone face down on the desk. "Good morning. How can I help you?"

"I'm here for Marcus Jones's arraignment. Can you please tell me where I need to go?"

The redhead tapped on her computer keyboard, hit enter twice, then said, "He's in courtroom 2A. The top of the stairs, then back to your left."

"Thank you."

I returned to the foot of the staircase and climbed

toward the second floor. When I peeked over the banister, the redhead had resumed phone surfing. My kind of job. I could get paid for writing. Or at least reading.

I turned left at the top and faced the double doors with a brass "2" on one and an "A" on the other. I pulled open the "A" door and entered the aisle between the rows of battered wooden benches on either side. A low, paneled wall with a gate in the middle divided the room.

A dozen people were scattered throughout the gallery, none of whom were Ingrid. I settled on the third bench of five on the right side. A Sutton County Sheriff's deputy, acting as the bailiff, stood left of the judge's bench in front, and a woman with brown hair and glasses had her own desk on the right. She shuffled papers and compared them to what she saw on her computer screen.

The door behind me opened, and two men in suits, engaged in a heated discussion, proceeded to the tables on the other side of the wall. Still no sign of Ingrid.

The bailiff stepped forward and announced, "All rise. This court is now in session, the honorable Judge Peter Simmons presiding."

Judge Simmons entered through a door behind the brown-haired woman's desk and climbed the steps to the bench, his black robe swishing around his ankles. "Please be seated," he said as he followed his own instructions. He turned to the bailiff. "Bring in the defendants."

Ingrid bustled through the entrance as the bailiff opened a door beside the empty jury box. I waved her over, and she slid in beside me. "What did I miss?"

"Nothing. They just got started."

Five men and two women in handcuffs shuffled into the courtroom and lined up by the wall near the jury-box door. Marcus glanced around from his position of third in line. Ingrid smiled and gave him a finger wave when he caught her eye. Without moving his arms, he waved back as much as his handcuffs would allow. His clothing drooped as if he'd lost ten pounds during his three days behind bars. Angus would have fun fattening him up again when he got out.

As disturbing as I found his disheveled clothing and three days of beard growth, the black eye and cuts on his puffy cheeks bothered me even more. A fight with another inmate? Or were the guards roughing him up? Neither option helped me feel better about Marcus's circumstances.

I glanced at Ingrid to see if she'd noticed, and a tear rolled down her cheek as she clasped and unclasped her fingers. I reached over to hold her hand. We sat that way through an armed robbery, a shoplifting, and a grand theft auto. Ted Winslow breezed by us and settled on the bench behind the barrier. Marcus must be up soon. Obviously, the prisoners weren't lined up in order of appearance.

The brown-haired lady handed a file to the judge and announced, "The State of South Carolina versus Marcus Jones. First-degree murder."

Ingrid inhaled sharply and covered her mouth with her hand.

"It's going to be all right," I whispered.

Ted slipped through the gate and stood at the defense table, digging through his briefcase. "Theodore Winslow for the defense, Your Honor."

The bailiff escorted Marcus over.

Judge Simmons flipped through the file, then looked at Marcus. "Mr. Jones, you are charged with murder in the first degree for the premeditated and willful murder of Travis Underwood. How do you plead?"

Marcus lifted his chin. "Not guilty." Despite his bravado, his voice carried a tremor.

"Very well. I'll hear the prosecution on bail."

The prosecutor rose and buttoned his jacket. "Your Honor, given the particularly heinous nature of the crime and the defendant's history of violent offenses and his current probation for his involvement in another murder last year, we request remand."

Remand? They wanted to keep Marcus in jail until his trial. If his face was any indication, someone was already harassing him. Would he make it to his trial date?

Ted slammed his briefcase shut. "Your Honor, my client has turned his life around since his release from prison and is an upstanding member of his community. Mr. Jones had no direct involvement in the incident last year and testified against the perpetrators in exchange for the probation he's currently serving. He has two young children at home with nobody to care for them. He's not a flight risk. We request he be released on his own recognizance."

The judge stared at Ted, tapping his pen on the desk. "I'm sorry, Mr. Winslow, but I have to go with the prosecution on this one. Mr. Jones is remanded into the custody of the Sutton County Department of Corrections for imprisonment in a facility of their choosing." He banged his gavel on the block. "Next case."

Ingrid and I exchanged glances and filed out of the courtroom.

"Are you all right?" I asked.

At the bottom of the staircase, she met my gaze, tears glistening. "No. You?"

Anything but. Anger was building in me like a volcano ready to erupt, but I had to remain calm for Ingrid. "No. You want to get some coffee and talk awhile?"

She inhaled deeply, appearing to steel herself. "I wish I could. I pushed my morning appointments so I could be here for the arraignment. I have to get back."

"No problem. I have some things to do, too." Like figuring out who murdered Travis. It was time for me to have another chat with Hank. "Catch up with you later?"

"Definitely."

I climbed into my Dodge and drove straight to St. Mary's. Lula didn't get off until noon, so that gave me a half-hour to take a priest's confession. Too bad I had no leverage on him. I could use those love letters as a bludgeon, if I knew who they were from. Not that I'd ever actually do anything with them, but he didn't know that.

My biggest challenge was broaching the subject in a way that wouldn't make Hank tell me to mind my own business and throw me out. I needed to channel the social twin, Daniel, for this one. Dana would barge in there and demand answers. Daniel used diplomacy to get what he wanted. Time for me to dig deep for that finesse gene I had to have somewhere, even if it was recessive.

I climbed the steps to the imposing structure, and the same sense of dread washed over me when I stepped through the doorway. Was the place haunted or something? I'd had no experience with psychic sensitivity before. Why now? And why here?

196

Shaking off the creepy sensation, I headed to Lula's office, hoping to find Hank in his. They were together, chatting in the hall between the two offices. *Jackpot.*

Lula turned as I hit the top of the stairs, and her eyebrows jumped up. "Oh, is it that late already?"

"Not quite. I'm a few minutes early." I glanced at the priest. "I was hoping Father Hank might have time to chat."

His broad grin crinkled the skin near his eyes. "I knew you'd come around. My office okay or would you prefer the confessional?"

I crossed my arms. "Your office will be fine, thanks."

He gestured for me to precede him into the room, then settled behind his desk. "What can I do for you today, Ms. Dawson?"

"Jen, please." *Come on, Daniel, give me a good lead-in.* Whatever he came up with would have to be a fib, though. I crossed my fingers and braced for a lightning strike. "I've heard that Travis Underwood came back to town for the sole purpose of speaking with you. I was wondering if you knew anything about that. Assuming it's not privileged, of course."

He propped his elbow on the desk and his chin in his hand. "Hmmm. I'm not sure what it might be. Unless it had to do with his desire to join the priesthood. His last few months in prison, he wrote me several letters asking questions on the subject. And we spoke for a few minutes when he picked up the holy water, but not about anything of consequence."

Travis wanted to be a priest? Prison did change some people. "I can honestly say that's the last thing I expected. Were you surprised?"

"Yes and no. He'd considered it as a boy, before he

started making bad decisions for his life. Of course, that was after I'd left for Idaho, so I'm not really sure what that was all about, either. Obviously he decided against the priesthood."

He'd given me the opening I'd been looking for. "Why did you relocate to Idaho, if you don't mind my asking? From what I understand, the move was kind of sudden."

"I don't know if I'd say sudden. I grew up in Boise, and my mother had been ill for quite some time. And there was a parishioner I was having some problems with, so when a position opened up in my home parish, I requested the transfer." He sat back and clasped his hands behind his head.

"Isn't solving people's problems sort of in your job description?"

He smiled. "It is, but in this case the problem was me. I take my vow of celibacy very seriously. Someone didn't understand that."

The letter writer? "I imagine that would make things difficult for you."

"It did."

"Did transferring solve the problem?"

Hank rubbed the back of his neck. "Yes and no. We corresponded while I was in Idaho, and she's still in love with me, but the situation is under control now."

My cocked eyebrow and tilted head made him laugh. Now I was really confused.

"She's been hospitalized for years. Delusions and hallucinations. Medication helps, and she could be released any time if she'd stay on it, but she prefers the controlled environment. She's happy there. I visit her twice a week."

"The homebound parishioner?"

He nodded.

"That makes sense. How is your mother now?"

His face darkened. "She passed away ten years ago."

I pried my foot out of my mouth. "I'm sorry."

"Don't be. She's with my father again."

Lula tapped on the doorframe. "I'm ready to go whenever you are, Jen."

"I'm ready." I stood and stepped away from the desk. "Thanks for your time. And don't stuff any more knives under your mattress. You might hurt yourself."

Lula laughed, but the puzzled look on Hank's face pushed my grin away. He had no idea what I was talking about. So, who put the knife under his mattress? And why?

We headed to the diner, but the Friday lunch crowd almost spilled over into the street. Angus handled the cooking, and Penelope wrangled the herd, assisted by a new server I hadn't met yet. I turned to Lula. "What would you like to do? It looks like it'll be a while before we can get a table."

She looked around, lips pursed. "I have some sandwich fixings at home. Why don't we just see what we can rustle up for lunch there?"

"You sure it's no trouble?"

"I'm positive. Come on. Follow me so you don't get lost."

Lula climbed into her beige, late-model Mercedes, and I started my silver Dodge. Fifteen miles of winding roads and near-circular turns later, we coasted to a stop in front of a freshly painted white farmhouse that had to have stood there since the turn of the last century. The building sat in a clearing surrounded by the remains of hay fields as far as I could see, the soil recharging itself for the next growing season.

On the opposite side of the clearing rested a relatively new—compared to the house—barn. An occasional horse's nicker penetrated the chirping chorus from the trees surrounding the structures. The idyllic scene instantly filled me with peace.

"You have a beautiful place here, Lula," I said as my car door closed behind me.

A proud smile crossed her face. "Thank you. We've worked hard on it. You should've seen it when we bought it. I don't think anyone had been near it for fifty years."

"Well, your hard work has paid off. It's lovely."

She led me up the board steps to the wraparound porch. "Let's go see what we can find to eat. I made fresh tea this morning. We can start with that."

"Sounds wonderful."

I followed her into the family-sized kitchen, which maintained its rustic atmosphere despite the modern appliances. Pale-green curtains decorated with roosters adorned the windows, and an eight-seat plank table covered with a red-and-white-checkered cloth dominated the center of the room. It seemed I was about to have lunch with the Waltons, except Mary-Ellen and Erin weren't shelling peas at the table. I suspected John-Boy wasn't in the attic writing his memoirs, either. Too bad.

Lula bustled around, pulling lunch meat and cheese out of the refrigerator and bread out of the wooden box on the counter with a rooster carved into it. She handed me a flowered plastic pitcher filled with sweet tea and pointed to the cabinet over the sink. "Glasses are in there, and you know where to find the ice."

I retrieved two glasses from the cupboard. "Is George joining us?"

"No, he went to Blackburn this morning to meet an old friend. He saddled the horses for us before he went, though."

"That was nice of him," I said, over the clatter of ice cubes on glass.

She set our plates on the table and pulled a tub each of potato salad and coleslaw out of the fridge. "I have trouble with my shoulder sometimes. He didn't want to hear me whine later."

I chuckled. "He's a true gentleman."

"Indeed."

Once seated, Lula prayed over our meal. I bowed my head in respect until the final "Amen," then reached for the potato salad. Although it wasn't the first time I'd participated in the ritual, this was one of the few occasions I didn't feel like the words were rote. I didn't know Lula well, but she seemed to live her beliefs. That was good enough for me. Not that my opinion on the subject mattered any.

Lula chattered about how much she loved her horses, and my stomach clenched a little more with every word. The prospect of climbing up on an animal with its own mind that weighed ten times what I did tightened my throat with each swallow. Did I really want to do this? Yes and no. I was always up for a new adventure, but this one had a fifty-fifty chance of being more disaster than thrill.

The more I thought about it, the more my belly threatened to send back my lunch. Time to change the subject. "Did you ever have any luck finding the name of that kid in the diner you told me about?"

Lula's eyebrows raised, and she formed a circle with her mouth. "Oh, yes! I forgot all about it." She jumped up and searched a drawer by the sink until she found a scrap of paper. "Here it is. I wrote it down for you."

I glanced at the note she handed me. The guy's name was Denny Holloway. "Do you know anything about him?"

Lula finished her sandwich. "Not really. Only what he said in the diner that night. I've heard rumors about him, but I don't know how true they are. I think he's worth looking into, don't you?"

"Definitely. I'll give his name to the detectives first chance I get."

She collected the empty plates and rinsed them in the sink while I recapped the leftover potato salad and coleslaw and returned them to the refrigerator. Drying her hands on the green-and-white striped dish towel, she smiled at me. "You ready to go for a ride?"

Not really. "Why not?"

CHAPTER TWENTY

The barn did double duty as a stable for the three horses and a storage area for farm implements. On the stable side, four giant rolls of hay took up one wall, and a rack full of tack boxes and assorted equestrian necessities covered the other. I had no idea what they used most of it for.

I also had no idea what kinds of horses occupied the three stalls. The two wearing saddles were small, brown females and relatively docile, while the third—a huge, black male with a white blaze between his eyes—was restless and agitated. Jealous because he wouldn't get to go this time? Did horses even think like that?

The more I watched him, the more my hands shook, and my belly twisted into knots. What was I thinking? My legs belonged on solid ground, not wrapped around a wild animal big enough to crush me just by rolling over.

"Are you all right?" Lula asked.

I started, having forgotten she was there. "I don't know. This might not be such a good idea."

"There's nothing to be afraid of."

"Easy for you to say."

She laughed. "I was where you are once. Of course, I was much younger, but I was still scared the first time. Whatever you do, make sure you stay relaxed. Lucy will feel your tension."

"Lucy?"

Lula gestured toward the first stall. "The smaller one. Remember, my three-year-old niece rides her. So can you."

My stomach disagreed, but I forced a smile. "I'll take your word for it."

"You'll be fine. I'll be there with you the whole time." She stepped toward the door. "I left my gloves in the house. I'll be right back."

"I didn't bring any gloves. Do I need them?"

"Not necessarily, but there are some extras in the tack box over there, if you want. Help yourself."

She ducked out the door, and I turned to the shelf area, which held three tack boxes. Which one did she mean? I slid the first one down and opened it—riding breeches and boots. The second was full of old papers. I dislodged a stack to ensure there were no gloves underneath. A Polaroid photo fell out.

After a glance over my shoulder to ensure Lula hadn't returned, I picked it up. It was a photo of a baby. A boy according to the blue knit cap on his head. Lula told me she had no children. Why would she have a photo of a newborn? Maybe one of those nephews she mentioned the other day. Maybe not.

I retrieved my phone and snapped a picture of the picture, tucked it back in the middle of the pile, then quickly slid the box back onto the shelf and grabbed the third. This had to be the one with the gloves in it.

Lula returned as I rifled through the assorted harnesses, halters, and bits, looking for the gloves hidden on the bottom.

"Any luck?" she asked. She'd donned knee-high leather boots in addition to her gloves.

I pulled out a pair of soft leather ones that seemed small enough for my hands. "I think so." I slid them on, and they embraced my fingers like a second skin. Forget the ride; I'd just wear the gloves. Reluctantly, I pulled them off again. "Yup. These are good."

"Terrific. Let's go meet Lucy."

She handed me a couple of peppermints and led the brown mare out of her stall.

Candy? "I thought horses liked apples or carrots."

Lula stroked Lucy's neck. "They do, but they have a sweet tooth, too. Lucy in particular."

Lucy nuzzled Lula's other hand, and Lula gave her a mint.

I watched in amazement as the horse crunched it down and poked her for another.

Lula led the mare over to me. "Now you try."

No, thank you. I liked my fingers just the way they were.

"Go ahead, she won't hurt you. She'll be your best friend."

Candy in the center of my palm, I tentatively held it in front of the horse's nose. She nibbled it out of my hand with her lips, her whiskers tickling my palm. I rubbed her between the eyes as she chewed. This wasn't so bad. I could do this.

Lucy poked my other hand as if she knew it held another mint. I offered it to her and stroked her neck. Horses seemed like big dogs. A few more pieces of candy, and she'd love me forever. Until Lula had to take her to the dentist.

Lula interrupted my musings. "You ready to try sitting on her?"

Not a chance.

Deep breath in, slow breath out.

"Sure. Why not?"

"I'll help you up."

I'd watched enough spaghetti westerns with Gary to know how to do this. Just stick my left foot in the stirrup and hoist my right leg over the back. I didn't need any help. "I got it."

"You sure?"

"Yup."

Lula smirked. "Okay, go for it."

I followed my own instructions: left foot in the stirrup, throw right leg over the saddle... And immediately slid off the other side, landing on my back. The air rushed out of my lungs, and pain sizzled through my ribcage. It looked a lot easier in the movies. Clearly, there was a knack to it. I clambered to my feet, feeling the blood rush into my face, and brushed off the back of my jeans. And my pride.

Arms crossed, Lula stood with her lips pressed together, doing a great job suppressing the laughter. "Did you break anything?"

"No, I don't think so. Nothing but my ego."

"Not the first time, I imagine."

No kidding. "Smart aleck."

She flashed her even, unusually-white-for-a-woman-her-age teeth. "Come on, let's get you up there."

I put my gloves back on, inserted my foot in the stirrup, and Lula supported my bottom as I slowly lifted my leg over the saddle. The cold leather sent a chill through my legs, and I shivered. At least the horse had a blanket.

Lucy shifted her feet, and I grabbed the saddle horn. "Easy, girl. You're all right."

The mare backed up a few steps. Sliding precariously close to the point of no return, I scooted back toward the saddle's center. They should make these things with Velcro.

Lula led her horse out of its stall and mounted her. "I don't know why she's so agitated. She must be feeling your anxiety. Try to be calm, and she'll settle down."

I *was* calm until she started dancing around. I had enough difficulty with a two-step on a dance floor. A four-step on horseback? Forget about it.

Deep breath in, slow breath out.

Lucy dutifully followed Lula's horse, Millie—according to the brass plate on her stall door—out the stable doors. My butt bones collided with the leather with each step Lucy took. I might survive this ride, but I suspected I'd spend most of tomorrow alternating between standing up and lying down.

When we hit the yard, Lucy sped up to walk side-by-side with Millie down the path that cut through one of the hay fields. I gripped the reins with one hand and the pommel with the other, my legs tight around the mare's sides. My heart pounded so hard, I could barely hear Lula when she spoke.

I turned my head. "I'm sorry, what did you say?"

"I asked if you were doing okay."

"I think so."

"Relax. Loosen up on the reins. Let her have her head."

I loosened my grip, letting blood flow back into my knuckles. My breath came in short gasps. I took a deep one to force myself to calm down. My muscles loosened a tiny bit, but my heart still raced. After a few minutes, I was finally able to look at something besides Lucy's twitching ears.

At the end of the hay field, the path entered the woods surrounding the property. The silence was all-encompassing. Pine scent filled the air. The real kind, not the phony stuff they put on car air fresheners to hang from the rearview mirror. I relaxed into the peace. My mind wandered, and I at last understood the appeal of being out in the middle of nowhere.

The panicked expression on Marcus's face when they led him away haunted me. No way for me to know what lay behind it, though. Concern for his children, sure, but definitely something else. Something to do with the bruises he wore, maybe. I had to get him out of there. But the police were satisfied they had the right guy. Somehow, I'd convince them otherwise.

The only way to do that, though, would be to replace him with someone else. But who? My only choices at the moment were Father Hank, who had explained away his sudden transfer to Idaho and the letter from Travis, thus eliminating his motive, and Denny Holloway, the kid with the knife in the diner. I'd checked into Father Hank as much as possible, so perhaps it was time to investigate Denny.

I'd give his name to Eric when I got home tonight, but did I trust him to do anything with it? Would Havermayer *let* him do anything with it? He lived under her thumb, and she seemed content to put Marcus away for the rest of his life. Even though all the evidence against him was circumstantial. They couldn't even prove Marcus saw Travis that night, let alone killed him. That didn't seem to matter, though. Marcus was an ex-con, so he must be guilty despite his lack of a history of violence.

I sighed out my frustration.

Lula turned her head. "Are you all right?"

"I'm fine. Just trying to figure out who killed Travis."

"You're supposed to be relaxing, not thinking about stressful things."

"I know, but Marcus looked so miserable in court this morning." I patted Lucy's neck. She'd turned out to be as gentle a ride as Lula had said. "What were the stories you heard about Denny Holloway?"

Lula scrunched up her face. "I'm not sure I should repeat things I don't know are true."

I laughed. "You're the one who brought him up to begin with. I didn't even know he existed until you told me about him."

"Yes, but that was based on my direct observation of his behavior in the diner. Repeating rumors is a whole different story."

Why the sudden bout of conscience? She'd already told me she'd heard about his two arrests for attempted robbery. Was there something else more felonious? "I understand. I'm only trying to keep an innocent man from going to prison. Even an unsubstantiated rumor might give me something to go on."

Lula stared at the rows of pines as we slowly passed them. After a minute, she looked at me. "Someone told me Denny was complaining about having lost his knife the morning after Travis was murdered."

Lost? More likely disposed of as incriminating evidence. "Did he happen to say where?"

"Not that I know of."

Something else for me to figure out.

The trees ended at a road's edge, but I had no idea where we were. We'd taken so many turns on the way to the farm, we could be halfway to Sutton by now. Or right outside of Riddleton. I'd need my GPS to find my way home tonight.

Lula grabbed Lucy's bridle and turned us around to head back to the farm. "You want to try going a little faster now?"

I shook my head. "I think this is good for today. Maybe next time?"

She shared a full-toothed smile. "I knew you'd love it."

Not sure I'd go *that* far. "It's peaceful. I can relax and let the horse do all the work. And I don't have to watch where I'm walking."

"That's true. It's always better to let the horse find its own way. Accidents happen when people try to take charge."

"How long is this trail?"

"We've never actually measured, but I'd say five miles or so."

I scratched Lucy between the ears with my gloved hand. "Do they need a break?"

"Oh, no. At this pace, in this weather, they can go for hours."

Huh. Maybe I'd learn enough about horseback riding for the twins to take a ride one day. Not in book three, but perhaps in the next one. Although, sending them through the tunnels on horseback could be interesting. I'd have to make the tunnels ten feet tall, though. Not very historically accurate. *Book four it is.*

I breathed in the pine-scented air and searched for designs in the white puffs drifting across the blue sky. My butt had gone numb three miles ago, so no more pain as long as I stayed in the saddle. I refused to think about what would happen when I dismounted.

I'd crawled into the deepest recesses of my mind when a loud bang sounded behind us.

A gunshot?

The horses whinnied and reared. I wrapped my arms around Lucy's neck and held on. They took off down the path at a gallop. Lula struggled to bring Millie under control, but they raced out of sight. Lucy had shorter legs and couldn't keep up. I was on my own.

Sweat covered Lucy's neck, my arms slid, and my feet came out of the stirrups. I bounced for two more strides, desperate to re-establish my grip. Lucy cut to the right, and I flew off her back, spinning in the air. I rebounded off the ground, then slammed into a tree.

Pain flashed through my head.

CHAPTER TWENTY-ONE

I drifted into consciousness and opened my eyes. A halftime band marched through my brain, and I grimaced against the agony. I was facedown in a bed of pine needles, and something hard pressed against the side of my neck. What happened? I searched my memory and found only random fleeting images of hanging off a galloping horse. What was I doing on a horse?

When I shifted onto my side, my entire body exploded in pain. That was a good sign, right? I could move and feel every limb. So far, so good. If you considered being run over by a truck good. Bit by bit, my memory came into focus. I'd been riding with Lula, and a loud noise had spooked the horses. Okay. Progress.

I sat up, which sent a wave of nausea up my throat, and leaned against the tree I'd apparently been thrown into. The bulk of the throbbing in my head radiated from the back. I felt around my scalp and found a golf-ball-sized bump. No blood, though. Another good sign.

Using the pine for support, I climbed to my feet,

every muscle in my body screaming. A surge of dizziness almost sent me back to the ground. I worked up a bit of saliva in my arid mouth and swallowed hard against the queasiness. Did I have a concussion? Probably, but I had to get back to civilization. A chill accompanied the setting sun. It would be dark soon, and I hadn't worn a jacket.

When I rested my weight on my left leg, the knee buckled, pain shooting in all directions. I looked down. Dirt, pine needles, and leaves covered me. A feeble attempt to brush some of it away only left streaks of dirt behind. A pointless endeavor and the least of my current problems.

I reached for my phone to call for help, but my pocket was empty. I had to find it before dark. No way I could walk several miles back to the farm on a leg that wouldn't hold my weight. Of course, my phone might not've had a signal to begin with. I had no reason to check. Either way, locating the thing was my top priority.

Feeling around in the straw at the base of the tree produced nothing, so I expanded the search radius, crawling on my hands and good knee while dragging the injured leg behind me. No cellphone anywhere in the immediate vicinity, but I'd added to the collection of detritus on my clothing. Another new fashion trend?

I pulled myself upright and hobbled to the path, glancing in both directions. Was Lula looking for me? I had no idea how long I'd been unconscious, but Lucy had surely made it back to the barn by now. Why hadn't Lula come back for me? Perhaps she couldn't stop Millie from galloping all the way home, and now she had to ride back in the semi-dark. The path wasn't wide enough for a vehicle. Regardless, for the time being, rescue was nowhere in sight.

No sign of the phone on the path, so I limped toward the other side. Perhaps Lucy had kicked it into the woods over there. It had to be somewhere. I couldn't spend much more time searching for it, though. The sun had fallen below the tree line. I shivered in the dropping temperature.

At the edge of the track, I caught a flash of something out of the corner of my eye. A surge of adrenaline pushed me in that direction.

Please be my phone.

As I maneuvered through the pine straw, the familiar blue protective case came into view. My swollen left knee stiffened, so I stretched my leg to the side and knelt on my good one to retrieve the cell. Spiderweb cracks covered the dark screen. From all appearances, Lucy had stepped on the thing before kicking it off the trail.

A desperate attempt to activate it produced no results, no matter how hard or often I pressed the side button. My cellphone had died a quick and painless death. Needless to say, I had no insurance on it. My only hope was that Lula would come back for me. Where was she? She should've found me by now.

I studied the path that grew more difficult to see by the minute. The rapidly cooling air had my teeth chattering. I couldn't wait. At least walking would help me stay warm. And help me feel like I was doing something about my situation. It was only a few miles, although exactly how many I had no idea. It didn't matter. I had to get moving.

A quick search of the area produced a fallen branch,

about two inches thick, I could use as a walking stick. It might help take some of the pressure off my bad knee. If it didn't break. A picture of me leaning on it, then ending up facedown on the ground, flashed through my mind. I shook it away. Besides, it wouldn't be the first time. At least there'd be nobody around to see my humiliation for a change.

The going was slow as complete darkness obscured all but the three feet right in front of me. My ears took over for my eyes, and every rustle in the woods became a critter about to attack in my mind. Although remote, the area was close enough to civilization to discourage major predators, right? I'd never encountered any. Then again, I'd never roamed the woods at night before. If nothing else, I was far enough away from water to eliminate alligators and cottonmouths. Two fewer things to worry about.

The walking stick added rhythm to my progress as I dragged my nonfunctional leg behind me.

Thump, step, drag. Thump, step, drag. Thump, step, drag.

Each round brought me a couple of feet closer to my destination. How many rounds back to the farm? I considered doing the math but quickly changed my mind. Arithmetic was never my strong suit, and I still didn't know how far I had left to go.

I continued for what I hoped was a mile when I heard an odd sound in the woods to my left. I froze, unsure of what attracted my notice. Then I heard it again. A low moan came from behind a tree.

I peered into the darkness. "Who's there?"

A whimper this time, barely audible.

"Hello?" I stepped closer to the path's edge, and a

boot came into view. A boot like the one Lula was wearing. "Lula? Is that you?"

"Jen! I'm over here," she said, a shade above a whisper.

I dropped my walking stick and scuttled toward the footwear. Lula was propped against the tree, her left arm limp in her lap. "Hey, what happened?"

"Millie started bucking. I couldn't hold on."

I took in her figure, searching for potential injuries. All I noticed was a lack of the debris that had covered me. How had she managed that? She either fell more gracefully or had spent her wait time cleaning herself off. "Are you all right? Did you hurt anything?"

She tried to lift the hand in her lap and winced. "I dislocated my shoulder. Other than that, I'm okay." She noticed the odd way I held my leg. "What about you?"

"I think I sprained my knee. The swelling has it pretty much unusable at the moment, but I don't think anything's broken." I shifted until I was sitting beside her. "My phone was smashed in the fall. What about yours?"

"I didn't bring it with me. There's no service out here, so I didn't see the point."

Terrific. "What about George? Do you think he'll come looking for you?"

Lula shrugged. "Possibly. It depends on how many bottles of wine he and Leroy taste-tested this afternoon. Leroy's an aficionado with a huge wine cellar he likes to show off. George usually has to take a nap on the couch before he can drive home. And then it's an hour drive."

"I guess we're on our own, then. You ready to go?"

216

Her eyes widened. "What? No. The safest thing to do is wait here until someone finds us. That's what all the rescue people recommend when you're lost or injured. Stay put and wait for help. So, that's what I'm doing."

I shook my head. "That's fine if someone's actually looking for you. We don't know that they are. We're on a straight path back to the farm. Since we know exactly where we're going, there's no reason to wait."

"But what about your leg?"

"I made it this far; the rest should be easy now that I have you to lean on."

"Me? But what about my shoulder?"

"The other one's okay, isn't it? Between that and my tree branch, we should be back in no time." I patted her good arm, hoping I was right. "Come on, let's get moving. It's cold out here."

Lula got to her feet, and with her arm wrapped around me, she helped me up. I propped my left forearm on her good right shoulder and hopped back to the path. After retrieving my walking stick, we set out toward the farm, the new rhythm much more efficient than the old one.

"What do you think the noise that spooked the horses was?" I asked.

"Probably a hunter, although it's unusual for them to be out in the afternoon."

"I wish they'd picked a different afternoon to be unusual."

She chuckled. "Me too."

I twisted my neck to ease a cramp and the pain in my head. "How much farther do we have to go?"

"I'm not sure. We should be almost to the fields, I think."

217

"Hope you're right. How's your shoulder?"

"It's okay as long as I don't move it. How's your knee?"

I gingerly tested it. "Still won't bend. It'll be fine once the swelling goes down. My head is killing me, though. I slammed into a tree."

"You might have a concussion. We'll have you checked out when we get back. George can drive us to the hospital."

Oh, boy. Eric would never let me live this down. I hated when he turned out to be right. I'd handled the riding fine. It wasn't my fault some hunter got stupid in the middle of the day. That wouldn't matter, though. He'd run with it for sure. If he'd talk to me long enough to hear the story. I wasn't his favorite person at the moment.

A slight breeze carried the aroma of hay. Almost there. How long had it taken us to get through the fields? Not long, I didn't think. Granted, the horses walked faster than we were now, but not much. Otherwise, I never would've made it past my fear to the woods.

When the rustling became audible, our pace sped up like we were the horses headed for the barn. Every step jarred in my head, and I gritted my teeth against the pain. We were almost there.

Suck it up, Jen.

When the house's lights appeared in the distance, Lula and I exchanged glances and smiled. Not much farther now. We would make it.

We hobbled into the house, and it sounded like someone was trying to start a balky chainsaw in the living room. George was asleep on the couch, mouth

218

open, snores reverberating with each breath. The lights from the fully loaded Christmas tree behind him bathed him in multicolored art deco. It seemed he hadn't completely slept off his wine-tasting afternoon before he drove home, which explained why he never came looking for us.

Each flash of light bored into my brain like a blind surgeon searching for a tumor. I lowered myself into an armchair and closed my eyes, basking in the room's warmth. Fatigue added ten pounds to each limb, and random thoughts floated around my mind. An overwhelming desire to sleep came over me. I gave in to it.

"Jen! Jen, wake up." Lula shook me.

I opened my eyes. "I'm sorry. I must've dozed off."

"I know, but you can't sleep. You have a head injury. We need to get you checked out."

I shook my head. Pain ricocheted through it. "I'm okay."

"You are not." She moved to the couch and poked her husband. "George, get up. You have to drive us to the hospital."

He opened his eyes. "What's going on?"

"Some idiot hunter fired and spooked the horses. We both got thrown off. Didn't you notice I wasn't home? I could've been bleeding to death, and you've been lying here sleeping. Get up!"

He sat on the edge of the couch and wiped a hand over his face. "All right, I'm up. Are you hurt?"

"I dislocated my shoulder again, and Jen has a concussion. Come on. Neither one of us can drive."

I stood, balancing on my good leg. "Lula, can I borrow your phone to call Brittany to meet us there?"

"Of course." She collected her cell from the counter and handed it over.

I punched in the only number I knew by heart besides my own.

CHAPTER TWENTY-TWO

Brittany stood by the curb at the Sutton Medical Center emergency entrance. She opened the car door and helped me out, shaking her head at my disheveled condition. "What did you get yourself into this time?"

"I had a fight with a horse. She outweighed me by a thousand pounds, but I held my own."

"Held your own what?"

I lowered my eyebrows in mock anger. "Very funny."

Lula remained in the passenger seat.

"Aren't you coming?" I asked her.

"I'll come in with George after we park."

"Okay. See you inside." I propped my forearm on Brittany's shoulder, and she wrapped an arm around me for support.

As I hopped through the automatic doors, the ten-foot Christmas tree dominating the corner by the reception desk jumped into view. Silver garlands, multicolored balls, and slips of paper decorated the branches protecting the piles of wrapped presents beneath.

When we approached the desk, the words on the sign beside the tree came into focus. The gifts were for the kids who wouldn't be able to make it home for

Christmas, and the slips of paper bore the names of the donors. Tears welled in my eyes. I chalked them up to fatigue and stress. No way I was *that* mushy.

Bright lights over the reception area slammed through my brain. Brittany intercepted the clipboard the nurse tried to hand me. Fine with me. She knew the answers to all the questions as well as I did. Probably better.

When she finished and handed it back, I asked, "Would you please call Eric for me? I can't remember his number."

"I already did. He should be here any minute." She gave me a side-eye. "I suggest you learn his phone number, though. He wasn't real happy you didn't call him first."

I sighed. "He's not real happy with anything I do these days. Besides, he should know better. The only reason I remember my own name is because I hear it every day."

"Yet you can recall every detail of your books while you're writing them." Brittany settled me into an orange plastic seat about as comfortable as the saddle I'd fallen off. I stretched my injured leg out in front of me and shifted until the pressure on my bottom was tolerable. The relatively empty waiting room signaled I might not have to deal with the discomfort for too long. The one advantage of being brought in by ambulance was I wouldn't have had to wait at all. I wouldn't trade it, though.

"Occupational necessity." My eyelids grew heavy, and my chin dropped onto my chest.

Brittany poked me in the ribs. "Hey! Wake up. No sleep until we know your head is okay. Get it?"

I opened my eyes and pulled my head up. "Got it."

"Good."

"Talk to me so I don't doze off. I feel like I just ran a marathon."

She snickered. "That'll be the day. From what I hear, one lap around the park does you in. And it takes you all day to boot."

"That's not true. I'm up to two laps now and home by noon."

"Yeah, but you start at six a.m."

"Not anymore. We start at eight in the winter." I stuck my tongue out at her. "So there."

Brittany sent an eye roll my way. "When are you going to grow up?"

"Growing up is overrated."

"So you keep telling me." She turned toward me. "Tell me what's going on with you and Eric. Why's he so unhappy?"

The tears threatened a reappearance. I blinked them back. "Honestly, Britt, I don't think I can give him what he needs. I can't open myself up to being hurt again."

"But you have to, Jen. You're too young to give up on love. You don't want to spend the rest of your life alone, do you?"

I shook my head and winced from the blinding pain. "No, of course not. But I don't want to get my heart broken again, either."

"Nobody does. I know you've had some bad experiences, but Eric is a good guy. Give him a fair chance. Who knows? He might even make you happy."

"Every time we get close, I panic and push him away. I don't know how much longer he'll put up with it. Even *his* patience has limits."

She took my hand. "I get it. I hope you can figure it

out before it's too late. Eric is good for you. He loves and supports you in every way that's important. That kind of thing is hard to find. Think twice before you let it slip away."

Brittany was right, of course. She was always right. A fact I found particularly annoying most of the time, but had to acknowledge she only wanted me to be happy. The question I struggled with, though, was why didn't *I* want to be happy? My life was a mess. My life was always a mess, and I seemed to go out of my way to ensure it stayed that way. *Why?*

"Sometimes I wonder if the reason I push Eric away is *because* he's good for me."

"I can see that. Maybe you don't think you deserve to be happy."

Thankfully, a turquoise-clad nurse called my name, so I didn't have to verbalize my response. Stepfather Gary had more of an impact on my psychological makeup than I wanted to admit to myself, let alone say out loud. His words burned in my subconscious like the Hindenburg after the explosion. Always there to scorch any positive thoughts I ever had about myself. Someday, somehow, I'd find a way to put the fire out. But not today.

Brittany helped me up, and we hobbled toward the brown-haired woman with the clipboard. A couple of hops in, she stopped us with a raised hand and grabbed a wheelchair. I settled in for the ride, far too comfortable with this process than I should be at my age. It'd been a tough year or so for my physical well-being. Mental too.

The nurse fumbled with the footrest, trying to accommodate my injured leg.

I stopped her. "It's okay. I can just hold my leg out, if you promise not to run me into anything."

She smiled. "I don't know. I don't have a license for this thing."

"I'll take my chances."

It turned out she would've passed her wheelchair road test with flying colors. I gave her an honorary driver's license as she helped me onto the bed. Pain seared my head when it rested on the pillow, and she raised the head of the bed.

"Is that better?" she asked.

"A little. Thank you."

"I'm sorry I can't give you anything for pain until the doctor examines you. Head injuries can be tricky."

"I'll be all right."

She retrieved a pen from her pocket. "Tell me what happened to you today."

My memory after the gunshot was still fuzzy. I had no idea how long I'd been unconscious or how I'd ended up on the ground with a bump on my head, to begin with.

She checked my vital signs, then flashed a light in my eyes and seemed satisfied with the results.

After the nurse's departure, I turned to Brittany. "I wonder where Eric is."

She shook her head. "I don't know. I called him right after I got off the phone with you."

"He must be really mad. Did I tell you he broke up with me?"

"No. What happened?"

I took a deep breath. "He made a comment about us getting married at my mother's last night, and I freaked out. He said he needed some time to think about things."

Brittany shook her head. "That's not a breakup, it's a break."

"I don't know, Britt. He seemed pretty serious about it. And he's not here." I swallowed my disappointment. No time for that now.

"Give him time. He'll come around. He loves you."

When the doctor came in, we had to table the discussion, so I never got the chance to tell her I wasn't sure if I loved Eric in return. That was an issue I'd have to grapple with on my own.

The dark-haired, average-built man settled on a rolling stool and used his feet to propel it to the side of my bed. "Hi, Ms. Dawson. I'm Dr. Martinelli." He reached over and shook my hand. First time for everything. "What's going on tonight?"

I filled him in on my equine adventure and its painful consequences.

"You had a run-in with a horse, huh?"

"Well, the horse did all the running. I did all the crawling and limping."

"I'll bet. How long were you unconscious?"

I shook my head, my face contorting when pain flashed through it. I had to stop doing that. "I don't know."

He stood, felt around the bump on the back of my head, then shined a miniature flashlight in each of my eyes. "Just look straight ahead for me."

I stared at the beige curtain surrounding my cubicle.

He went back and forth with the light several times, then said, "Excellent. Pupils are equal and reactive."

"What does that mean?" Brittany asked.

"For starters, it means she's not dead." He grinned.

She returned a wry smile. "We figured that much out. Thanks."

"It also means there isn't any undue pressure on the brain, so probably no subdural bleeding." He held out two fingers on each hand. "Squeeze my fingers as hard as you can."

I wrapped my hands around his fingers and squeezed.

"Excellent," he said, and I let go.

"You have a very mild concussion, Ms. Dawson, so you're going to need to take it easy for a couple of days. No running, jumping, or heavy thinking. Your brain needs time to heal. What do you do for a living?"

"I'm a writer, and I own a bookstore."

"Well, no writing, and no sampling your own product for at least two days. You're going to have a whopper of a headache, so you probably won't feel like it, anyway."

Brittany took my hand. "Can she have something for the pain?"

Dr. Martinelli nodded. "I'll have the nurse bring you some acetaminophen. But let's take a look at that knee first." He handed me a bedsheet. "I'll step out while you take off your jeans. Do you need a nurse to help you?"

Brittany moved forward. "I'll help her."

He left, and Brittany undressed me like I was a two-year-old. I focused on not moving my head any more than necessary.

She folded my pants and laid them on the chair. "He seems nice. Not stuck-up like a lot of doctors. Think he's single?"

I cocked an eyebrow. "Getting tired of Olinski already?"

"Not for me, silly. For you."

"When did you start playing matchmaker?"

She shrugged.

"Besides, I have enough problems right now. I still have to figure out what's going on with Eric, remember?"

"I remember. I have a feeling there's nothing going on there, though. You're not going to let it happen."

"I want to."

She pressed her lips together. "I know you do. You just can't help yourself."

The nurse slipped through the curtain holding two cups: one tiny and paper, the other plastic. She handed me the paper one, which had two white pills at the bottom. I glanced at her.

"Acetaminophen for your head."

"Thank you." I tipped the pills into my mouth and reached for the other cup, which held water to wash them down. I settled back on the pillow and closed my eyes.

No sooner had she left than the doctor came in.

"All right, let's see what's going on with that knee." He pulled the sheet back to expose my lower left leg. He whistled softly. "Very colorful."

I tilted my head up slightly to sneak a peek. The swollen purple blob in the middle jumped out at me. "Yeah, it's from my blue period."

"All right, Madam Picasso, let's see how well it works." He gently ran his hands over and behind the knee and manipulated the kneecap. "Where does it hurt?"

"Mostly in the back."

"Were you able to put your full weight on it when you were walking?"

"I didn't really try. It was already stiff, and I didn't want to make anything worse."

"Good thinking." He flexed the knee slightly, then straightened it a couple of times. "Everything seems to be working as it should be. I think we're looking at a PCL sprain."

Brittany frowned. "What's that?"

Dr. Martinelli framed my leg with his hands, gesturing as he spoke. "Since Ms. Dawson doesn't remember what happened, I can only speculate. I think she landed on the front of this knee when she fell off the horse." He pressed his finger on the bone right below my kneecap. "When she hit the ground, the top of the tibia was pushed back into the posterior cruciate ligament, which supports the back of the knee, causing it to stretch. The bruising and swelling is all from the impact."

"Will I need surgery?"

"I don't think so. If there's a tear, it's a small one. You should be fine after some rest. I'll give you a brace to wear and some crutches to keep you off it for a week or so. If you still have problems after that, I can refer you to an orthopedist for a follow-up."

"Thank you, Doctor."

"Take care." He smiled. "And next time, you ride the horse instead of the other way around, okay?"

Everyone's a comedian. "I'll try to remember that."

The nurse came in with the brace, the crutches, and my discharge instructions. We got me suited up, and I

229

clomped around the room a few times until I adjusted to crutch-walking. Finally, I was ready to go, and, for once, I didn't have to ride in a wheelchair.

CHAPTER TWENTY-THREE

I awoke a little after ten on Saturday morning with my arms covering my head and my cheeks wet with tears. My heart pounded. I must've been dreaming about the accident. Focusing on my breathing to slow things down, I reached for Savannah, but my other half was still at my mother's. Probably a good thing since my left leg throbbed the drum solo for a heavy-metal song with no melody.

On the plus side, my headache had dulled to a tolerable level, and I slowly pushed myself into a sitting position. No reaction. The knee brace they'd given me at the hospital sat on the nightstand—an offer of hope for a semi-functional day. I strapped it on and reached for my crutches, girding myself against the cacophony of pain my stiff, sore muscles were about to raise. When I hoisted myself upright, the marching band screeched as expected.

A few deep breaths turned down the volume, and I shambled to the bathroom. Now I just had to figure out how to do my business without falling over. Perhaps I should've taken that gymnastics class my mother wanted me to when I was six, after all. Of course, if I had, the embarrassment would've started earlier and lasted longer.

I gave up and ditched the crutches altogether. Maneuvering in the tiny bathroom was like dancing *The Nutcracker* in a refrigerator box. All I could do was pirouette. Thanks to the brace, the injured knee tolerated my weight with only a little extra complaining. I reached for the acetaminophen and swallowed two tablets with a handful of water from the tap.

The coffeemaker had long since brewed its pot and shut off, so I poured a cup and nuked it in the microwave. Savannah's half-full water bowl and empty food dish accused me from the corner. I hadn't planned on leaving her for so long, but my mother was well-prepared for such occasions. My German shepherd had her own dishes and food supply at Grandma's, along with an array of toys to keep her occupied. Assuming Gary ever let her off the couch.

Coffee fixed to my liking, I retrieved the icepack I had left over from my broken nose last summer from the freezer and stretched out on the couch to ice my knee after removing the brace. The acetaminophen reduced my headache to a slight annoyance. The doctor warned me against reading or writing for two days, but he only mentioned *heavy* thinking. I wouldn't be doing any calculus in my head. Or anywhere else, for that matter.

My mind drifted behind closed eyes in a form of makeshift meditation, something I'd never been very good at. Random thoughts floated through, and I pushed them away, only for others to immediately replace them. Finally, I gave up, and they coalesced around a theme. Who murdered Travis Underwood?

I didn't have many options to choose from. Travis had never married, so no spouse to automatically accuse. His release from prison was only a few weeks ago, so no business associates or friends to investigate. The only former inmate from his time in Broad River Correctional the police had any interest in was Marcus, and I had no way of knowing who else might be swimming in that particular suspect pool the detectives weren't paying any attention to.

That left me with Ingrid, the veterinarian Quincy Felton, Hank Mathews, and Denny Holloway, the kid with the knife in the diner.

In my mind, Ingrid fell into the same category as Marcus—no way she'd risk everything unless she was threatened. Would she do it if Marcus was threatened? She'd help him if she could, but murder? I didn't know her well, but my gut said, *No way*.

I'd learned nothing helpful about Quincy Felton, and neither had Brittany. All I knew was he went to medical school for two years and then became a veterinarian. He was familiar with human anatomy, had surgical experience, and access to ketamine. Not much to go on. I had to put Charlie to work unearthing more information about him. If anyone could find a link between the vet and Travis, Charlie could.

My phone lay upside down on the coffee table, where I'd dropped it when I came home last night. I grabbed it, and the smashed, black screen stared back at me. *Crap!* I'd forgotten. Looked like I had more than one reason for a visit to Charlie. Besides the fact I hadn't been in my bookstore in two days. No need to worry, though. Lacey had everything under control.

Did Eric tell her about my accident during their run

this morning? Probably not. If he didn't care enough to show up at the hospital, he wouldn't bother to tell anyone why I wasn't there. If anyone even asked.

I shook my head, causing a momentary flare of pain. I *really* had to remember not to do that. Eric wouldn't be that petty. Lacey and Angus would undoubtedly have asked him where I was. He couldn't give them any details, though, unless he got them from Brittany. I picked up my cell to check for missed calls. The screen's spider cracks reminded me of *Charlotte's Web* without the messages. *Good grief!* Why couldn't I remember my phone was dead? Blame it on the concussion.

Okay, so I'd eliminated Marcus, Ingrid, and Quincy, for the moment. Who did that leave? Hank and Denny Holloway. I'd developed a solid case of circumstantial evidence against Hank. He knew Travis both when he was a child and since he got out of prison. He left town abruptly around the same time Travis stopped going to church, and he returned to Riddleton after being accused of having an affair with a parishioner in Idaho.

He told me he left town to care for his ailing mother and he'd returned because Father Preston had retired. Those seemed reasonable explanations, but what about the cut he had on his hand around the time of the murder and the letters he'd received from a possible love interest? A woman had pined away for him for years. He claimed he didn't return the feelings, but how could I know for sure?

And then there was the knife Lula had found under his mattress. When I'd mentioned it, he'd seemed totally bumfuzzled. He was either an award-winning actor, or he knew nothing about it. If he didn't put the knife there, who did? Who had access to his private rooms in the rectory?

Actually, anybody could've put it there. I had no trouble getting into his suite. Nobody else would, either. Hank didn't lock the doors, and if he was out, the rectory was unoccupied. Anyone could've snuck in and planted the knife under his mattress. But if someone was going to frame him, why put the murder weapon somewhere only Lula or Hank could find it? To be honest, I didn't even know if the knife had anything to do with Travis's murder.

And I still hadn't mentioned Denny Holloway to Eric. In my defense, I'd been a little preoccupied, what with the arraignment and falling off a horse and all. I needed to tell him, though. If Denny had killed Travis, Marcus was off the hook. He could go home to his girls and resume living his life.

All the pondering made my head hurt. The doctor said I had to rest so my brain could heal. I'd be willing to bet this mental merry-go-round I rode didn't come close to what he had in mind. I closed my eyes and allowed my attention to wander again, doing my best to ignore any thoughts about the murder.

I floated in the gray space between being fully asleep and fully awake. The melted icepack slid off my knee, and I made no move to catch it before it landed on the floor. Pictures from yesterday's ride drifted through: Lucy and Millie in their stalls, Lucy crunching on a peppermint, Lula in her riding habit, Lula leaning against the tree clutching her shoulder...

My eyelids flew open. Lula and George never came into the emergency room after parking the car last night. Brittany and I waited at least twenty minutes before I was called for examination. They never showed. I had to call and make sure she was all right. I snatched my cell off the coffee table. Screen still black. Still cracked, only this time I could swear it was laughing at me.

That's enough. Apparently, I was incapable of functioning without a phone. Time to see what Charlie could do with it. But how would I get there? My car was still at the farm, and I couldn't call anyone for a ride. The bookstore was only two blocks away. Was I strong enough to get there on crutches? Guess I'd find out in a few minutes.

I strapped on my knee brace and threw the icepack back in the freezer. I swallowed a couple more acetaminophen, grabbed my crutches and the spare apartment key out of the kitchen, and headed out the door. The stairs were tricky, but I'd watched Brittany maneuver them several times when she was on crutches last summer. I made my way down one step at a time and only slipped once, the banister saving me from tumbling to the bottom. And I wasn't in the mood for another trip to the hospital.

By the time I reached the sidewalk, my arms vibrated with fatigue, and sweat chilled my face in the cool December air. I shivered, then dried it off with my sleeve. I shuffled past the Goodwill, trying to keep time with "Deck the Halls" but hadn't yet found my rhythm.

Sidewalk Santa rang his bell at me. "Hey, what happened?"

"I fell off a ten-story horse."

"You shoulda used the elevator."

I started to shake my head, then remembered, grateful to have dodged the lightning strike that would've accompanied it. "Next time. Definitely."

My cadence picked up as I passed the town hall, and it finally seemed I was progressing. I zipped along the sidewalk, reaching the bookstore in record time. For a sloth. Exhaustion hummed through my arms, and I had to force my fingers open when I released the grip to grasp the door handle. Perspiration soaked the inside of all my clothing. No sweatshirt sleeve would alleviate the chill this time. I had to get inside where it was warm.

I negotiated the entrance, only getting whacked by the door twice, and found three customers browsing—a thirty-something woman and two gray-haired men. Fewer than I'd hoped for at noon on a Saturday a couple of weeks before Christmas. I suspected most Riddleton shoppers had visited the malls in Blackburn and Sutton. The last place I'd want to be in December. It could've been worse, though.

The light crowd gave me easy access to Charlie, however, which was just what I needed. I hobbled to the coffee bar, where he was restocking the coffee supplies.

"Hey, Charlie. How's it going?"

He looked up, showing no surprise at my condition. Eric must've told Lacey, who'd told Charlie. "Hi, boss. Heard you had an adventure yesterday."

"Don't I always?" I rested the crutches against the counter. "Any time I try something new it goes haywire."

"You like to get the most out of all your experiences."

"Yeah, something like that."

Lacey exited the stockroom, holding two books. She waved and carried them over to one of the gray-haired men. He smiled and thumbed through one of them.

She came over to where I was propped. "Hi! I see Eric wasn't exaggerating."

I scowled. "How would he know what shape I was in? He never showed up at the hospital."

"I'm sure he had a good reason. Did he call you at least?"

I retrieved my phone and showed it to her. "No idea."

"Oh, wow! What happened to it?" Charlie asked.

"I'm not sure. I think Lucy stepped on it."

"Who's Lucy?"

"The horse." I handed the cell to him. "Think you can fix it?"

Charlie laughed. "I'm good, but I'm no miracle worker." He pulled a set of tools someone had left in the dryer too long out from under the counter. "I'll look at it, but I'm pretty sure it's toast. Do you have a backup? I think I can get your SIM card out and transfer it."

I gave him a stink eye. "A backup? Really? Who has an extra phone lying around?"

He reached into his laptop case. "Lucky for you, I do."

Leave it to the computer geek. "Is it compatible?"

"We have the same carrier, so it should be. Are your contacts on your phone or your SIM card?"

"SIM card, I think. I have an SD card too. There's a photo I'd like you to take a look at. Maybe do some investigating if you have time." But only if he could retrieve that baby picture.

He pilfered through his toolkit. "I'll see what I can do. Now go away, so I can work."

"Yes, sir!" I fired off a salute, then went to find Lacey, who was helping the thirty-something find a book in the History section.

One of the gray-haired men stood at the register,

238

waiting to check out. I hopped over to help him. "Did you find what you were looking for?"

He smiled and handed me a copy of *Double Trouble*. "I did. Looks like I got the author too. Would you mind signing it for me? My wife will be thrilled."

"I'll be happy to." I fished a pen out from under the counter. "What's your wife's name?"

I wished Janice a happy holiday on the title page, rang up the sale, and slid the novel into a bag.

"There you go. That should keep her from peeking before Christmas."

"Thank you."

New customers coming in kept Lacey busy on the sales floor. Charlie worked on my phone between pouring coffee and doling out pastries. The safest place for me seemed to be where I was. I checked people out and retrieved bookmarks and reading lights from the display case, feeling useful for a change. There were worse ways to make a living, right?

A flow of people in and out occupied us nonstop for an hour. I reveled in our success, though I knew things would likely return to normal come the new year. The bells over the door jingled again. I looked up to greet the new customer, who turned out to be Eric. I dropped my hand back to my side.

How dare he come strolling in here after blowing me off last night?

He caught my eye and headed in my direction. I made a show of rearranging the bookmarks in the display case. I was still too angry to talk to him. We had our problems, yes, and he wanted some time to sort them out. I understood that. However, I never would've ignored him when he'd been injured. No matter how

239

mad I was. I couldn't think of a single reasonable excuse he might have for his behavior.

Eric changed directions and helped himself to coffee instead. He chatted with Charlie but never took his eyes off me. My face heated, and I searched for something to keep me busy while pretending I didn't know he was watching me. In my peripheral vision, I saw him refill his cup and amble in my direction.

I met his gaze, firing daggers at him from my eyes, which made my head hurt. But I was fuming, and I wanted him to know it. To his credit, he never looked away. The guy had guts. I had to give him that. And he didn't show up with flowers as if that would magically make everything all better.

"Hi, Jen. How are you feeling?" Concern filled his eyes. Was it real, or did he know he was in trouble?

"I'm all right."

He nodded. "I know you're mad, but I can explain why I didn't pick you up last night."

"It's no problem. Brittany was there for me. Brittany's always there for me. Unlike you."

"Come on, Jen, you know that's not true."

"Do I? I don't remember seeing you at the hospital."

Eric reached for my hand. I pulled away. He sighed. "I was already at the hospital when Brittany called me. Marcus was stabbed in jail."

CHAPTER TWENTY-FOUR

"What?!" I reached over the counter and grabbed Eric's arm. "What do you mean Marcus was stabbed?"

Eric took my hand. "Somebody got him on the way to the mess hall, but he's going to be okay. They found him quickly."

"This time."

"What do you mean?"

"Someone's been after him since you transferred him over there. Didn't you see his face?"

He frowned. "Yeah, but I assumed it was part of the same attack."

"Nope. He got beaten up his first night there. Do they have any idea who stabbed him?"

"If they do, they're not telling us. Sutton County's kinda tight-lipped about stuff like this. They worry about their reputation."

"Too bad they don't worry more about the inmates, instead."

He looked away.

"I need to see him, Eric."

"I don't know if that's possible."

"Why not? He hasn't been convicted of anything."

"No, but he's accused of a capital crime."

"One you know he didn't commit. Or at least you should."

He scowled, and his eyes flashed. "I don't know that at all, Jen. And I wish you'd stop saying that."

A chill ran down my spine, and my dander rose. "I say it because it's true. There's no way he murdered Travis and left his body behind my bookstore. Deep down, he's a good person. Even during his checkered past, he never hurt anyone. And he wouldn't do that to me. I saved his life once, remember? He wouldn't put me in that situation."

Eric pressed his lips together. "Look, I don't want to fight. I just wanted you to know why I didn't come see you in the hospital. It wasn't because I didn't care."

"Well, thanks for telling me. I'll figure out my own way of getting into the hospital to see him."

"And get yourself into trouble again."

I shrugged. "Maybe, maybe not. Either way, it's worth the risk. Somebody has to let Marcus know he matters and we haven't forgotten him."

"There might be a way." Eric studied his fingernails for a moment. "I can go with you. They may let me in if I tell them I need to question him."

"What about me?"

"I'll say you're a witness. Then they have to let us see him. We can go this evening."

"Thank you."

"You're welcome. I'll pick you up around five." He topped off his coffee and headed toward the door.

I remembered Denny Holloway. "Eric, wait!"

He turned and came back to the counter. "What's up?"

"Lula Parsons gave me the name of the kid with the knife who was in the diner bragging about going after the 'new guy in town' the night Travis was murdered. He was Denny Holloway. Do you know anything about him?"

"I had a few run-ins with him when I was on patrol. Mostly petty stuff. A couple of attempted robberies. I don't think he's capable of killing anyone, though. He's just mixed up."

"Maybe one of his attempted robberies got out of hand. What if Travis fought back?"

"I can see that happening, but five perfectly placed stab wounds? No way. That's someone who's organized, not a frantic kid."

I sighed out my frustration. "You're probably right, but what happened to the 'no stone unturned' guy who wanted to become a detective I used to know? I'm handing you a stone. Turn it over and see what's under it."

He studied the tops of his shiny new detective shoes. "All right. I'll see what I can do. At least find out if he has an alibi."

Finally. "Thank you. Since you mentioned the perfectly placed stab wounds, what did the second autopsy show?"

"The results were identical to Ingrid's."

"So, she's off the hook?"

"She was never on the hook." Eric waved and went back to work.

Not his, maybe, but somebody's or they wouldn't have gotten a second opinion on the autopsy.

The rush had died, so I crutched to the coffee bar to check Charlie's progress. He was studying his laptop screen.

"What did you find?"

Charlie turned the computer to face me. He had the baby picture loaded onto it. "I assumed this is what you wanted me to look at? Unless, of course, it was one of the two-hundred pictures of Savannah you've got on that SD card." He arched an eyebrow.

"What? She's cute."

"Yes, she is, but I have a feeling this baby picture is a little more important."

I studied the photo. "I think it could be. Maybe the rumors were true, and Lula *did* have a baby in high school."

"It's possible. It doesn't necessarily mean anything, though. It could be a relative or the child of a friend."

"You're probably right. You mind checking into it for me, anyway? You know how I hate loose ends."

"Sure. I'll see what I can dig up."

"Thanks. Well, you retrieved the SD card. What about the phone itself? Any hope for it?"

He shook his head. "'Fraid not. It's a paperweight. I did get the SIM card out, though. I had to finagle a little, but it'll work in this other phone if you want it."

"Just until I can buy another one. I discovered this morning I'm one of those people who can't live without a phone."

Charlie showed me his five-thousand-dollar smile. "I know what you mean. I can't imagine not having mine." He handed me his backup. "It's all set up for you. Ready to use. Keep it as long as you like."

"I appreciate it. I need to call Lula and make arrangements to get my car back. The other thing I've discovered I can't live without. Any chance you might give me a ride out there later?"

"Sure."

I scrolled through the contacts, hoping I'd saved Lula's info to the SIM card, not the phone. Otherwise, I'd have to meet her at the church in the morning. I had no other way of contacting her.

The second time scrolling through the list, I spotted her name and tapped the phone icon. She answered on the second ring.

"Hi, Jen. How are you?"

"I'm okay. A little bit of a headache and my leg hurts, but other than that no major problems. Except my sore butt, of course, but I knew that was coming."

"Good. I'm glad to hear it. I've been worried about you. I tried calling, but it went straight to voicemail."

I settled into a wingback chair in the front of the store to take the strain off my leg. "Yeah, my phone is dead. Charlie lent me his spare until I can get a new one."

"That was nice of him."

"It was." I hesitated. "I thought I'd see you at the hospital last night."

"George and I talked a while in the parking lot, and by the time we came in, you'd already gone back to see the doctor."

"How's your shoulder?"

"It'll be fine in a couple of days. They popped it back into place and gave me a sling. It's happened a few times before, so I'm used to it."

I shifted in my seat to take the pressure off my tailbone. Horseback riding didn't seem to agree with me. In more ways than one. "Are you going to be home later today? I need to pick up my car."

"Actually, we were just coming to town. Why don't we bring it to you?"

245

"You sure it's no trouble?"

"None at all."

"The keys should be in the ignition. I'll wait for you at the bookstore."

"See you soon."

"Thanks." I ended the call and settled back in my chair. My headache flared, and my leg ached. I needed some ice and another round of acetaminophen, although that wouldn't help with my drooping eyelids.

Lacey ushered the last customer out the door and dropped into the other wingback opposite the couch. "Are you okay?"

I replied without opening my eyes. "I'm fine. Just tired. It's been a long day after an even longer night."

"Thanks for your help today."

"I should be helping all the time."

She chuckled. "We don't usually need it, and you have a lot going on. I get that."

"Still, I should make more of an effort. Focus on the important things, instead of being distracted all the time. I'm sorry. I'll do better."

"How's your investigation going? Figure out whodunit yet?"

I opened my eyes. "No, but I need to. Eric told me somebody stabbed Marcus in jail last night. I have to get him out of there."

Lacey covered her mouth with a hand. "Oh! Is he all right?"

"He's stable. Eric and I are going to visit him in the hospital this evening. I'm hoping this will help convince Eric the situation deserves more than the cursory once-over they gave it. Maybe then he'll help me find something to prove Marcus is innocent."

"I'm sure he will. You always come through in the end. I have faith."

I lifted one eyebrow. "Thanks. It would be nice if I didn't have to, though. Wouldn't it?"

"Yeah. A little normalcy around here wouldn't be terrible. Although, your adventures seem to be good for business."

"I vote we try to drum up some customers the usual way for a change."

Lacey laughed. "I second. But right now, I'll take them any way I can get them."

I closed my eyes and dozed a little, running through those two hundred pictures Charlie mentioned. I missed my little girl. Had she fully recovered from the thong incident yet? Dr. Felton said…

Oh! I'd forgotten to ask Charlie to check into him, too.

Wide awake, I gathered my crutches and returned to the coffee bar, my arms quivering. How had Brittany done this for six weeks? Maybe Olinski would let me borrow that wheelchair he'd found for her last summer. That would make getting around a lot easier.

Charlie was so deep into his computer screen, he never noticed my approach. I cleared my throat. He continued to scroll. I tapped him on the shoulder, and he jumped.

"What's so interesting?" I asked.

"I'm checking adoption records. Obviously, Lula didn't keep the baby if it was hers, so maybe someone adopted him."

"Good thinking. I have another project for you, though. One that could be directly related to Travis's death."

He perked up. "Oh? What's that?"

"Can you look into the vet, Quincy Felton?"

"I guess so. Why? You think he killed Travis?"

"Probably not, but he's capable of making the stab wounds Ingrid found, so we should rule him out, if nothing else. He spent two years at MUSC before switching to vet school. That means he's familiar with human anatomy, and he's a skilled surgeon. Can you see if there's any connection between him and Travis? Brittany couldn't find anything, but she doesn't have your voodoo skills."

"Voodoo skills?"

"You know. Dark magic."

He tipped an imaginary Stetson, though he wasn't in his cowboy suit today. "My hat is always white. I only use my powers for good."

"I know. But where you find your information is another story, isn't it?"

"Hypothetically speaking, I might bend the rules a little from time to time."

"Your secret's safe with me. Let me know what you find out."

He tipped his hat again. "Will do, ma'am."

"Thank you."

Before I could make it all the way back to my perch, my new phone rang. I pulled it out of my pocket and dropped into the chair. MOM decorated the screen. I swiped.

"Hi, Mom."

"Don't you 'Hi, Mom' me. I've been trying to call you all day. I've probably left fifteen messages. Why haven't you called me back?"

I sighed and counted to ten. She had a right to be

angry today, but that didn't stop me from taking a trip back to the bad old days when she was like this all the time. "I'm sorry. My phone was broken. Charlie lent me one of his. That's the only reason I'm talking to you now."

"What happened?"

Once she was satisfied I'd suffered no permanent consequences from my adventure with Lucy, my mother laughed hysterically. I could see the tears streaming down her face in my mind. Empathy wasn't one of my mother's most vital qualities. Must be where I got it from.

When the hilarity subsided, and her breath hitched, I asked, "Are you done?"

She giggled. "I think so. I kept picturing you bouncing around on that horse, and I couldn't help myself. But I really am glad you're okay."

"Sure you are. Well, now that you've had your entertainment for the day, why have you been so frantically trying to reach me?"

"I wanted to know what time you and Eric were coming for your birthday dinner tomorrow. I have a surprise planned."

My birthday. I'd forgotten about it in all the commotion.

I had a surprise for her too. "Eric's not coming. We broke up after we left your place the other night."

"What did you do?"

Nice to know you're on my side, Mom. "Nothing. That's the problem."

"What does that mean?"

"He kept making all these comments about us getting married, and I didn't react the way he'd hoped. In fact,

I kinda panicked. After that, he decided we needed some time apart so he could figure things out."

"It seems like he left the door open, at least. How do you feel?"

Good question. "I don't know yet. With everything that went on yesterday, I haven't had time to think about it. I know I'm not ready for the kind of commitment he's looking for. And I'm definitely not ready to get married. To anyone. Maybe I never will be."

She scoffed. "I refuse to believe that."

"That's only because you want grandchildren. Even if I do decide to get married someday, I still might not want any children. You should be prepared for that possibility."

"I'll cross that bridge when I come to it. Right now, I want you to be happy. Are you happy?"

I thought about it for a minute, then still had no answer. "I don't know. In some ways I am. I'm happy with my career and the bookstore. That's a start."

"There's more to life than work. You need someone to come home to at the end of the day. Someone with fewer than four legs."

I smiled. "How's my girl doing?"

"Savannah's fine. Curled up on the couch with Gary, watching a movie."

"And what about him? Is he feeling any better?"

"He loves having her around. She makes him happy. I don't suppose you'd consider letting her stay here a little longer?"

No! But I had to be pragmatic. I was in no condition to take care of her. "How about you keep her until my leg is well enough to walk on without crutches? Does that work?"

"Thank you. We can iron out the details tomorrow at your party. Can you be here around four? That'll give us time to visit before we eat."

"Sure. Sounds great." I laid the phone down on the side table, knowing I'd just lied to my mother. Turning thirty didn't sound great to me at all.

I glanced out the door in time to see Lula park my car in front of the store. I hobbled out to greet her.

She handed me the keys. "Here you go. Sorry we took so long."

"No problem, I appreciate you bringing it to me. I wasn't looking forward to the long trek back home."

"Happy to help. I feel terribly guilty about what happened yesterday. It's all my fault."

"It is not. You didn't fire that gun behind us and spook the horses."

"No, but still…"

"Don't worry about it. We'll both be fine in a few days, and it'll be like it never happened."

"Thank you." Her face brightened. "Hey, maybe we can try it again sometime."

"I'll have to think about that. Maybe sometime in the distant future."

Lula laughed. "Fair enough." She got in the car with George, and they drove away.

I waved and turned back toward the bookstore. As I opened the door, it dawned on me she wasn't wearing her sling.

CHAPTER TWENTY-FIVE

I said goodbye to Charlie, and Lacey escorted me to my car.

"Are you sure you're okay to drive?" she asked, brow furrowed in concern.

"I'll be fine. My right leg works, and it's only two blocks."

"Right, so it's only two blocks for me to walk back after I drive you. And you have the steps to negotiate after you get there."

My every instinct screamed, *No! I can take care of myself*, but I knew she was right. No sense in being stubborn. "That would be helpful, if you're sure you don't mind."

"Not at all."

Lacey ran back inside to tell Charlie she was leaving for a few minutes. Then she helped me into the passenger seat, lifting my leg so I wouldn't bump it against anything. She tossed the crutches on the back seat and took her place behind the wheel.

"Are you comfortable?"

"I'm good, thanks. It's only two blocks, remember?"

She adjusted the seat and mirrors, being a few inches

taller than Lula, and put the Dodge into gear. A minute later, she steered into the empty space beside Charlie's Ford. She reversed her process to unload me and helped me up the stairs into the apartment.

I had to admit it was much easier than it would've been if I'd done it all on my own. Another sign of personal growth. If I wasn't careful, I'd become a grownup after all. I was still a big Peter Pan fan, though. And I had one day left until I was an official adult. Today, I was still twenty-nine.

"Do you need anything before I go?" Lacey asked.

"No, thanks. I'm just going to ice my knee and rest awhile."

Lacey went to the kitchen and opened the freezer for the icepack. "Go ahead and get comfortable. I'll get you set up."

"Don't worry about it. I can handle things. You need to get back to the store."

"Shut up and lie down. Let somebody help you for a change."

A warm place grew in my chest. Did I have another friend like Brittany? I didn't deserve the one I had, let alone a second, but my head hurt too much to argue. I settled on the couch. "Yes, ma'am. Can I have some acetaminophen too, please?"

"Absolutely." She helped me remove the knee brace and positioned the icepack. "Coming right up."

I swallowed the tablets and washed them down with the bottle of water she'd brought me. "Thank you. Now, get back to work. I'm not paying you for babysitting," I said with a smile.

"You're not paying me for working, either." Lacey laughed as she headed out the door.

"Minor detail," I called after her.

I vegged out on the couch and waited for the pain meds to kick in. I had about an hour before Eric was supposed to pick me up, so I let my mind wander at will until I remembered I hadn't even thought about the Davenport twins in days. Which meant still no perfect first line. However, I'd changed the victim from a dead cheerleader to a frat boy murdered in the tunnels, so I could begin the story anywhere I wanted.

Since the fraternity Daniel wanted to pledge had become the story's focus, what if I opened with Dana teasing him about it? She wouldn't even consider joining a sorority and would think Daniel was being silly. *Note to self: research fraternities to find the best fit for someone like Daniel. He's intelligent but sociable and gets along easily with others. Not athletic. Doesn't drink or do drugs.* I suspected this would be tougher than I expected. There had to be a good one for him out there somewhere, though.

I personally didn't know how it all worked. I'd avoided Greek Week like the plague when I attended the University of South Carolina. I'd heard enough stories to wing it, though. I only needed enough detail to make the scenes realistic. I could do that.

After forty-five minutes or so, I gave up. The first line still hovered out of reach, but the story had taken shape. Enough for a loose outline, anyway. Not that I'd be working on that today. I had fifteen minutes to get ready before Eric arrived.

I pulled myself into a sitting position, using the back of the couch for leverage. The acetaminophen had dulled my headache, and the ice had done the same for my knee. The brace would take care of the rest. I limped

254

to the bathroom to check out the damage my waking nap had done to my hair.

The face staring back at me in the mirror resembled an overstuffed, blue-eyed scarecrow. My black hair stuck out all around my head, and I beat it into submission with a brush. As much as it ever capitulated, that is. My multiple cowlicks left me looking like Alfalfa with a tail sticking out each side. No time to wash it, so I ran my fingers through to make it stylishly messy and gave up. I'd long since accepted I was having a bad-hair life.

Eric tapped on the door a little after five. Fatigue aged his face, and his rumpled jacket made it seem as if he'd been getting fashion tips from Olinski. A flash of guilt tightened my chest. He needed to go home and rest, and here I was, dragging him off to Sutton. I should tell him to forget about it. That would be the right thing to do. But Marcus needed me, and Eric was the only one who could get me in to see him. I had no choice.

"Are you okay?" I asked, putting on my jacket. "You look tired."

"It's been a long day. You ready to go?"

I loaded my pockets with my keys and phone. "Yes. Thanks for doing this."

"I'm just trying to keep you out of trouble."

"I know. Thank you."

He helped me down the steps to his black Jeep Wrangler. After settling me in the passenger seat, he climbed in the driver's side. He'd had to clear clutter off the seat before I could sit in it, which had never happened before. Detective work clearly demanded more of his time than patrol did. I'd often teased him about how much energy he dedicated to caring for his car. The mess had to be driving him crazy.

The road to Sutton was congested with Christmas shoppers returning from the malls. The last place anyone would ever find me in December. While they were great places to search for characters, I would never step foot in one this time of year. Crowds weren't my thing.

The silence in the car felt like a weighted blanket in the summertime. Normally, I enjoyed a companionable quietude, but this was different. Was it fatigue, or did Eric not love me anymore? Could I handle that prospect? Perhaps, but losing his friendship would be a different matter altogether.

I put out a feeler. "My mother called today. She wanted to know what time we were coming over for my birthday dinner tomorrow. I told her you probably wouldn't be there."

"Why would you do that?"

"You told me you needed space. I didn't want to presume."

His hands tightened on the steering wheel. "Do you want me there?"

"Yes, but not if you'll be uncomfortable."

"Let me think about it. I'll let you know in the morning."

Not what I'd hoped for, but at least it wasn't a rejection. "Okay."

I pushed back a twinge of irritation. How could he claim to love me and not want to spend my thirtieth birthday with me? Except, I'd pushed him away every time he tried to get close, so I had no right to expect him to keep coming back for more. Someday, my warring emotions would call a truce. Sooner rather than later would be nice. After the lifelong struggle, I had a serious case of battle fatigue.

Time to change the subject before we ended up in another fight. "You look pretty worn out. A lot going on at work today?"

"I told Havermayer about Denny Holloway, and she wasn't impressed. She told me to leave it alone."

My eyebrows dove for the bridge of my nose. "It figures. Talk about tunnel vision. She doesn't want to admit she might've made a mistake."

"She doesn't think she made a mistake. All the evidence points to Marcus."

"All the circumstantial evidence."

"Either way. But when I told her I didn't feel comfortable not investigating the possibility the kid had something to do with the murder, she let me run with it."

Color me surprised. "That's unexpected."

"Not really. You don't know her. She's a good detective."

"So people keep telling me."

Eric clamped down on the steering wheel again, jaw working. "Do you want to know what I found out, or do you just want to criticize my partner some more?"

I'd made him angry again. When would I learn to keep my mouth shut?

"Please tell me what you discovered today."

He relaxed his grip. "I checked into his record, and all his arrests were before he turned eighteen, so they're sealed. I had a chat with a detective who arrested him once, and he told me the kid was bad news."

"That's pretty much what Lula said."

"Yeah, so I went to see him. I asked him about what

he said in the diner, and he said he was just showing off for his friend. Trying to look tougher than he is. Plus, he has an alibi for that night. His uncle came in from out of town, and the whole family went to dinner together. I talked to his parents, the uncle, and the server from the restaurant, who remembered them because the uncle looked like that mountain man, Grizzly Adams. So, it couldn't have been him. I'm sorry."

I swallowed my disappointment. "Thank you for trying. You went out of your way to look into it for me, and you didn't have to. I appreciate it."

Back to the drawing board.

The Sutton Medical Center parking lot was packed, and Eric dropped me off at the entrance, so I wouldn't have to make the trek from the hinterlands. I'd been here so many times in the last couple of years, between my adventures and Gary's illness, the place almost felt like home. And, like during my childhood, my first instinct was to run away. No escape this time either, though.

A gray-haired woman in a pink jacket with a hospital volunteer patch perched behind the information desk, where I waited for Eric. Her expression settled into a poker face when she brought up Marcus's information on her computer and told us his room number. We thanked her and ambled past the angel-topped Christmas tree to the bank of elevators.

All the units were in use, and it took a couple of minutes for an elevator to open and discharge several passengers. Eric held the door for me to crutch my way in, then pressed the button marked seven. My stomach roiled as I considered what we'd find when we arrived. Would Marcus even be allowed to talk to us?

The seventh-floor bustle clashed with the elevator's silence, and my senses recoiled. Scrub-clad staff and visitors clogged the hallway, but we had no difficulty spotting Marcus's room. It was the one with a uniformed Sutton County deputy sheriff seated beside the door. As we approached, he glanced up from his phone, and Eric flashed his badge.

"What can I do for you?" the deputy asked.

"Detective O'Malley, Riddleton Police Department. I need to speak with your prisoner."

"You're okay, but who's your friend?" The deputy checked out my knee brace and regions higher up.

Hey, buddy, my eyes are up here. I bit back a nasty comment.

"Um…" Eric blushed and fumbled to explain my presence.

I bailed him out with a fib. Well, an out-and-out lie. "I'm an assault victim." I gestured toward the knee he'd shown so much interest in a minute ago. "And I have to see if this guy is the one who attacked me, so they can put the no-good bum in jail."

Eric choked on suppressed laughter and coughed to cover it.

I slapped him on the back hard enough to make him stumble. "You okay? You need some water or something?" I whacked him again just because he could do nothing about it. That would teach him not to be mad at me all the time.

He sniped a side-eye at me and put up his hand. "I'm okay now." He glanced at the deputy with an embarrassed grin. "Can we go in? It'll just take a minute."

"Yeah, sure. Knock yourself out."

"Thanks."

Eric held the door for me to hobble through. A pallid and frail version of Marcus was sitting up in the hospital bed, his left wrist handcuffed to the rail. On the table across the bed in front of him sat a tray with a plate holding a brown glob, a white glob, and peas. Beside it, a cup of green Jell-O, and apple juice. He unsuccessfully attacked the mystery meat with a plastic fork. They'd given him no knife, and he only had one hand to work with.

He gave up as we approached. "Hey, what are you two doing here?"

Eric put a finger up to his lips until the deputy closed the door behind himself. Then, in a voice loud enough to be heard in the hall, he said, "I need to ask you a few more questions."

When I was certain we couldn't be overheard, I whispered, "How are you? What happened?" I took the tiny pocketknife I carried on my keychain and used it to cut his meat. Not the most hygienic solution, but at least he wouldn't starve.

"I'm okay. The doc says I should make a full recovery." Marcus looked away. "Then I get to spend the rest of my life in prison for something I didn't do."

I took his hand. "No, you don't. I'm not going to let that happen." If only I knew how I'd stop it, though. There had to be a way. I refused to give up. "Who did this to you?"

"One of Travis's buddies from Broad River was in lockup with me and decided to get revenge for me killing Travis. I tried to tell him I didn't do it, but he wouldn't listen."

A flurry of grief, regret, and determination ran across Eric's face. "I'm sorry this happened to you, Marcus."

Anger flashed from Marcus's eyes. "Yeah, right. You're the one who put me in there."

"I had no choice. Give me something to work with, and I'll do everything I can to get you out. I've followed every lead we have. There's no evidence against anyone else."

"I got nothing to give you. I was home with my kids and Mrs. Washington. I didn't know I needed more than that for an alibi. I damn sure would've had one if I did."

Eric clenched his jaw. "I get that, but there's nothing I can do without new leads to follow. And Havermayer considers this case closed."

I stepped in. "Marcus, I found that note you hid in your daughter's bedpost. What was that all about?"

He stared out the window. "When Travis started spreading stories about me killing that guy in the shower room, the other guys took sides pretty quick. That was just one of them letting me know he was on mine. When I heard Travis was murdered, I went home and looked for anything bad the police might find. I knew I'd be the first suspect. I stuck the note in the bedpost, so the cops wouldn't find it. I don't even know why I kept it."

I glanced at Eric, suppressing a grin. "Well, the cops didn't find it, I did, but I had to tell them about it. Sorry."

"It's okay. I didn't do anything wrong then, and I didn't kill Travis. I just wish somebody would figure out who did, so I can go home to my girls." Frustration lined his face.

It occurred to me there was one lead we hadn't looked into yet. "Marcus, why did Travis have a slip of paper with my name on it in his pocket?"

"I gave it to him. He told me he needed to find someone, and I thought you might be able to help."

"Who was he trying to find?"

"He never said. Just that it was important."

I looked at Eric. "I think we just got another lead to follow. Maybe that person didn't want to be found."

CHAPTER TWENTY-SIX

Eric cranked up the car and stared out the windshield.

"Are you okay?" I asked when he made no move to back out of the parking space.

"Yeah. It was just tough seeing him that way. I wish I could do something for him."

"You can. You can believe in his innocence and find the person who *really* killed Travis."

He put his Jeep into reverse and rolled past the vehicles on either side. "If only I could believe him. He didn't say anything he hasn't already said a hundred times. But none of it is proof. The evidence doesn't lie."

"It doesn't tell the whole story, either. You know that."

"Either way, I'm not the one he needs to convince. It's Havermayer, and she's not even listening. It's going to take undeniable proof to persuade her to reopen the case. And I'm not seeing anything like that."

It was my turn to stare out the window. "Maybe you should interview the guy who stabbed Marcus. He might be able to shed some light on who Travis was trying to find in Riddleton. I have a feeling that person may be at the center of all this somehow."

"Could be. It's worth a shot. I'll have to convince Havermayer, though. It'll take someone with a lot more pull than I have to induce Sutton County to let me talk to him. The assault is in their jurisdiction."

"What about Chief Olinski? He has more influence than anyone else."

Eric snuck a quick glance at me. "I don't know, Jen. Going over Havermayer's head could be career suicide for me. I'll try her first. If she doesn't go for it, I'll consider going to the chief. But I'm not making any promises, okay?"

"That's fair, I guess." If I didn't consider that Marcus's life was at stake. Still, Eric would try. About all I could ask for. "Have you learned anything about Father Hank? He seems like a viable alternative to me."

"There's nothing there other than the few things you brought to our attention. He's a priest. We need more than circumstantial evidence to accuse him of anything."

Anger bubbled in my belly, forcing bile into my throat. "Unlike Marcus, right?"

"Marcus has a history of criminal activity. That, along with his issues with Travis, makes him a plausible suspect. You know how things work."

"Yeah. Guilty until proven innocent. And you don't even have to try to prove him innocent. Must be nice to have your case all tied up in a little bow because someone made a mistake fifteen years ago."

His fingers strangled the steering wheel, but he said nothing.

We rode the remainder of the way in silence. I didn't dare broach the subject of my birthday dinner again. He said he'd think about it. I had to give him time.

Me, too. No point in pushing for a relationship I wasn't sure I could handle. That wouldn't be fair to either of us.

Charlie heard us laboriously climbing the stairs and came out of his apartment. "Need a hand?" he asked when we were halfway to the top.

"I think we got it. Thanks, though."

He followed us up, patiently waiting on each step until I cleared the next. How long did the doctor say it would take my knee to heal? Whatever he said, it was too long for me. With luck, I'd be able to ditch the crutches in a few days. At least the brace would be manageable.

Eric waved and left me alone in my apartment with Charlie. A year ago, I'd never have allowed that to happen. When Charlie had first moved into the place downstairs, he'd constantly hounded me to go out with him. After a few months of him refusing to take "no" for an answer, I'd avoided him any way I could, usually without success. Then he'd helped me find Aletha's killer and volunteered to work at the bookstore for almost nothing. I'd cringed at the concept but agreed since I couldn't afford to hire anyone to run the coffee bar. We made a deal. He'd stop asking me out on dates, and I wouldn't hold his head in the full coffee urn until he drank his way out. So far, neither of us have had any complaints.

"Can I get you anything?" I asked him as I gathered my icepack and acetaminophen.

"I'm good, thanks. I just stopped by to fill you in on my progress."

Charlie carried my supplies, while I crutched over to

the couch, removed my brace, and settled back against the pillows with my leg outstretched. "Okay, I'm ready. Whatcha got?"

"I couldn't find any connection between Quincy Felton and Travis. In fact, I didn't find any dirt on Felton at all. The vet's cleaner than any of his patients."

Not at all what I wanted to hear. "What about his sudden transfer out of med school?"

"According to his social media posts, he wanted to work with animals and only went to med school in the first place because his father refused to pay for anything else. I guess his dad had a change of heart."

I inhaled and let the air out slowly. "That lets him out. Thanks for trying. Any luck on the baby? A birth certificate or adoption records maybe?"

"Nothing yet, but I'm still working on it. I'll let you know as soon as I find something."

"Thanks, Charlie." I closed the door behind him.

One fewer alternative to Marcus in Travis's death. Today alone had eliminated Denny Holloway and Quincy Felton. The only suspects left were Father Hank and Marcus. And Eric had made it clear they wouldn't accuse the priest unless they found the bloody knife in his hand. It didn't look good for Marcus. I'd failed him.

I swiped at the brimming tears and reached for my laptop. The doctor had warned against writing, but I needed a distraction. The only mystery I could solve now was the one in my head. Not that I'd give up on finding Travis's killer. I needed fresh ideas, and they only came when I wasn't thinking about the problem. I had to let my subconscious work on it for a while.

My headache skulked like a rattlesnake coiled behind a rock, prepared to strike at any moment. Perhaps researching those fraternities would be better than actually trying to write anything. I typed "fraternities at U of SC" into my search engine. After a couple of clicks, I found a list of twenty-eight fraternities in alphabetical order. More than I expected.

I began the laborious process of selecting each one to learn what they were all about. After eliminating the ones whose websites didn't work, the ones whose mission statements were so generic they didn't actually say anything, and the ones who were openly anti-hazing, I settled on Alpha Phi Alpha for Daniel. A fraternity dedicated to social justice. A perfect fit.

Daniel would be against hazing too, but I couldn't have a frat boy lost in the tunnels if someone hadn't sent him there. I'd have Daniel decide that the mission was more important than the inconveniences he had to go through to get in. And, frankly, having the guys navigate the tunnels was much less dangerous than pouring bottles of vodka down their throats. The kid who would get lost could get drunk before going down there without help from his future fraternity brothers. Problem solved.

By this time, my head was splitting, and I opted for another round of acetaminophen and a nap. Enough work for today. I still hadn't had my brainstorm, so I closed my eyes to rest until the meds kicked in. Maybe my subconscious would spit out something useful. I could only hope, since my options for getting Marcus out of jail had dwindled to almost none.

My thoughts immediately turned to the person Travis wanted my help to find. Marcus had no idea who it might be, and the only other person I knew Travis had spoken with since his return to Riddleton was Hank. The priest had only mentioned the discussion about Travis joining the priesthood. Did they talk about the mystery person? He said they spoke of nothing else important, but maybe he didn't consider it consequential. I hadn't known to ask about a mystery person. I did now, though. I put that on my to-do list for tomorrow.

My headache ebbed, and fatigue weighted my eyelids. I debated whether to give up and go to bed, though it was only eight thirty. Apparently, in my world, thirty was the new sixty. A knock on the door interrupted that thought. I sat up and reached for my crutches.

Brittany opened the door a crack and poked her head in. "Hey, Jen, you decent?"

Olinski must be with her. Otherwise, she wouldn't care. "No, but I'm fully clothed."

"Perfect." She pushed through the doorway, followed by Olinski carrying a grocery bag he unloaded on the kitchen counter. "We brought you some snacks."

"Thanks."

She tossed me a pack of Ding Dongs and flopped on the couch beside me. "How are you feeling? Headache any better?"

"It comes and goes."

"You're following doctor's orders, right?"

Olinski snickered in the kitchen. "That'll be the day."

"Hey, I'm doing what I'm supposed to."

Brittany picked up my laptop. "Really? What's this doing here?"

"He said I wasn't supposed to write. He didn't say anything about research."

She shook her head and watched Olinski park in the

cracked-leather recliner by the sliding doors. "Why do I bother?"

I stuffed half a Ding Dong in my mouth and smiled. "Because you love me."

"That's debatable."

After aiming my chocolate-coated tongue at her, I turned to Olinski. "How's it going, Chief? Have you guys found who murdered Travis yet?"

He lifted his furry caterpillars. "Yes. Marcus Jones is in custody awaiting trial."

"He didn't do it."

"Show me the proof, and I'll be happy to recommend the DA drop the charges."

"I don't have your resources."

"From what I understand, we looked into every lead you've given us, even though we didn't have to. None of them went anywhere. What more do you want us to do?"

My fingernails dug half-moons into my palms. "I don't know. I'm frustrated. Marcus is innocent, and I can't prove it."

Olinski rested his forearms on his knees. "Maybe you don't know him as well as you think you do. Have you even once considered the possibility he's guilty?"

"No, and I never will." I propped my injured leg on the coffee table. "Eric has a new lead to check out, anyway. Marcus said he wrote the note in Travis's pocket because Travis wanted me to help him find someone, but he doesn't know who."

"I hope Eric finds something. I don't have anything against Marcus personally, you know. He seems like a terrific guy."

"I know. I'm sorry to be so stubborn about it, but my gut is screaming, 'He's innocent,' and I can't ignore

269

it. Especially since my instincts about these things are usually right."

Olinski gave me a half-smile. "Maybe, but some-times—"

Brittany interrupted. "I think we should table this discussion for now. You're both convinced you're right and nothing the other says will change your minds. So, it's pointless."

I couldn't disagree. Besides, she was always right. One of her more irritating traits. "Okay, I'll change the subject. Are you two coming to my birthday dinner at Mom's tomorrow?"

"I wouldn't miss it, and neither would you, right, Olinski?"

He cleared his throat. "Yes, dear. I can't wait to spend the evening with Jen's parents. We got along so well when I was in high school, I'm looking forward to picking up where we left off."

Brittany threw an empty Ding Dong wrapper at him. "Knock it off. It won't be so bad. Besides, Eric'll be there. You can just hang with him."

I blew out a lungful. "Not necessarily. I don't know if he's coming or not."

Her eyebrows shot up. "What do you mean?"

"We haven't been getting along lately. He might not show up tomorrow."

"What's going on?"

Olinski stood. "I'm gonna take off and let you ladies chat. You'll be more comfortable without me here."

Brittany laughed. "You mean you'll be more comfortable." She slid her arm around his waist and walked him to the door. "Thank you. I'll call you in the morning."

He kissed her cheek and made his escape.

Brittany raided the kitchen for a bottle of wine and two glasses. "You're not on anything stronger than Tylenol, are you?"

"No, that's it. Wine sounds good. And I'm not going anywhere tonight."

She filled our glasses, handed me one, and settled beside me on the couch with her legs tucked beneath her. "Talk to me."

I took a large swallow of the white Moscato, and a flood of words poured out. All the mixed feelings I'd struggled with, Eric's allusions to marriage at dinner the other night and my reactions to it, and his desire for space as a result. "I don't know what to do, Britt. We're just in really different places right now."

"Sounds like it. Do you love him?"

"I think so, but honestly, I'm not sure. It's not like it was with Russell or Scott. Being with them was like riding the biggest rollercoaster in the amusement park. Giant ups and downs and always exciting. Being with Eric is more like hanging out on the train that goes around the perimeter. Slow and steady and always where it's supposed to be when it's supposed to be there. I'm not sure I'm ready for that yet."

Brittany drained her glass and poured a refill. "I get it. Everyone loves the excitement of a new relationship, but it rarely lasts. Everything's wonderful and raging hormones hide all the flaws. Then you wake up one day and have no idea who that stranger is across the breakfast table from you. That won't happen to you and Eric. You've been friends for a long time. What's wrong with that?"

"Uh, I'm thirty, not eighty. I want that excitement."

"Even though you know you'll probably end up being hurt in the end?"

"Not necessarily. Why do you assume I'll get hurt?"

She looked at me over the top of her glass. "Because you need stability in your life, whether you realize it or not. You crave the rollercoaster because your childhood was so volatile. It's what you're used to, and you know how to deal with it. But it'll never make you happy. Eric will, if you let him."

My instinct was to argue with her, but I had a sneaking suspicion she was right. Again. Nobody knew me better than she did, including me. Besides, Brittany was always right.

CHAPTER TWENTY-SEVEN

"Jingle Bell Rock" blared its way into my sound sleep Sunday morning, and I slapped the alarm into silence. Why did I even set it last night? Brittany and I were well into our second bottle of wine by the time she left, so no telling what I was thinking when I crawled into bed. Assuming my brain actually functioned.

A bomb went off in my head when I moved, but I suspected it was more hangover than concussion. Drinking so much wine was a bad idea, but the conversation with Brittany had helped. She always gave me clarity when my brain filled with Mulligan stew. And she understood the source of my confusion. Sometimes better than I did.

I patted the bed where Savannah was supposed to be and came up empty. That settled it. My little girl was coming home tonight, no matter what. My recovery had progressed well—I could bend my knee for the first time in two days. With the brace's assistance, I could take care of her with no trouble. And, most important, I missed her.

But she made Gary feel better. Contributed to his healing just by being there. How could I take her away from him? Maybe we could work out a shared-custody arrangement until he recuperated. I could get him a dog of his own to fill the space, but my mother would have to take care of it, and she had enough to worry about already. More mixed emotions to deal with. Perfect. Sometimes, it seemed my whole life was a no-win situation.

The coffeemaker did its thing while I limped to the bathroom to do mine. The aroma of freshly brewed coffee always perked me up, no matter how bad my morning started. Someday, when I was rich and famous, I'd treat myself to a pound of Jamaican Blue Mountain, one of the most expensive coffees in the world. I wouldn't hold my breath for that day, though; I'd end up as blue as the mountain the coffee beans grew on.

I chased a couple of acetaminophen down with a bottle of water and grabbed the icepack out of the freezer. The swelling in my knee had gone down considerably, but I might as well put it to rest altogether. If Savannah came home tonight, I had to be well enough to walk her using only the brace.

The coffeemaker hissed its last, and I carried my full mug to the couch. Between the drugs, the water, and the caffeine, my head should clear soon. As much as it ever did, anyway. Book three was near the top of my to-do list, though. *Twin Terror* was due for release in April. Only four months away. I had four months to create a follow-up to help my publisher decide whether they wanted to continue the series or let it die a natural death. *No pressure there.*

My headache dulled to an annoying presence. Like a relative who came for the weekend and stayed for a week. I'd have to learn to live with it. About the same time, the icepack dissolved into a portable lake, so I had no more excuses. Time to get to work.

I retrieved my laptop from the coffee table and started it up. Lying on the couch wasn't the best position to work in, but my leg needed support. I opened my outline for the novel and saved it as "Book Four" since I'd taken off on a whole new tangent. I wasn't sure why I even bothered with an outline for my novels since I never followed them anyway. Somewhere along the way, I always had an idea that changed everything. Still, it gave me a starting point. After that, anything could happen.

The first chapter began with the twins arguing the merits of Daniel joining a fraternity. Still needed a first line, though. I could only assume one would come before I finished. Opening with dialogue might work too, but that would be a last resort. I'd much rather begin with something witty or philosophical. For the moment, though, I'd have to settle for just getting started.

I'd banged out brief summaries of the first three chapters and the opening bars of the twins' discussion when someone knocked on the door. I called out, "Come in!" and then remembered I hadn't taken Savannah for a walk this morning, so the door remained locked. I limped over and opened it.

Charlie stood on the other side, wearing jeans, a gaudy red Christmas sweater covered with reindeer, and an ear-to-ear grin. "Good morning! I didn't wake you, did I?"

"No. I've been up for a while." I gestured for him to come inside. "What're you so happy about this early in the morning?"

He helped himself to coffee. "Wouldn't you like to know?"

I rolled my eyes. "As a matter of fact, I would. Especially if it has something to do with that photograph."

He waggled his eyebrows. "Maybe it does. Or maybe it doesn't."

"Of course it does. Sit down and spill it."

"Party pooper." He moved my laptop to the coffee table and dropped onto the couch. "I found a birth certificate for a baby boy named Jonathan born to Lula Wilcox and an unnamed father in 1987. Then I did a social media search on Jonathan Wilcox. There are almost a hundred on Facebook alone!"

"Do I really need the play-by-play?"

He scowled. "This is my story. I get to tell it any way I want."

I suddenly missed the days when I could be mean to him and get away with it. I settled in for the duration. "Proceed."

"Anyway, I realized that wasn't going to work. It would take days to check them all. So, I created an algorithm using the info on the birth certificate. And you know what I found?"

"He's your long-lost twin brother?"

"Ha ha. Nope. I found nothing at all. The Jonathan Wilcox on that birth certificate doesn't exist."

"What do you mean? The birth certificate's a fake?"

He sipped his coffee. "Patience, my dear. Patience."

Not something I was known for. I swallowed a retort. "Go ahead."

"I ran the algorithm through adoption records."

"I thought those were sealed."

He shrugged.

"How many laws did you break? You know I can't afford to bail you out, right?"

"Stop worrying. Do you want to know what I found or not?"

"Yes, unless it makes me an accomplice."

"Relax. We won't get caught."

Not crazy about his use of the word "we."

When I didn't reply, he continued, "Jonathan Wilcox was adopted by Steven and Mallory Underwood. And they changed his first name to Travis."

I froze with my coffee cup halfway to my mouth. Jonathan Wilcox was Travis Underwood. In an instant, Charlie had added two more suspects to the list: George and Lula Parsons. His birth mother, Lula, had to be who he was trying to find. Did Lula know? More important, did George know? Lula couldn't have subdued a man Travis's size without help. But George could.

"Thank you, Charlie. That was definitely worth waiting for."

He thrust out his chest. "I thought so. Glad you agree."

I checked the time on my phone: 9:35. If I hurried, I could catch the Parsons before they went in for the ten o'clock mass. I jumped up, balancing on my good leg. "I have to go. I need to talk to Lula Parsons."

Charlie stood and swallowed the last of his coffee. "Do you need a sidekick? I'll be happy to go along."

"No, thanks. I can handle it. Besides, don't you have to work today? If we're lucky, Lacey will need the help."

His face fell. "I guess. I'd rather go with you, though. I'd like to see the look on Lula's face when she learns we know her secret."

"I know, but we don't want her to feel like we're ganging up on her."

"Fine. But I want to hear all about it later, okay?"

"Definitely. I'll be there as soon as I'm done."

I rescued my jeans from the worn-but-still-clean-enough-to-wear-again pile and pulled a red sweatshirt out of a drawer. The nearest thing I had to seasonal attire. My mother gave me an itchy green elf sweater one year, but I accidentally put it in the dryer with my jeans. It came out the size of an infant's onesie. Oops.

The morning chill hadn't yet given way to the midsixties temperatures the weatherperson had forecast. I shivered as my Dodge warmed up. I'd rather have walked the two blocks to the church, but my knee vetoed the idea. Just as well, though. I had to go to the bookstore, too. This was the next-to-last weekend before the holiday, and I was hoping for a banner Sunday.

Main Street was clear of traffic, and I made the left turn onto Oak without having to stop. Another left onto Riddleton Road brought me to the church parking lot, which hadn't filled up yet. No sign of either Lula's or George's vehicle, so I settled in to wait. I had no doubt Lula would be here this morning. Rumor had it she never missed a service.

I watched folks drift in one car at a time until, sure enough, at nine fifty-five, Lula's Mercedes turned into the lot with George behind the wheel. I hobbled over to where they parked.

Lula removed her seatbelt. "Hello, Jen. I'm surprised to see you. Are you here for mass?"

"Not today. I wanted to talk to you about Travis Underwood."

"Did you find Denny Holloway?"

"The detectives did. He has an alibi for the night Travis was killed."

She got out of the car. "Then what did you want to talk about?"

"Did you know Travis Underwood was your son?"

Her face paled, then reddened as my words sank in.

"I get the feeling you did."

George scowled his way around the front of the vehicle. "What's this all about?"

For starters, they could be suspects in Travis's death, but if I said that, they wouldn't speak with me. "Nothing really. It just seemed strange that in all the times we discussed his death, you never mentioned it."

Lula met my gaze. "It's a painful time in my life I prefer not to talk about. And I especially don't want to discuss it here, in public, in front of all my friends."

I glanced around the deserted parking lot. "There's nobody else here."

"Still, someone might come out."

She and George conversed with one exchanged glance.

He nodded at the end of it and smiled at me. "Listen, Jen, I know this seems important, even though it isn't, so how about you come out to the farm, and we can discuss it in private?" He turned to Lula. "My wife can fix us up a nice brunch, and we won't have to worry about some gossipmonger overhearing us. It's really nobody's business."

Did I want to go back to the farm? Nope, but they'd made it plain they wouldn't discuss the situation anywhere else. Niggling doubts hovered in the back of my mind. I couldn't imagine Lula or George being dangerous, but nobody suspected Ted Bundy of being a serial killer, either.

I had to take the chance. This might be my last opportunity to free Marcus. However, I'd call Eric on

279

the way to have him meet me there, just in case. I was desperate, not stupid.

As soon as I fell in behind the Mercedes on Main, I pressed the icon next to Eric's picture and put the phone on speaker. It rang five times, then went to voicemail. I left a message informing him of my plans and hung up.

What should I do now? If he didn't get the message in time, I could be in trouble.

I tried Brittany next. Same result. Didn't anyone answer their phones on Sunday morning anymore?

My mother was my last resort. I couldn't expect her to come to the farm, but at least someone would know where I was if I didn't come back. Well, three someones, since my messages to Eric and Brittany included my whereabouts. With luck, I was overreacting, and nobody needed to know where I'd gone. Fingers crossed.

When we reached the twisty-turny part of the trip, I turned on the voice recorder and dictated the location of each direction change. Although my robot-woman GPS should be able to steer me home, I wasn't taking any chances.

George parked next to his gray Tahoe, and we entered through the kitchen door.

Little had changed since the other day. The wooden plank table still lacked Mary Ellen and Erin, and the roosters still watched me from the curtains. George disappeared, and a chill ran down my spine. Another lunch with the Waltons, only this time, I was pretty sure John-Boy *was* locked in the attic.

I glanced at my phone, hoping for a response to one of my messages. No luck. My thoughts waffled between

I was about to be murdered and my paranoia was getting the best of me. For once, I wanted to be paranoid. Best to take my mind off it altogether.

Lula bustled around the kitchen, making coffee and scrambling to prepare the unexpected meal. From the look of things, she'd settled on omelets.

"Is there something I can help you with?" I asked, to avoid looking at my phone again.

"Oh no, you just relax. The coffee will be ready in a minute."

Relax. Fat chance. "You don't have to go to all this trouble."

"It's no trouble at all. Really."

"Do you want to talk while you're working?" The sooner I got the facts, the sooner I could leave. I'd enjoyed my visit the other day, but for some reason, I had the yips this time. Maybe it had something to do with the way our horseback ride ended. No chance of that happening again, though.

"No. Let's just wait until we're all together. Then you can get the whole story and put your mind at ease."

"Where did George go?"

She shrugged. "I think he went out to the barn to check on the horses."

"How are they doing after our little adventure?"

"They're fine. They came straight back to the barn and waited for us."

"I'm glad they weren't injured. It was a scary situation. Did you ever find out who fired the shot that spooked them?"

Lula cracked eggs into a bowl and beat them with a fork, adding mushrooms, onions, and peppers as she went. "No, we never did." She poured the mixture into the preheated pan. "It could've been anyone, really. It's hunting season after all."

"True." The coffeemaker finished gurgling. I rose to pour, and Lula pointed to the cabinet beside the sink where the cups were stored. I filled three cups and added cream and sugar to mine. "How do you like your coffee?"

"Just cream for me. And black for George."

"Got it." When I was finished, I carried the cups to the table. "Who sits where?"

She layered ham and shredded cheese across one side, then deftly covered it with the other. "George prefers the end by the door, and I usually sit beside him to his right. But you can have that seat if you'd like."

"The other side is fine with me." I placed the cups down and took my seat.

George returned and washed his hands at the sink.

"How is everyone?" I asked him.

He grabbed a towel and faced me with a puzzled expression. "Who?"

Weird. "Lula told me you went to check on the horses."

"Oh, yeah. They're fine."

"Glad to hear it. They're beautiful animals."

He nodded and occupied his place while Lula doled out eggs and toast and carried the plates to the table. We joined hands, and I bowed my head when George blessed the food. The aroma of freshly buttered toast teased me, and my stomach rumbled. I blushed, hoping nobody else had heard.

Thankfully, he wasn't the long-winded type. My toast was still warm when I dug into it after we said, "Amen." I was savoring the melted butter surrounding my taste buds when I felt a sharp pain in my right thigh.

I looked down in time to see George pushing the plunger on the syringe he'd buried in the muscle. I jumped up. "What are you doing? What is that?"

He smiled. "It's Special K. Relax and enjoy it. It's very popular with the younger crowd."

Special K? I'd heard of that. He'd injected me with ketamine. "You shot me up with street drugs? Why?"

"Oh, no. I'd never do that. You don't know what you're really getting that way. We get ours straight from the vet. For the horses."

His words came from far away. Then Lula's voice emanated from the echo chamber. "Remember, George, you're not to hurt her. I won't stand for it."

"Yes, dear."

My body buzzed, and I was floating like people describe when they have a near-death experience.

Is this what it feels like to die?

CHAPTER TWENTY-EIGHT

Every muscle in my body relaxed, and I fell back into my chair. A nap would be great, but an overwhelming sense of well-being made me determined to stay awake. I didn't want to miss a minute of it. I couldn't remember ever feeling this good.

I smiled when George and Lula moved to either side and lifted me to my feet. My headache was gone, and my knee was ready to do jumping jacks. I glanced down at the brace. "Hey, I don't need that anymore." I ripped it off and dropped it onto my plate. A piece of toast skittered off and landed on the floor. I giggled. My stomach didn't want food, anyway. In fact, it tried to return the little I'd already eaten.

A warning voice whispered in the distance of my mind, reminding me I was in trouble. That someone had dosed Travis with ketamine too. I pushed it away. I couldn't possibly be in danger and feel this good. No pain anywhere. I danced a soft shoe as Lula and George led me toward the door. Where were they taking me?

My heart pounded as if running a race all on its own. I had to catch up, so I skipped ahead. The Parsons trotted along beside me, steering me into the barn.

Yay, I'd get to see the horses again! I liked the horses, even if they didn't like me very much.

Lucy, Millie, and the boy horse poked their noses over the stall doors as we entered. "Hi, guys! Miss me?"

Lucy nickered softly. She'd missed me!

Lula guided me down the wall to the dirt floor, and I drew pictures with my finger. A house with two stick-figure people holding hands with a little one in between. I signed my name below it with a flourish.

George approached with a coiled rope and a roll of duct tape. He bound my wrists and ankles, tied them together, and slapped tape over my mouth. The drug quickly quelled a flash of fear. It was a game. It had to be. George had no reason to hurt me. I leaned my head against the wall, and my eyelids fell.

When the door to the outside closed, I opened them again. George and Lula were gone, leaving only the horses for company. I watched them watch me. Necks growing longer and longer, they stretched slowly in my direction. They were coming to see me! Around the halfway point, their faces morphed into three-eyed creatures with gnashing teeth that closed the distance with lightning speed. I screamed into the tape and ducked my head, my heart threatening to burst out of my chest.

My pulse and breathing slowed, and I dared a peek. The horses, looking like horses again, placidly munched hay in their stalls. No sign of the toothy monsters. I heard a noise to my left and turned my head. A double-sized George, his bald head almost scraping the ceiling, crept toward me, holding a serrated knife like the one used to murder Travis. When had he returned? How did he get in without my hearing him?

I jerked my wrists and ankles, trying to free myself before

he reached me. When I couldn't get loose, I scrunched my eyelids together and screamed again. Nothing happened. I peered through semi-closed lids and found myself alone.

Deep breath in, slow breath out.

This time, when the heaviness came, I slept.

When I awoke, Eric stood over me, calling my name. "Jen, wake up!"

Relief flooded through me, though I was still woozy from the drug. "I didn't think you'd come." My hands and feet were free, and I tried to stand.

He placed his hands on my shoulders and pushed me down. "Of course I came. It's my job."

I blinked back the water pooling in my lower lids. "Is that the only reason? Because you had to?"

"Well, yeah. What else is there?"

"I thought you loved me."

Eric laughed from deep in his belly. "What? That's crazy. Where'd you get that idea?"

My breath caught. "You told me you did."

"That doesn't sound like me. Maybe you misunderstood."

My heart shriveled into an over-dried prune. Tears poured down my cheeks. "I guess so."

He squatted and grasped my upper arms. "You don't love me, do you? You've made that pretty clear. So, why should I love you? That would be dumb."

"But I *do* love you," I whispered.

"Go back to sleep now." He shook his head and drifted away.

"Eric, wait!"

But he was gone.

*

286

This time, when I woke up, my head had cleared, and for the first time, I fully grasped my situation. I was bound and gagged in the Parsons' barn with no idea what they planned to do with me. My wrists and ankles were raw and bleeding from when I'd tried to free them while under the influence of the drug. I still had a fantastic sense of well-being, but pain had returned to my consciousness. Everything hurt.

I had to find a way out of the mess I'd gotten myself into. Had Eric and Brittany heard my messages? Clearly, the earlier visit from Eric had been a hallucination, so he might still turn up. In the meantime, I searched for something to cut the ropes with. Nothing jumped out at me. I pushed back my frustration.

This was a working farm. The barn had to have something I could use to free myself. A table sat against the back wall of the building. Could there be cutting tools on it? Possibly, but my hands and feet were tied together. Even if I could get to it, would I be able to see what was on it? I didn't know, but I had to try.

I fell onto my side and used the toe of one Nike to turn myself away from the wall. It took forever, but eventually, my back pointed toward the table. I dug my heels into the dirt and pushed off, sliding on my butt like an upside-down inchworm. My progress was limited to the slack in the rope tying my hands to my feet. With one eye on the door, praying nobody would come to check on me, I scooted toward the table a fraction at a time. To call it "slow going" would be like calling Hurricane Katrina a breezy day.

I'd progressed around two feet when I heard a car pull up, then voices in the yard. I froze, trapping the air in my lungs, desperate to make out what they were saying. No luck, though. The voices were calm and controlled. If someone had come looking for me, they weren't particularly concerned about it. Why would they be? George and Lula could simply tell them I'd come out for brunch, ate, and left.

But my Dodge was parked near the house... Unless one of them had moved it during my delirium. A property this big would have plenty of hiding places for a small car. My belly dropped when I heard a car door slam and the visitor drive away. All visions of Sir Eric riding in on his white steed to save the day disappeared. No rescue for me today.

I dug my heels in for another slide. My butt ached from the friction, but I had to keep going. Not much farther now. I still had no idea if there was anything on the table of use, but what choice did I have? The Parsons could easily talk their way out of any attempt by someone else to save me. I had to save myself.

Dig scoot, dig scoot, dig scoot.

I could see the table leg in my peripheral vision when I turned my head. Almost there.

The door opened. George and Lula strode in, then stopped when they saw me.

"Where the hell do you think you're going?" George asked. He held up another syringe and closed the distance between us in three strides.

Lula followed close behind. I tried to wriggle away, but she held me down as George jabbed another dose of ketamine into my thigh. The left one this time. I had matching pinholes in each leg. My last coherent thought: *Here we go again.*

George grabbed me under the arms and slammed me

back against the wall where I'd started. My head bounced, but the pain didn't follow. My wrists and legs no longer ached, either. Next stop: hallucinations. Who would visit me this time? I didn't care as long as it wasn't the toothy monsters again. I glanced at the horses. Nope. Still horses.

Lula stood with the knuckles of one hand pressed into her lips, doubt plain on her face.

George stormed toward the exit. "Are you coming?" he asked Lula.

"I'm going to stay with her a while. To make sure she doesn't hurt herself." When she shook her head, it moved in slow motion, appearing to be in several places at once.

I snickered. Lula was a five-headed monster. At least she didn't have gnashing teeth.

George stretched out the doorway, eventually snapping through it like The Flash. Lula picked up a stool and floated to where I sat.

"Are you all right?" She removed the tape from my mouth so I could answer.

My smile felt wrapped around my head like an old-timey toothache bandage. "Yup. Why are you doing this to me? Did you kill Travis?"

"Absolutely not!" Her eyes bugged three inches out of their sockets. Wiley Coyote stepping off the cliff. "He was my son. You were right about that." Tears glistened in her eyes. She wiped them away.

"Then let me go. I won't tell anyone."

She laughed, her lower jaw falling all the way to her chest. "I couldn't possibly let you go in your current condition, dear."

"You can untie me, though."

"George wouldn't like that."

"George doesn't have to know." I held my wrists up, and my feet followed, pushing me over on my side. "Oopsie! I fall down."

"You should take a nap. You'll feel better in a little while."

Feel better than I did right now? Not a chance. "Tell me a bedtime story. Tell me about Travis."

Her face crumpled, and she fought to control her emotions. "I've never told anyone the whole story."

"Then tell me. You need to get it out, and I probably won't remember when I sober up anyway, right?"

Lula glanced back toward the door. "All right."

I struggled to focus. To remember every word she said.

She took a deep breath. "Jonathan was born when I was in high school. I couldn't keep him, though I desperately wanted to. My parents wouldn't allow it. His father wouldn't allow it, either. It would destroy his life if it ever got out. Neither of us wanted that."

The letters I'd found in Hank's desk floated through my head like dancing feathers, but Hank insinuated someone other than Lula had written them. Had the priest lied? "It was Hank, right?"

Her eyebrows lifted, briefly hovering above her head. "Do you want to hear the rest of the story or not?"

Sounded like a "yes" to me. Hank's letters materialized in front of me, bobbing and weaving like prize fighters. *Come on, Jen. Focus!*

"I'm listening."

"The Church set up a private adoption and Jonathan became Travis Underwood. His family belonged to the church, and I got to watch him grow up. It wasn't a

perfect solution, but we could all live with it until…"
She stopped, wearing a sad smile, and ran her fingers through her hair.

"What went wrong?"

Lula tried to meet my gaze, but my eyes wouldn't stay still, no matter how hard I worked at it. She gave up. "When Travis hit puberty, he took on a resemblance to his father. So much that people started to notice. Travis started to notice. By then, he knew about the adoption, so he asked questions that nobody wanted to answer. That's when Hank knew he had to leave."

"He made up the story about his mother being sick."

"No, his mother had fallen ill, but he moved to Idaho permanently to quell the rumors. He believed if he and Travis could no longer be seen side-by-side, eventually the uproar would die down. And he was right. Everyone forgot about it but Travis. He couldn't let it go and started getting into trouble. Eventually, he went to prison."

"What made Hank think it was safe to come back to Riddleton?"

Lula shifted on her stool and stretched her legs. "Nobody ever mentioned it anymore. Travis was gone, and his family had moved to Blackburn, so he had no reason to come back here when he got out."

"But he did. Why?"

"The Underwoods disowned him when he was convicted. He spent his prison years trying to find his birth parents. They'd sealed the adoption records, of course, but he managed to discover that St. Mary's had arranged it. He already suspected Hank was his father, so he only had to figure out who his mother was."

"How do you know all this?"

A tear rolled down her cheek. "He found me. The day he died. We had tea in the kitchen, and he told me his story. He was alive when he left, though. I didn't kill him."

"Who did?"

"I don't know." She blinked back a tear.

I tried unsuccessfully to sit up. Lula reached over and helped me. "Thank you." My head cleared faster than it had the first time George injected me. Perhaps my efforts to concentrate had helped. "You must have your suspicions, though."

She looked away. "I can't imagine anyone involved in the situation killing him over it. That's why I was so sure it had to be Denny Holloway."

"But Denny's been cleared, so someone else did it. Someone like Hank. He still has as much to lose as he did before. I never saw Travis alive. Did he still resemble his father?"

Lula wiped her eyes. "Not like when he was a teenager, but enough for people to notice. Hank wouldn't have murdered him, though. He isn't that kind of man. He would've left the priesthood first."

"Who killed him then?"

An odd expression flitted across her face. "I told you, I don't know. Maybe it *was* your friend Marcus. Just because you refuse to believe it, doesn't mean it isn't true."

Huh. The heat of her denial suggested maybe she *did* know. "And just because you refuse to believe it might be Hank, also doesn't mean it isn't true. And he doesn't have an alibi. Marcus does, but the prosecutor won't accept it because it's his family."

George burst into the barn before she could reply. "What are you doing?"

Lula stood, toppling the stool. "We were just talking."

"You need to learn to keep your yap shut." He pushed her aside and grabbed me by the ropes that bound my hands, forcing me to my feet, but I couldn't straighten up. "You're gonna put a needle in both our arms."

"I didn't say anything, George. I swear! You promised you wouldn't hurt her!"

Gravity pulled me heels over head, and I landed on my side in the fetal position, George's words pounding in my ears. Had George Parsons murdered Travis? Possibly, but what about the odd placement of the wounds? He wasn't medically trained. Then I remembered the photo of George in uniform on Lula's desk. He wore an armband with a red cross on it. Perhaps he had some medical training after all.

I forced my eyes to focus on George. "You killed Travis! Why? He was no threat to you. He only wanted a family."

He raised his fist. "Of course he was! He wanted *my* family. You don't understand."

"Explain it to me, then."

"I worked my whole life to build a reputation in this community. He would turn me into a laughing stock. And he wanted money I don't have."

What reputation? I'd never heard of the guy until a few days ago. I had to keep him talking, though. "Nobody would blame you for something your wife did before you married her. That's crazy."

His face darkened. "I'm not crazy."

"No. Of course not. I only meant—"

"I know what you meant. You think I'm a nobody.

Well, I'm not." He puffed out his chest. "I'm an upstanding member of this community. I will *not* have my name dragged through the mud!"

The guy was a legend in his own mind. I had to calm him down somehow, or I'd be joining Travis in the hereafter.

"Okay, George. I get it. You're obviously smarter than people give you credit for. Nobody else would've thought to plant the murder weapon under a priest's mattress. Or leave the body on my doorstep just because he had my name in his pocket. That was a brilliant move. You had the police looking at everybody but you."

"You're patronizing me."

"No, I'm not. Untie me and we can talk about it."

He gave me a Chucky smile and jabbed a syringe into my butt. Not ketamine this time. Everything immediately went black.

CHAPTER TWENTY-NINE

Opening my eyes made no difference. It wasn't the dark of my bedroom when I woke up with my head under the covers during the night. More like the complete absence of light in a place that had never seen it. Or the black of total blindness.

Waving a hand in front of my eyes produced nothing. Panic-laden bile rose from my gullet. Had George's drugs blinded me somehow? My heart hammered, and I hyperventilated, pulling in moist, cool air that smelled like mildew. I was underground. Trapped in the tunnels under the church? Like the frat boy who was never seen again?

Oh, God, I'm gonna die!
Get a grip, Jen.
Deep breath in, slow breath out.
And repeat. And repeat.

When I could think again, I sat up to take stock of my situation. First off, my hands and feet were no longer tied together or to each other. The ketamine's numbing effects had dissipated, and my wrists and ankles cried out from the damage I'd inflicted on them while under the influence. My injured knee throbbed, and I suspected

I'd contributed to that too, but couldn't remember how. It didn't matter, though. I had to figure out where I was and find my way back.

Or I could relax here for a while and wait for someone to find me.

No, that was the ketamine talking. Despite my earlier panic, I still had an overwhelming sense of well-being. As if everything would be fine, even if I did nothing. No way was that true. I had to get moving.

I pushed myself into a sitting position, ignoring the pain shooting up my forearm. My phone pressed against my bottom. Huh. Why didn't George take it? On the other hand, would it work this far underground? He obviously didn't think it would, but it was worth a try.

I pulled it out and pressed the side button, lighting up the screen. The time and date showed, but I had no idea how accurate they were. Plenty of battery life. No bars.

Emergency calls only scrolled across the top of the screen. Well, this was an emergency.

I dialed 911 and waited. It didn't even ring, so I hung up and tried again. Still no response. So much for that theory. Apparently, emergencies below street level didn't count.

Now what?

I turned on the flashlight. The tunnel stretched to infinity in both directions. Moist soil all around, broken up every few feet by rotting wooden boards used for support. Terrific. Not only did I have to find my way out, I had to do it before it all tumbled down on my head.

Sitting here waiting for rescue became more appealing every minute. However, I suspected the only people who knew I was here were the people who left me here: the Parsons.

What would Dana do? How would I write the twins out of this situation? I'd get them moving, that's for sure.

I climbed to my feet, putting as little weight on my damaged knee as possible. It was only sprained initially, but what condition was it in now? It didn't matter.

I drew an "X 1" on the wall where I stood with my finger so I'd know where I started if I ended up wandering around in circles, and set off to my right. Since there seemed to be no difference in either direction, it was as good a way to go as any.

Somewhere above my head, Riddleton bustled. Too bad I had no way to orient myself. I could be anywhere from directly under the church to halfway to Lake Dester, which didn't even exist when these tunnels were built. For all I knew, the nearest exit was under water.

I didn't get very far before I had to make a decision. A tunnel branched off to my right. Should I take it or keep going? On one hand, I should probably clear one tunnel before turning into another. On the other hand, George wouldn't have left me someplace I could walk straight out of. Would he? No. That would defeat the purpose of dumping me down here to begin with.

I drew an "X 2" on the wall opposite the passage entrance and made the right turn. The flashlight showed the standard dirt and boards as I limped along. Damp, mold-scented air filled my lungs.

Before long, I encountered another passageway that extended out in both directions. Now I had three choices: left, right, and straight ahead. Which way should I go?

Eenie, meenie, miney, moe selected left for me, and I drew "X 3" and "X 4" on the walls, indicating the direction I'd come from and the way I was heading. I might get lost, but I wouldn't repeat myself. Not without knowing it, anyway.

It turned out to be a short tunnel that ended in a right turn that took me away from my original path. I had no choice but to follow the zigzag pattern. Lefts and rights at roughly ten-foot intervals, as if I were an aircraft carrier evading a submarine. I had no idea where I was in relation to where I started. I suspected that was the point.

Eventually, the dizzying turns led to a solid left, which led to a cross tunnel. I made my marks—"X 5" and "X 6"—and turned left, my stomach roiling. Fear made its first appearance. I did my breathing exercises and soldiered on.

It wasn't long before I saw the big "X 1" I'd drawn on the wall at my starting point. I'd come full circle.

Disappointment added a hundred pounds to my limbs. I squeezed my eyelids against the tears, breathed through it, and limped on. No way George Parsons would beat me.

With no idea how long I'd traveled the seventh circle of hell, I stopped when the ground sloped toward the surface. My pulse raced. An exit had to be close. Why else would the builders have done that?

I hobbled as fast as possible, ignoring the pain shooting through my leg. Any minute now, I'd be out. I panted and sweated as I climbed. Almost there. Had to be.

The light illuminated an empty tunnel for at least another twenty feet. I puffed like I'd climbed Mount

Everest to get this far. How deep were these tunnels? Designed to be deep enough to discourage the most dedicated of slave catchers, apparently. The area under the church must've been the pool's shallow side. George, however, had dumped me in the deep end.

When the tunnel finally leveled off, I searched for an exit. Nothing in the walls or the ceiling. I kept going forward, enthusiasm waning. Discouragement returned the lead weights to my feet. Dana wouldn't quit, though. She'd plod on until she couldn't move her legs anymore. And then she'd crawl.

Was my main character stronger than me? Yup. But she was a part of me, and I'd follow her lead. If I didn't, the twins would never find the dead frat boy.

I played the light along the walls as I went. The entrance in the church had steps leading to it. Perhaps this one did too. Unless it led directly outside, in which case, there'd probably be a door. Either way, if it was here, I'd find it.

Around a hundred feet down, I found an opening in the left wall, barely wide enough for an adult to fit through. Could this be it?

I flashed the light through the crack. The foot of a steep wooden staircase, identical to the one at the church, popped into view. Footprints in all directions littered the dirt, but no indication of how long they'd been there. Even more critical, no sign of any other living things running around inside.

A deep breath slowed my racing heart while I summoned enough courage to step into the gloom. No matter what I might find inside, it was the only way out. Could snakes climb stairs? Maybe, but not as fast as I could.

I slipped through the opening, showering soil over myself, and froze, listening for any sound of movement.

Nothing. Excellent.

I examined the area with the flashlight, finding only dirt, tiny tree roots sticking out of the walls, and small shards of wood from the steps. In the corner beneath the apex of the staircase, clothing sat in a heap. An odd place for someone to leave their clothes, but whatever. I was getting out of here.

The rickety staircase had no rails, so I stashed my phone in my pocket to free up both hands. I gripped the steps above to maintain my balance and hopped on my good leg in the dark. When I ran out of handholds, I retrieved my phone and lit the area over my head. A two-foot wooden square, the same as the one in the church kitchen, was directly above me.

I clamped my cell in my teeth and pushed on the door. Earth fell in my face. I rubbed it out of my eyes and tried again, but the hatch wouldn't budge. I played the light over it, searching the cracks between the boards. No luck. I pushed again, treating myself to another dirt shower. If—no, when, I got out of here, I'd take a long, hot bath. I'd had enough showers today.

Since the wood had almost two hundred years to rot, I picked at a corner of the cover. Tiny pieces came away in my fingers, but not enough to make any progress.

I moved to the other side and discovered somebody else had done the same with more success. A small gray patch was visible behind the lumber. When I poked my finger in the hole, my heart sank. The cool, rough feel of concrete was instantly recognizable. Someone had cemented over the entrance. Nobody was getting out this way. Not without a jackhammer.

Tears created mud tracks down my face as I hopped back down the staircase. When I reached the bottom, I collapsed against the wall and sobbed into my hands until my nose ran. I wiped it on my sweatshirt sleeve, not caring how it looked. The odds of anybody ever seeing it were now much lower than before.

My sobs hitched to a halt, and I wiped my nose again. My stomach rumbled. I hadn't eaten since before I met Lula and George at the church. How long had it been?

My phone screen showed the exact date and time it had when I first checked. No help there.

I clambered back to my feet and flashed the light again, settling on the pile of clothing. Something about the layout pushed me in that direction. As I approached, the pile took on the shape of jeans and a plain white T-shirt, still covering a skeleton curled into a fetal position. I took an involuntary breath. Was this the missing frat boy after all this time?

My brain seemed clear to me, but I couldn't discount the possibility I was still hallucinating. I inched closer and reached toward the jeans' cuff. My hand recoiled without instructions from me. While I'd seen dead bodies three times before, including at Chief Vick's autopsy, I'd never actually touched one. Still, I had to be sure. I shot my finger out and held it on the material just long enough to be sure it wasn't my imagination.

Nobody would believe I'd found him, so I tried to take a picture to make it easier to find later, but when I started the camera, the flashlight went out. I'd have to take a shot in the dark. Literally. After activating the flash, I snapped photos from every imaginable angle, hoping at least one would be visible.

Now I needed to get myself out, so somebody could see them. Which way to go, though? I had to approach this logically. A cement slab covered this entrance. That meant it was likely in a building, which was likely in town. Unless it was a shack in the woods that'd been part of the Underground Railroad. If so, I could be anywhere. Miles from the next exit, even. I could wander around for days without ever escaping. Like the guy in the corner.

Nope. I couldn't think of it that way.

Okay, so I'd assume I was under Riddleton. What other buildings existed before they built the downtown area in the forties? The original stagecoach rest stop had the church, a stable, and the caretaker's house, which doubled as the traveler's rest area. Where would those buildings be now? Somewhere near the church. The buildings would be close together for safety.

St. Mary's shared the block with its parking lot and Ingrid's office. The parking lot was asphalt, not concrete, so that left the doctor's office. Could I be close enough to the church right now to throw a rock at it? Possibly, if I was on the street. And I could throw. The tunnels crisscrossed each other, though. And I'd yet to see one that branched off the tunnel I was in.

Basically, I had to make a giant "U," ignoring all the tunnels meant to be distractions. If I was under Ingrid's office, I had only to find a shaft that crossed over to the passageway that led to the church. So, basically, hang a left out of the opening, a left into the crossover tunnel when I found it, and another left back to St. Mary's. Piece of cake. If I was where I thought. If not, well, I didn't want to think about that possibility.

I slipped out of the opening and traced "X 7" on the

opposite wall to mark the spot. The light showed nothing significant ahead, but I limped on with my fingers crossed. I had to be right about my calculations. If not, I'd end up another hidden skeleton remembered only in folklore.

With no sense of passing time, I couldn't tell how long I'd been traveling or how far I'd gone. All I had was the uniformity of the endless dirt walls and a growing sense of doom. And still, I trudged on. What choice did I have? I couldn't give up. Dana would never allow it.

The going became difficult when the path tilted down again. My feet slid beneath me, and I had to use my injured leg more than I wanted. I braced against the wall to take some weight off it, which helped a little, but not enough. With each step, agony drowned the constant ache like a tidal wave.

A new challenge presented itself when loose soil and rocks littered the trail. I sensed something was about to change. I prayed it was for the better. Perhaps this end of the tunnel was often-used, creating the debris. The idea lifted my spirits, and I kept the light trained on the left wall, searching for the crossover tunnel.

I turned it forward again when I stepped into a deep pile of dirt. I'd reached a dead end. A wall had collapsed, blocking the way ahead. I had nowhere to go except back the way I'd come.

CHAPTER THIRTY

My body slithered to the ground, and I bit my lip to hold back the tears. Arms and legs aching with fatigue, my mouth felt like my dentist had extracted all the moisture with his suction hose. I had to rest.

I dozed for a few minutes until it occurred to me that the longer I was down here, the more time the Parsons had to get away, leaving Marcus in prison for a crime I could finally prove he didn't commit. I hoisted myself up and hobbled as fast as I could back down the tunnel to where I'd started.

When I reached the "X 7," I whispered into the opening containing the frat boy's skeleton, "Don't worry, I'll be back for you." Although, since he'd been in there for almost a hundred years, I couldn't imagine he'd be concerned about it now. Plus, he was dead. Nothing bothered him anymore.

"X 2" marked the circular tunnel, which I ignored. It took a while to make it back to "X 1," where my journey had begun, and I blew right past it. The crossover tunnel had to be up here someplace. One way or the other, George's plan to leave me here to die would fail, if I had anything to say about it. He wasn't the

304

first person to underestimate me. Probably wouldn't be the last, either.

The passageway popped up on my right, and I was so lost in my thoughts I almost missed it. I marked it "X 8" and charged forward, ignoring all cries from my legs. The doctor's office was only a couple hundred feet from the church, so it shouldn't be much farther. Unless the other tunnel ran at an angle away from it.

I stopped to check my phone, and the time still hadn't changed. Still too far away to pick up the Wi-Fi from the church or the doctor's office, which was blocked by the concrete. I slogged on.

A passage appeared on my left. I flashed the light down it. Should I try that way? I was almost certain the church was back to my right. What if I was wrong, or this was a shorter way out? More likely, this was how people got lost. Better to stick to my plan. If it didn't work out, I could always double back.

An eternity later, I reached the tunnel I'd hoped led back to the church and flashed the light toward the ceiling. The string of bulbs the rumrunners had hung reflected in my phone LEDs. I turned right into the new passageway and scurried toward the exit at St. Mary's. I could only hope I'd get there in time.

George and Lula couldn't escape. Of course, there was always the possibility they believed I was gone for good and weren't even trying to get away. I couldn't take that chance, though. Marcus's life depended on it.

It took forever to retrace the distance from the crossover to where I thought the church should be. When I saw the storage room on my right, I broke into a run, every footstep shooting fire through my legs. The stairs to St. Mary's were just ahead. I was almost free.

I burst into the alcove containing the staircase, and everything was exactly as I remembered it. The hanging switch dangled above my head, and I flipped on the lights. They didn't illuminate the steps past the first few feet since there were no bulbs in the alcove itself, but I felt better having them on. I looked up into the dark. No square of light at the top this time, but I knew the trapdoor was there. I put my phone in my pocket and climbed, using the steps above for handholds as I'd done the last time.

After pulling myself up a half-dozen steps, I reached for a handhold and found only empty space. Perhaps a step had broken. I stretched farther. Still nothing. I retrieved my cell and shined the light up the ladder. Someone had sawed off a bunch of the boards in the staircase. Too many for me to reach the next one. My heart dropped into my belly.

What now?

Tears prickled behind my eyelids. I shook my head. No time for that. Dana wouldn't cry; she'd figure out what to do next. *I'd* figure out what she should do next.

My options were limited. I could climb back down and follow the lights to the exit in the woods, or I could find a way around the obstacle before me.

My arms and legs vibrated with fatigue. I had no clue how far the trek to the trees would be. Would I make it before I collapsed?

The only way to reach the top from here was to shimmy up the side like the rope my middle school gym teacher always encouraged me to climb. I never reached the top back then. What made me believe I could do it now?

Necessity.

While it was good to know I had an alternative, my physical condition would only decline the longer I remained down here. If the exit to the woods was impassable after all this time, I wouldn't have the strength to make the ascent when I got back. If I even made it back. I had to try now.

Using the side rails for support, I climbed until my feet were on the top remaining step. Then, I swung my leg around and hugged the rail like a koala in a tree. Pulling myself up set off a firestorm in my biceps, but I held on with my legs until it passed. I was a foot closer.

I continued the painful process a bit at a time. Pull, clamp, rest. Pull, clamp, rest. The breaks became longer with each effort, but I forced myself up with sheer willpower. Being stubborn came in handy sometimes.

When I busted a knuckle on a step, I knew I'd make it. I wrapped my arm around the rail and pulled my upper body onto it with my legs swinging below me. My flashlight illuminated the few remaining steps to the top. No light showed between the cracks of the hatch. Either the church kitchen was empty, or the rug covered the floor.

Grabbing the next board gave me enough leverage to hoist my knee onto the first one. From there, it was a cinch to stand. Adrenaline and determination drove my every move. I felt no pain. No fatigue.

One more step up, and I could reach the two-foot square trapdoor. I gave it a nudge, and it moved. I sighed in relief. At least George hadn't thought to block it. Perhaps he assumed I'd never get this far. Or maybe he had another surprise waiting for me.

I took a deep breath and pushed the door open.

The rug slid away, and I ascended into the darkened kitchen. No light shined beneath the door leading to the rectory dining room. According to my newly reactivated phone, it was almost midnight. Hank was away or in his chambers. No problem. I'd let myself out.

When I opened the door to the nave, I heard whispers near the front of the church. A parishioner in distress here for counseling in the middle of the night? Must be something serious.

I stepped through the doorway straight into a tree branch. Lula or the parish children had been busy. Probably both.

On the wall next to the kitchen stood a Christmas tree the size of a minibus. A glass ornament rocked on the branch. I grabbed it. The crash when it fell would give me away for sure. Until I knew who else was in the building, stealth was my word of the day.

I tiptoed along the wall. The whispers became clearer, although I couldn't actually see anyone yet. Sweat dripped into my eyes, and I mopped it away with my sweatshirt sleeve. Then remembered I'd wiped my runny nose with the same sleeve. Yuck.

About halfway to the front, I noticed flashing lights coming through the stained-glass windows at the top of the double doors. Perhaps Zach Vick had stopped a speeder who'd pulled into the parking lot for safety. The closer I got, the louder the whispering voices were. And the more recognizable. I couldn't be sure, but it sounded like George and Lula Parsons.

What are they doing here?

I dropped between the pews and duck-walked toward the aisle, gritting my teeth against the sting in my leg. At the opening, I fell on my belly and peeked around

308

the pew. The Parsons huddled by the double doors, George peeking out every so often. Were the cops here for them? How did they know?

Either way, I had to escape without the Parsons seeing me. I'd be safe once I hit the parking lot. Not much they could do with the police out there.

Did the church have a back door? Not that I'd seen. I could scoot around the wall to the front of the building, but I could figure no way to get out the door unseen with them standing in front of it.

I needed a distraction. If I could throw something large enough to draw their attention, they might investigate. Other than my phone, I had nothing on me, though. I searched the back of the pew beside me. It had kneelers but no bookracks. No help. What did the church have that I might use to distract George and Lula?

The kids had slathered the Christmas tree with glass ornaments. I could throw one of those and hope the Parsons would investigate the noise. Would it be loud enough? Maybe. Maybe not. I needed them to think someone dangerous to them had breached the sanctuary somehow. They would have to check it out then.

What else did the church have in it? Candles. Not the candles themselves, necessarily, but a brass candle holder would make a loud clatter when thrown across the room. Unfortunately, the candles were in the back by the altar. That meant slinking back the way I'd come without getting caught. The Parsons seemed absorbed by whatever was happening in the parking lot. It was worth a try.

I scuttled back to the wall on all fours, bad knee throbbing. If I kept my head below pew level, I might have a chance. Adrenaline pulsed in my ears, and I held my breath to slow my racing heart. When I could breathe again, I made my way to the kitchen doorway and eased into the room. I needed time to think.

The massive spruce blocked my view of the candle table, but I knew it was there. How to get to it, though? Squeezing past the tree ran the risk of knocking off an ornament and exposing myself before I was ready. That might mean certain death. Nope. Not an option.

I slipped into the sanctuary to get a closer look at the Christmas obstruction. The branches lapped over the first pew. No way to get past them safely. However, the bottom limbs rested about a foot off the floor. I might be able to slither under them.

Dropping to my belly, I stretched out on the floor. My pulse pounded in my ears. Chin on the ground, I inched forward by shifting my hips back and forth. When I lifted my head to get my bearings, I ended up with needles up my nose and a mouthful of tinsel. An ornament bumped off and landed on my back. I froze.

When I was certain the glass wouldn't crash to the floor, I gently worked the tinsel out with my tongue and pinched my nostrils to suppress a sneeze. Half the problem solved. Now for the ornament.

Holding my breath, I pressed my arm tightly against my side and tipped my opposite hip up until the ornament rolled into the space between my arm and my ribs. Then I slowly increased the gap until the ornament eased soundlessly to the floor. I released the air from my lungs.

I was certain I'd reached the eligible age to collect Social Security by the time I cleared the tree and reached the altar. Tinsel and spruce needles had accumulated in the waistband of my jeans, but I could do nothing about it. I steeled myself against the discomfort. The candle table was four feet away. Four feet during which I'd be exposed. I had to risk it.

The foot-tall candle holders were brass and glass. Perfect. I slithered on my stomach, gathering more debris and listening for any sign someone noticed me. Nothing by the time I reached my destination. I snagged two unused holders off the table, tucked them under my sweatshirt, and scrambled back to the altar. Now I only had to get back around the wall to the front of the church and hope my throwing arm had improved since high school. A big question mark. I'd never been much of a ballplayer.

I wiped the sweat out of my eyes, ducked into the aisle, and scuttled behind the first pew to bypass the Christmas tree. Too bad I hadn't thought of that in the first place. It was much easier than sliding along the floor gathering my own personal Christmas tree with my pants. I followed the wall to the front corner.

George and Lula debated their options by the double doors. Lula wanted to surrender and take her chances. After all, as far as I could tell, she hadn't done anything wrong. George wanted to escape through the tunnel and run to someplace with no extradition treaty.

When I was sure they were absorbed in their discussion, I reared back and threw one of the candle holders as far as I could toward the opposite corner. It landed with the hoped-for crash.

George took off running in that direction, but Lula didn't follow.

I threw the second holder toward the kitchen, burying it in the spruce and bringing multiple ornaments crashing down. Lula jerked her head toward the sound but still didn't move. What should I do? I had to take my chances. Lula hadn't harmed me in any way. As far as I could tell, it was all George.

I bolted toward the door. Lula's eyes widened, and she covered her mouth with her hands. I put a forefinger to my lips and opened the door. "Lula, come with me. You don't have to go down with him."

She shook her head and waved me out. "Hurry. He'll be back in a minute."

"Lula, please!"

"Go!"

I opened the door and immediately raised my hands above my head.

Eric called out, "Stand down! Don't shoot, it's Jen!"

Zach Vick ran to me, grabbed my arm, and escorted me out of the line of fire.

Brittany waited behind the police line. She wrapped me in a hug. "I'm so glad you're all right. What happened?"

"Take me home, and I'll tell you all about it."

CHAPTER THIRTY-ONE

I maneuvered through the yammering throng in Ravenous Readers, holding my plastic cup above my head so nobody would dump my white Moscato all over me. Decent turnout for a party on the Saturday before Christmas.

Brittany and Lacey had ganged up on me, insisting the town needed an injection of joy only we could provide. The joy part, I understood. Why it had to be us, not so much, but it made them happy. Even I had to admit they'd done a spectacular job putting everything together in such a short time.

A twelve-foot Douglas fir replaced my *Double Trouble* display by the door after I assured Lacey I would survive the disappointment of no longer accosting every visitor with my cardboard face. Leftover ornaments donated by anyone who had them, a garland, and strings of colored lights provided by the Feed and Seed covered the massive tree.

Christmas carols drifted down from the ceiling speakers, and homemade, beribboned wreaths hung on every bookcase and door, complementing the strategically placed mistletoe. Potluck platters of ham,

313

green bean casserole, and more chocolate desserts than even I could sample in one sitting lined the coffee bar.

I plopped onto the couch next to Brittany. "You guys did a great job on this party."

"Thanks. I'm glad you're enjoying it. Especially since you fought so hard against it."

"You know how I am. Look how far I went to avoid going to my birthday party."

Brittany rolled her eyes. "Yeah, that was the reason you scared us all half to death. Just so you didn't have to go to a party."

"That and I had to be the one to find that lost frat boy."

"Of course you did. Did you hear Lula is testifying against George?"

My jaw dropped. "Seriously? That's a surprise."

Brittany sipped her wine. "In exchange for probation. Olinski told me Lula wanted to welcome Travis to the family, and George wouldn't have it."

"How did Father Hank feel about welcoming Travis to the family?"

"I think he felt bad about running away from the kid when he was younger. He was willing to give up his career to make it up to him."

"It's nice that he didn't have to give up his career, but his being willing to explains why George tried to frame him for the murder."

She carried her empty cup to the table and returned with the bottle. After topping me off, she said, "I still don't understand why George killed Travis, though."

"When they had me tied up in the barn, he was ranting about his reputation and how Travis was trying

314

to ruin his life. It didn't make much sense to me, but I was still under the influence of the ketamine."

"What does Eric say about it?"

I grunted. "Not much to me. He interviewed me a couple of times to get my statement and ask follow-up questions, but other than that, we haven't spoken. He did ask me once if I knew anything about Travis blackmailing the Parsons. I think I remember George saying something about Travis asking for money, but he never mentioned blackmail per se. All I can say for sure is he seemed to think he was a lot more important than he was. I don't think anyone would've given it a second thought if they'd decided to make Travis part of the family."

Olinski and Eric came in and filled plates for themselves. I moved to one of the chairs so Olinski could sit next to Brittany. When I gestured to the other chair for Eric, he nodded and walked back toward the kids' section. I swallowed against the boulder in my throat, watching him chat with Santa Angus and his elf Charlie. At least he'd talk to someone. Just not me.

Brittany threw a crumpled napkin at me. "You need to go mingle."

"Yeah, 'cause I'm such an expert at that, right?"

"Practice makes perfect."

I took a hefty swallow of my wine and stood. "If you say so."

Laughter erupted from a group in the back by the kids' section. Might as well check out what was so funny. I channeled my inner social butterfly, Daniel Davenport, pasted on a smile, and moved through the crowd in that direction.

As I squeezed past Romance, a short woman with

curly black hair grasped my arm. The counter clerk from Bob's Bakery whose name I could never remember.

"Merry Christmas, Jen! Terrific party."

"Thanks. Glad you're enjoying it."

"I hear your new book's due out soon."

The rumor mill was in overdrive. "April."

"I can't wait!"

"Me either." Especially if it would make the questions stop.

Another burst of laughter urged me toward my destination. Marcus and his girls were chatting with the Winslows. My face split into a grin, and I threw my arms around Marcus.

He winced and pulled away. "Careful. I'm still healing up."

"I'm sorry. I'm just so happy to see you. When did you get out?"

"Day before yesterday. I guess it took a while to convince the DA."

Pissant. "I'm sorry they held you so long. I did my best, but nobody would listen to me."

He drew me into a gentle hug. "Thank you for everything. You saved my life twice."

"You're welcome."

Five-year-old Latoya wrapped her arms around my leg. "Thank you for saving my daddy again, Miss Jen. I missed him bunches and bunches."

I squatted to her level. "I'd bet he missed you more."

"Nuh-uh!"

The mayor-elect, Veronica Winslow, fished her phone out of her purse. "Almost time for me to announce the winner of the Christmas Decoration Contest."

I surveyed the room. "Is Anne-Marie Vick here? I haven't seen her."

"Me either, but the announcement's scheduled for eight, so ready or not, here I come."

Eric helped me carry a kiddy table to the middle of the store. I climbed up on it and cupped my hands around my mouth. "Hey, everyone, can I have your attention, please?"

Revelers poked each other, gesturing toward me. Silence rolled out from where I stood, eventually reaching both ends of the room.

When all eyes were on me, I said, "I'd like to introduce our mayor, Veronica Winslow, who will announce the Christmas Decoration Contest results."

I hopped down, and she took my place.

I took a chance and grabbed Eric's hand. "Come on, let's go check on Brittany."

"I think you should stick around up here."

"Why? Anne-Marie's gonna win. She always wins."

He shrugged. "Okay."

A cheer erupted from the throng behind us, followed by applause.

I turned for a better look and found a flock of faces staring at me. "What's going on?"

Brittany laughed. "Ravenous Readers won the contest, silly."

"What? That's impossible. Anne-Marie always wins."

"Not this year. Carry your butt up there."

What in the world?

I turned to head back toward Veronica. The clapping grew louder, and the people parted like the Red Sea. I reached a hand out to Lacey. "Come on, you too."

She shook her head. "Why me? It's your store."

"But you did all the work. You deserve the credit."

She took my hand, and we followed the path to Veronica's table together. Eric trailed us, wearing a huge grin. His disappointment at my refusal to remain at the table with Veronica made sense now. Somehow, he'd known this would happen. Who else was involved in this conspiracy?

When we reached the back of the store, Lacey and I did a one-eighty and raised our joined hands in a victory salute. A chant of "speech, speech" rang out.

I lowered my hands, palms down. "Thank you, everyone." I threw my arm around Lacey's shoulders. "And a particular thanks to Lacey for her brilliant artistry. My stick figures never would've impressed anyone."

Laughter greeted my pronouncement.

I gave Lacey a hug. "Did you want to say anything? I warmed them up for you."

She chuckled and shook her head. We waved, and everyone resumed their carousing.

Veronica hopped off the table and wrapped her arms around our waists. "Congratulations, you two. I'm proud of you."

Charlie approached and whispered in Lacey's ear.

She nodded and turned to Veronica. "Thank you. If you'll excuse me, I have to situate Santa and his elf."

When she left, I said, "Thanks, but how did this happen?" I tugged on my earlobe. "Anne-Marie's display was fabulous, as always."

"You're right, of course. The council did vote to give it to her. You came in second, though."

"There's no second place in this contest."

"I know. When I told Anne-Marie she'd won again,

to ensure she'd be here tonight, she withdrew her entry. She wanted you to have the victory. For saving Riddleton from another killer." She hesitated. "And I think it brought back too many memories."

I nodded, my heart swelling. "Who knows about this?"

Veronica met my gaze. "Only you, me, Anne-Marie, and the council members."

Maybe Eric didn't know. Or at least he wasn't supposed to.

"I'd like to keep it that way. I want Lacey to believe she won outright. She worked hard decorating our store, and she deserves the reward."

"You got it." She dipped her chin and winked. "I'll make sure everyone else keeps their mouths shut."

"I appreciate it."

Eric came up and stood by my side.

Veronica pointed to the ceiling and stepped away. "I'll talk to you later."

We glanced up. Directly above our heads was a sprig of mistletoe. Warmth spread up my neck into my cheeks. We'd met several times this past week to discuss my interactions with George Parsons, but all the meetings were strictly professional. We'd yet to talk about our issues with each other. Could we salvage our relationship? For the first time in a while, I was sure I wanted to. But how did he feel?

Eric gazed into my eyes. All the words we couldn't seem to say to each other hung between us.

"Eric, I—"

He placed a forefinger on my lips. "Shhhh…"

"But—"

He kissed me. A deep, passionate kiss that left me

wanting so much more. Every nerve in my body fired, and I leaned into it.

When we broke apart, Olinski and Brittany were standing beside us, grinning.

Olinski punched Eric in the shoulder. "Good man. About time you came to your senses."

Eric flushed, the red blending with his freckles.

Olinski turned to me while Eric gathered himself. "I just heard back from the lab in Blackburn."

"Oh yeah? What did they find?"

"That skeleton you found died around five years ago."

My eyebrows soared up. "So it wasn't the frat boy or a runaway slave."

"Definitely not. And don't you dare even think about investigating this one."

I gave him a sideways grin. "Who me? I'd never do that. I've absolutely learned my lesson this time."

Yeah, right.

ACKNOWLEDGEMENTS

A special thank you to:

My agent, Dawn Dowdle, and my editor, Rachel Hart, for all their support, enthusiasm, and assistance.

Ann Dudzinski, Julie Golden, JJ Grafton, Suzanne Oldham, and DL Willette for helping me turn straw into gold.

Sadie for always being there and asking for almost nothing in return.

She can write the perfect murder mystery...
But can she solve one in real life?

Crime writer Jen returns to her small hometown with
a bestselling book behind her and a bad case of
writer's block. Finding sanctuary in the local
bookstore, with an endless supply of coffee, Jen waits
impatiently for inspiration to strike.

But when the owner of the bookstore dies suddenly
in mysterious circumstances, Jen has a real-life
murder to solve.

The stakes are suddenly higher when evidence places
Jen at the scene of the crime and the reading of the
will names her as the new owner of the bookstore...
Can she crack the case and clear her name, before
the killer strikes again?

Don't miss Sue Minix's debut cosy mystery –
available now!

**I wrote murder mysteries. I didn't investigate them.
Until now...**

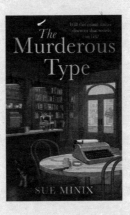

Crime writer turned amateur sleuth, Jen, has taken
over the running of the local bookstore in her
hometown of Riddleton.

But balancing the books at Ravenous Readers is
nothing compared to meeting the deadline for her
new novel.

Dodging phone calls from her editor takes a back
seat, however, when the local police chief is poisoned.
To solve the murder, Jen must dust off her detective
hat once more.

With everyone in town seemingly a suspect, and
evidence planted to incriminate local police officer
and close friend Eric, Jen is working against the
clock. Can she find the killer and beat her own
writer's block before it's too late?

**Don't miss the second instalment in this cosy
mystery series – available now!**